Re-enchanted

FEY CREATIONS BOOK 3

A.R. Miller

Mass-Market Edition - 2016

ISBN-10: 0-9914933-5-4
ISBN-13: 978-0-9914933-5-7

The Fey Creations Series

Disenchanted
Unenchanted
Re-enchanted
Shadow Play

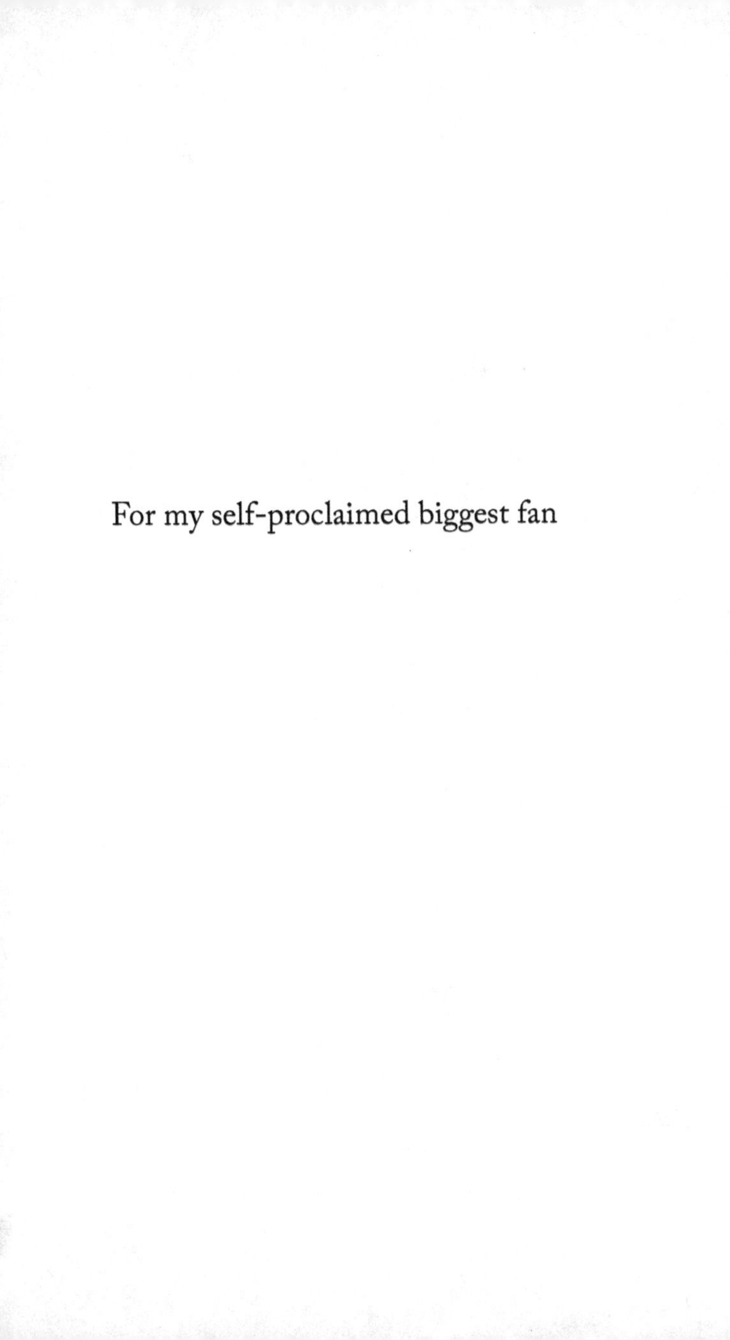

For my self-proclaimed biggest fan

Chapter 1

Var Royd—a.k.a. the biggest pain in my ass, a.k.a. the god Frey—sits behind his ornate desk, his attractive face twisted with annoyance. " Contract?"

"Yes, contract, I want the job."

Irritation disappears behind amusement, laughter reverberating across my flesh. Heat rises in my cheeks and my stomach drops to the lobby, my feet wishing they could follow. Laughter is not what one expects when offering to sign off on their soul.

"The job?"

"Yes, the job," I don't even bother fighting the eye roll, "the one where I take Einen's place as your Shadow."

"Ah, *that* job, what makes you think there is a contract?"

"I can't see you doing anything without a written document to cover your ass, so stop toying with me." I think I like his anger better, at very least it keeps mine in check.

A one-sided smirk graces his face, but at least he's not laughing anymore. "Who says this contract is in writing?"

"Fine, what do I have to do, get down on one knee and pledge fealty to you?" I can feel the darkness creeping in, the familiar tingle riding my skin as I watch it stir in corners behind him.

"That would be a start," his eyes narrow, "but for the moment, I would ask you rein in your Talent, before one of us pays the ultimate price for this little discussion."

"Then stop playing games and tell me what I have to do."

"Let us start with why the sudden change, what makes you so desperately want the position of my Shadow?"

"I had a visit with Stasia Athory this morning."

"And she persuaded you to take the position?"

"Not exactly, it was more what she intends to do that made the decision for me."

"And what might that be?"

"If I don't go into business with her, she thinks she can get Einen to agree."

The annoyance of laughter is back and the tingle builds to the pins and needles pain of disused limbs. "Why on earth would a cosmetics manufacturer wish to do business with that…thing?"

"That…*thing's* Talents are the same as mine, making his bodily fluids as usable as mine for her little serums."

"This is what brings you to the decision of taking the position? Idle threats?"

"Maybe you should take what you can get, because I'm not going to take the job because it sounds so *awesome.*"

"I'm well aware of that, Miss Fey, and exactly why I question your sudden change of mind."

"I need my Talents back. I can't stop her from getting to Einen without them."

He stands, fists braced on the massive desk, leaning toward me. "That is why entering into this relationship would be less than beneficial."

"And Stasia Athory getting to Einen would be? If even half of what everyone says about him is true and she lets him out—"

"Your fears are unsubstantiated. There is no chance of that ever happening. I've made certain of it, no one will ever *get to* Vereinen without my knowledge or consent. And if an attempt is made, it will be dealt with." A thunderstorm of angry certainty flashes in his eyes. The unspoken, *and that includes you*, hangs just below the surface.

He manages to dismiss my fears and threaten me all at once. Arrogance, thy name is Var Royd. One of these days I'm going to find out what he is, the answer might lead to why he's confident no one will cross him. I'm not as confident. It may have gotten Einen banished, but he still managed to cross Var. It can be done and Stasia might have the balls under that designer skirt to try again.

"Fine, if she can't get to Einen, she'll just turn

her attention back to me. With my Talents, I stand a chance, without them what the hel do I do to protect myself? Buy a gun?"

He sits, clasping his hands on the desk, the thunderstorm in his eyes quelled for the moment. "I gave you my Shield for such a purpose. Use him."

"Wow, if I were Teiran I'd feel so honored. I get to protect the thing I abhor." I don't bother holding back the sarcasm, but as expected it's lost on him.

"He will do his duty."

Yeah, that's comforting.

"Speaking of, if you feel this woman will force you into *business* with her, why do you insist on not utilizing his services?"

"For starters, I wouldn't have found out what she was up to, Teiran would've never let me meet her. Then there's the whole privacy issue, I have none."

"Privacy should be the last item on your list of what is important, if this woman's intentions are to harm you."

"I don't doubt her intentions."

"You mentioned bodily fluids and serums. Would this have anything to do with our last discussion about Miss Athory?"

"Yes, there were succubus tears in that mixture."

"That explains the aphrodisiac effect on the therians and the First Arrow. I wonder why it did not produce the same reactions in you and the nixie."

I shrug. "Don't know, don't care, all I care about is keeping my blood from being the main ingredient in a wrinkle cream."

"I reiterate, use the tool you have been given. Keep Teiran by your side." He picks up a pen and begins shuffling through the pile of papers on his desk, an obvious dismissal, punctuated by the elevator door sweeping open.

I don't think our definitions of tool are the same, at least when it comes to Teiran Rand. Teiran may be a big ol' pain in my ass, but he doesn't deserve to be treated as something to be used and put away when done. Var Royd is even more callous than I imagined.

Chapter 2

The elevator ride enhances the sinking feeling in the pit of my stomach. His rejection leaves me back at square one, with a very real threat and no way of defending myself. Might as well paint a big ol' target on my back.

The pretty blonde vamp nods and smiles as I pass, a constant stream of chatter and tapping of her ear piece. I wonder what Royd has on her to make her work on the weekend, or is this is business as usual. I'm tempted to come by tomorrow and try the door. Between dodging the light, let in by the glass front of the building and neglecting her sleep, the job must pay well to have her go against nature.

"Not all with fangs are vampires as you know them, Miss Fey," says Frank, as he swings the door open.

"Damn, was I using my outside voice again?"

He smiles and shakes his head. "No, it was very much your inside voice."

Shit, a mind reader.

"Not exactly, I pick up bits and pieces."

"So, you can't read minds?"

"As I said, bits and pieces, my Talents aren't

strong enough for more than a word or two, here and there. I specialize in emotions and intent. Call me the first line of defense."

"Clever. Who would think a doorman was anything more than a doorman?"

"Mr. Royd is not a stupid man."

"No, no he's not. How did you know I thought she was a vamp?"

"I picked off something about light and sleep, and of course you've seen Celia's fangs. The way you kept glancing between her and the streams of sunlight as you were leaving. I put it all together."

"Mr. Royd's not the only clever one here."

"Thank you, Miss Fey. By the way, if your shields are up and strong enough, I can't hear any stray thoughts."

"Not that I don't appreciate it Frank, but why would you tell me that?"

"Because I've already judged your intent, I don't think you'd do anything to intentionally harm Mr. Royd."

Those words make me smile as I strengthen the walls keeping my Talent at bay, extending it outward to surround my thoughts. "Thank you, Frank."

"My pleasure, Miss Fey." He tips his hat, with a smile that rings true, not a hint of fear in his hazel eyes.

The welcome change from the cold, calculating,

or fearful gazes I usually garner puts a little skip in my step. Until I see a leather encased body leaning against an oxblood Valkyrie at the curb. How in hel, does he manage wearing black leather in Iowa's July heat?

The stern set of sensual lips is offset by the amusement in amber eyes. "Miss Fey."

"Mr. Brand."

"Care to explain what you are doing downtown and without your guard?"

"The *Tool* was still in bed when I left."

His golden brow rises. "Tool?"

"Not my word choice." I motion to the penthouse behind me. "His."

Ric shakes his head, the corners of his mouth turning downward, the light in his eyes dimming. "I will not ask."

"It's not worth it. Why are you here, have meeting with the big guy?"

"No, I came at the behest of the *Tool*."

I cringe. "Like I said, his word, not mine. Should I ask why Teiran sent you instead of coming himself?"

"In his words, 'I do not know what I will do when I find her,' hence my offering to come in his stead."

Crap, what waits for me at home is going to be even more fun than expected. Running off without him again is bad enough, but Ric finding me here… Well, I essentially screwed Teiran over by letting Var know I left the house without him.

"Come, Miss Fey, I shall escort you home."

"I'm not exactly dressed for a long distance motorcycle ride."

His eyes scan the length of me, from t-shirt—lingering on the stone dangling from the collar—to sandals and all the bare skin between. I manage to fight the urge to shield myself with my hands, but can't contain the shiver following the goose bumps rising along the path his eyes take. "No, you are not. I shall take you to your vehicle and follow you home. Where is your car?"

"The ramp on 4th and Grand."

One fluid movement and he's astride the powerful machine, inclining his head to the space behind him. It's been a while since I've been on a bike. A long while, like high school. I may not be as graceful as Ric, when climbing aboard, but I do remember to keep my legs away from the hot bits.

"Would you mind if we make a stop along the way?"

"Nope." He's driving, so what else can I say?

I'd forgotten how much fun it is to ride on a motorcycle. Similar to riding in the 'Stang with the top down, but even more invigorating, fear coupled with invincibility. The glares and longing stares along the way only intensifies the feeling and I wrap my arms a little tighter around Ric's waist. Yeah, having a reasonable excuse to touch him doesn't hurt the situation.

My smug little smile disappears as he slows down,

pulling into an open spot outside the Hessen Haus. Sure, it's easy to act like I'm hot shit while we're moving, but now that we're stopped, that's a whole different story. He waits for me to dismount before following suit.

Head dipped, brows raised questioningly, he smiles. "Lunch?"

"Um, sure, why not." What's one more delay before going home to face whatever it is I have coming to me?

Chapter 3

That he picked a German restaurant doesn't surprise me, nor does the unified shout of his name by the staff as we enter. That it trails off as they take me in, does. It shouldn't, but it does. Once they pick their jaws up off the floor, the bartender snickers.

"Ric's got a new girlfriend. Looks like you're out of the running, Jane."

The rest of the staff laughs as a shapely brunette tries to hide her red face behind the pretense of gathering menus. "Whatever, Jake. Hey, Ric, want your usual table?"

He has a usual table and an escort? Wow, I'd heard it was a seat yourself kind of place. He must practically live here. I guess it makes sense, with his boss's office downtown and all.

We follow Jane to the last four-top before the long hall toward the kitchen. Ric takes the side facing outward into the room, swiveling the inside chair so his back is partially to the wall. Not unexpected, I've observed him—and Teiran— enough to know he will never take a seat that places his back to the room.

I hate high tables. The chairs are just tall

enough—even with a thirty-four inch inseam—only my tiptoes touch the floor, cutting off the circulation in my legs. This one at least has a rung to place my feet on, so I keep my mouth shut. I'm in enough trouble, adding complaints about the furnishings in Ric's favorite restaurant won't win me any points.

"Know what you want to drink?" I think I'm included in Jane's question, but she only has eyes for Ric.

The list of beers is daunting, I haven't heard of three-quarters of them. "Go ahead, Ric, I think I'm going to need a minute."

"Give us a moment, Jane."

Over the top of the menu, I see the usual sexy smile, this time tempered with a bit of indulgence. I'm not sure if it's for me and my lack of beer knowledge, or Jane and her teensy-weensy crush.

"So, tell me, Keely, what type of beer do you prefer? Lager? Stout? Ale?"

"In the colder months I prefer stout, but when it's warmer I usually go for something lighter."

"That narrows it a bit, can you give me examples?"

"Nothing too hoppy, I'm not fond of bitter beers. What's the kind you put fruit in?" I tap my fingers against the table, trying to remember the domestic brand I ask for at the club.

"Lambic?"

"No, not made with fruit. The one people usually put orange slices in, but I almost always substitute lemon."

He flinches at the suggestion of adding a lemon, so I push it a little further.

"I also like to put olives in light beers. Light colored, not *light* beer, that's a waste of time."

He laughs. "I am glad we can both agree that *light* beer is nothing more than colored water. Shall I order for us?"

I nod.

He scans the list again, then motions to Jane.

"Two Hefeweizen, Jane." Hefeweizen rolls off his tongue in an almost seductive manner and Jane's pen skips across the pad. "And a slice of lemon for the lady, please."

Jane is all smiles for Ric, but makes no attempt to hide her animosity toward me, once her back is to him. Yeah, she's got it bad for him, but then again so does every other woman who comes in contact with him. I smile sweetly in return, sadistically savoring her pinched-lipped scowl.

"Nice girl, that Jane," I say, perusing the lunch menu. "Gator Fingers? Interesting choice for a German restaurant."

"The proprietors own several establishments, those are a carry-over from their Cajun restaurant. Have you ever tried alligator?"

"No, is it good?"

He nods and smiles. "Yes, if prepared correctly."

"What's it taste like? And don't you dare say, *like chicken.*"

He laughs. "I would never say such a thing."

Jane returns with our drinks, setting mine down with a little more emphasis. A raised eyebrow dares me to say something as the cloudy, golden liquid splashes onto the table.

"Jane, would you bring us a plate of Gator Fingers?"

"Sure, Ric." Adoration masks her disdain, until she's behind him, then she turns and lets it all hang out.

"Wow, I think she likes me." I wipe as much of the spilled beer the small napkin can hold, ball it up and set it to the edge of the table.

"It would seem so." Ric frowns and stands.

"Hey, no worries, I'll just ask for another napkin when she comes back."

He ignores me and heads to the bar, returning with a stack of napkins and a dish with lemon wedges.

"Thanks." I grab one of the slices, give it a squeeze and drop it into my stein.

He says nothing, but the faint tick in his jaw hints that he might be a tiny bit irritated with the service.

"It must have slipped her mind, it's not like it was a normal order." I don't know why I feel the need to defend a girl who was so damn rude to me. Tentatively, I take a sip of the hazy liquid, letting it roll across my tongue. "Nice."

His smile returns. "I am glad my choice meets your approval."

"Seriously, it's good." I take another sip and look around. "All the years I've lived in the area, I've never been here."

"I shall have to bring you here on a weekend evening. The polka bands are wonderful and I could teach you to polka."

"Uh…yeah, that sounds good."

He laughs, plucking my hand from the table. "Do not humor me, Keely, I know you would much rather spend your Saturday night in a dance club."

"Um…no…I mean…I've got no problem listening to a band and I'm sure they're very good if they're playing here." The slow circles his thumb makes across the back of my hand is downright distracting. The functionality of my brain lowers considerably when whenever he's around. It drops another ten notches when his full attention is on me and his touch leaves me a dithering idiot.

The plate hovers over our hands and I pull away from him. His hand remains in the center of the table, the tick in his jaw returning.

"Your Gator Fingers."

"Thank you, Jane."

"Can I get you anything else?" She puts

the plate between us and takes a step back, head lowered, bottom lip quivering. Maybe she's finally figured out he's a bit upset.

"That will be all, for now."

"I think you hurt her feelings." I watch her take a left toward the bathrooms. The next time we see Jane, I'm betting it will be with red-rimmed eyes.

"I do not tolerate rudeness."

"You do realize she's got a crush on you, right?"

"That does not give her the right to act unprofessionally."

I shake my head. "Maybe not, but she's only human and you're, well, you." I wave a hand up and down in front of him.

"What does that mean?"

"Look, all I'm saying is that you're sweet and kind and come wrapped in a pretty package. Most women are going to have a hard time not falling for you, Jane's no exception."

"And you, Keely, do you have a hard time not falling for me?"

Damn, I really stepped in it this time. "We're not talking about me."

"You do not find this,"—he waves his hand up and down—"a pretty package that is hard to resist?"

I rest my elbows on the table, cupping my head in my hands and he laughs.

"I am sorry, I could not resist teasing you. Eat your Gator Fingers; they are not as palatable once they are cold." He pushes the plate toward me.

Glaring, I take one of the batter dipped chunks of meat feeling incredibly insecure as he watches me take the first bite. A flush hits the tops of his envy worthy cheekbones and he looks away, clearing his throat. Seems the tables have turned, but I keep the smile that wants to emerge pushed way down deep.

"You're right, they don't taste like chicken."

"I'm glad you like them. Now, what brought you downtown, Keely?"

Chapter 4

"How about you tell me how it is a vampire can walk in the sun?" I quickly stuff the last of the crispy coated meat into my mouth and shrug. This conversation was bound to happen, but it doesn't mean I have to like it, or participate. I almost long for Jane and her ill-concealed envy to swing by the table.

"It is because of what I am."

"So, some kind of genetic thing because you're a light elf?"

He nods. "Now, if you would kindly answer my question, I know you did not have an appointment with Lord Royd."

"For crying out loud, can you stop calling him Lord? This isn't the middle ages."

"Fine, I know you did not have an appointment with *Mr.* Royd, so why did you come downtown, Keely?"

"Is this where you start playing bad cop to Teiran's good cop?"

He sighs, shaking his head. "No one is playing at anything. We are simply doing our best to protect you."

"Whatever." I scratch my nose with my middle finger, hoping he'll interpret the true meaning of whatever.

"Stop being such a child. Have you forgotten that you are defenseless?"

"I'm not defenseless, at least not any more than I was before all this started."

"That may be, but with the emergence of your latent Talent, you became a target for all who would see you as a threat. Especially those who knew the other Schattenkind."

"Why does everyone keep pointing that out? I'm my own person and just because we share a Talent, it doesn't mean I will make the same decisions."

Not that I know what those decisions were. Everybody just keeps hinting that Einen was the bad guy back then. From the way I see it, Var Royd is the bad guy now. Maybe he was back then too, and Einen was the only one who saw it.

"It has nothing to do with you being your own person and everything to do with you sharing the same Talent. Because of that, they will continue to make the correlation."

"Well, it's not fair."

"Nor is it fair that you continue to make things more difficult for Teiran."

"Um, yeah, like you didn't ask me to ditch him so we could have coffee."

"That was different. I was there to watch over you."

"You go ahead and tell yourself that, because in the end it really isn't any different."

Those sensuous lips pinch and turn downward. "Perhaps you are right."

He's admitting I'm right? I nearly fall off my chair.

"All I ask is that you consider those around you and how your actions affect them."

My head lowers and a sigh escapes. I know I've gotten Teiran in trouble with each excursion, trouble that he doesn't deserve. Sure, he'd rather I was dead, or at least not his problem. Unintentional or not, I've made our situation worse. "I'll try."

"Now, why did I find you downtown?"

"I wanted to go to the Farmer's Market."

"Keely, please, do not lie to me."

"Fine, I was here to meet with Stasia Athory." I pull back in my chair, waiting for the fireworks.

He sits up straight, amber eyes darkening and that little tick in his jaw throbs. "Why?" he asks through clenched teeth.

"She asked me to meet her for coffee."

"This is exactly what I was talking about; you need protection from your own foolhardy choices. I thought you understood that Stasia is not to be trusted."

"Ya think?" I roll my eyes.

"There are times I question your common sense. Why do you insist on putting yourself into such situations?"

"Look, I know she's bad news, knew it the moment I laid eyes on her, but no one else was willing to find out what she's up to."

"And did you?"

"Oh, yeah." I take a sip of my beer, taking my time setting it back on the table, because here is where I eat crow. "You're right, I need protection."

"From Stasia?" He sits back in his chair, the fleeting appearance of shock crossing his features.

I nod.

"Did she threaten you?"

"Well, not exactly."

"What *exactly* did she do?"

"She wanted to buy something."

"What is it she wants to buy from you?" Irritation is starting to creep through his stoic façade. I'd be a liar if I said it didn't amuse me, but there's only so far I can push him if I want help.

"Body fluids. Specifically, blood, but tears will do if I don't want to part with the red stuff."

Darkness descends across his features. He pulls back, not physically, but emotionally. "Did she elaborate on what she intends to do with your... blood?"

"Remember those lovely serums she produces? One of the main ingredients is the body fluids of

Ens. Mine would be used in an anti-aging formula, since I supposedly have the power to regenerate dead cells."

"There is no *supposedly* about it, you do have that Talent."

Sarcasm may be my second language, but it's apparent he and his counterpart don't recognize it, or maybe they chose to ignore it and me.

"What did you tell her?"

"Seriously? You have to ask? I said, no, of course."

"Is this when she threatened you?"

"Maybe threatened is too strong, she didn't actually come out and say, give me what I want or else. It was more implied that she could take what she wanted." I take another swig of liquid courage. "She said if I didn't want to play, let's make a deal, she'd go to someone who would."

Ric shakes his head. "No, that is not even a possibility."

"That's what I said, but she insists she has a *key*."

"Is this what you spoke with Lor—Mr. Royd about?"

"Yep, and he pretty much pooh-poohed the idea of anyone getting near Einen."

I don't bother mentioning my true intent was to sign up for his little club. I have a feeling the other two legs of the tripod won't be privy to my conversation with Royd. Yeah, I'm just special that way.

"Can I get you anything else?" Attitude knocked down a couple of notches, Jane managed to pick the perfect time to invade. I almost feel sorry for her, until she turns her red-rimmed eyes on me. If looks were daggers, I'd be shish-kebabbed. Like I said, almost.

"Just the check, Jane."

She opens her mouth to say something, but one look at Ric's austere expression changes her mind and she scurries off.

Pity a gator had to lose its fingers for my lunch and I didn't even have the decency to finish them. Guess I could ask for a box, but the thought of holding on to them on the back of a bike sounds even less appealing than finishing them. Besides, I have one more stop I want to make before heading back to The Meadows, someplace they don't allow food.

Chapter 5

"Would you mind making one more stop before you take me to my car?"

"That depends on the level of trouble you can get into with this stop."

"It's a public library, so the best you can hope for is getting tossed out for flipping off the librarian when she shushes me."

With an overly exaggerated sigh, he straddles the bike. "We shall stop at the library, if you promise to keep your middle fingers off display."

A little piggy snort of a laugh escapes as I climb on behind him. "Sorry, can't make that kind of promise, they often have a will of their own."

As we round a corner, I find myself scooching forward against him. Not sure if it's momentum, or I'm just taking advantage of the situation, either way, I'm not complaining.

I like the feel of leather and blue jean against the inside of my barely covered thighs. The broad back, I'm pressed against. The taut stomach my arms are wrapped around. The vibration of the cycle and road beneath me. I close my eyes for a moment, reveling in the sensations and then we come to a stop, probably not a moment too soon.

Reluctantly, I unwrap my arms and climb off the bike onto jellified legs, the copper and glass monstrosity of the Des Moines library before me. Those of us who loved the old world charm of the building that previously housed the library have a love hate relationship with the new one.

I understand the need for a new building—well, not really, considering it was renovated and now houses the World Food Prize—the design is what I have a problem with.

Where the old building was warm and scholarly, this one is mod and cold. And speaking of cold, whoever had the brilliant idea to put not only a flat roof, but one with a garden, on a building in Iowa should have been shown the door. Snow, people, lots of snow and it's heavy.

Ric follows me inside and my disdain for the building disappears as I try and figure out where to start. The card catalog is probably my best bet. I can imagine the look of horror on the reference librarian's face if I asked for what I need.

Can I help you?

Where do you keep the books on necromancy?

Yeah, that's gonna fly. Probably should've looked this stuff up online, but then I would've had Teiran hanging over my shoulder.

"Something in particular you are looking for, a romance perhaps?"

"Nope, don't do bodice rippers." I manage to keep from smiling at the clueless look on his face as I find the nearest catalog terminal.

Subject, necromancy. Wow, that was helpful. Mostly fiction and a couple of supremely outdated books on witchcraft. I'm going to have to rely on the Internet after all.

"Necromancy?" His warm breath tickles my ear. "Why would you be interested in necromancy?"

I delete the search and try again with necromancer. More fiction. I clear out my search history, no reason for the next person to see what I attempted to lookup. "Because, Mr. Smarty Pants, that's what I am and I want to know more about it."

He frowns. "Who told you that you are a necromancer?"

"None of your bee's wax, now let's go, there's nothing here to help me."

It sounds like someone letting the air out of the room with all the shushing. I tried to keep it quiet, but it galls me he's pretending not to know what I am.

Throwing my shoulders back and raising my head, I stalk past the glaring librarians, banding together as if their collective shush will reduce me to a quivering ball of flesh on the floor.

Silence follows as I meet each with a glare of my own. A secret, unkind smile growing as I reach the doors, I can't help turning and backing my way out of the building, a final sneer to those still staring through the glass. The urge to give them the double flip squashed by a you-better-not glare from a perturbed, vampire elf. Talk about sucking the fun out of everything.

Hysterical laughter bubbles out onto the sun-soaked pavement. Bent over, hands resting on my thighs, I go with it, not caring about the curious looks. Dusty boots come into view and I slowly stand. Flat, darkened amber eyes, pursed lips and crossed arms rip the last trace of merriment from me.

"I will give you points for keeping your fingers at bay, but you need to learn to control your temper."

"I pushed a little attitude, big deal, it's not like I was harming anyone."

Fingers run through hair, made even more gorgeous by the midday sunlight. "Did you not notice the movement?" He taps the collar.

Reaching up, I judge the distance between it and my neck, there's a slight difference in position. Damn. "Did you see it move? I didn't use my Talents."

"You did not realize you had called upon your Talents?"

"No, how did you know? There weren't any self-mobile shadows. Hel's Realm, I didn't even feel the usual precursors."

He flinches. "Your eyes changed, and please

stop saying *her* name. We do not need an unexpected visit."

"Sorry." Crap, creepy black eyes, no wonder the room silenced so quickly. As for *her*, I highly doubt the mistress of the dead will show up on the streets of Des Moines. She's more likely to show up in my nightmares, but he's right. Why take the chance.

"I suggest we leave, before anything else unexpected happens."

"No arguments here."

He stares at me for a moment, then shakes his head before climbing onto the bike.

"What, I can't agree with you?"

"Oh, you can agree, it just comes so rarely I was taken aback." The smile I love is back, amber eyes dancing with mischief.

My own lips curl in answer as I swing my leg over the purring machine, situating myself behind him, arms wrapping around his waist as we pull out into traffic.

Chapter 6

Entering the ramp onto I-235, I crank the music and merge into traffic. The 'Stang begs to go faster than the fifty-five limit, but I'm not in the mood for a ticket in my mailbox. She'll have to wait for sixty-five until we hit I-80.

A glimpse in the rear view mirror tells me the hot blond on the oxblood Valkyrie is still there. Like there's any doubt he'd keep up. The urge to lose him tickles at the back of my brain, but why court trouble I don't need? I have plenty without even trying, like the stinking pile I have to deal with back home.

Home. My shoulders slump with the weight of dealing with Teiran. Yeah, I created the problem, but it doesn't mean I want to deal with it. I'd rather crawl into bed, pull the covers over my head and wish it all gone. Or grab a bottle of red, sit on the couch and ignore whatever comes from between those plump, sensual lips of his. I squirm in the seat. *Bad, Keely, bad.*

I flip through the stations on the radio. Whiny ballads, blah. Crappy boy bands, even worse. Head banger's ball, not in the mood. Finally, something I can get into. Oldies or classic hits from the eighties. Oldies, sheesh, it hasn't been that long. That's probably how the Baby Boomers feel about what I call oldies.

Merging onto I-80, I check the rear view again; Ric continues to hang at a safe distance behind me. Hopefully, he'll stick around once we reach The Meadows, it'd be nice to have a little backup with Teiran. Little being the key word. I know he won't interfere with the tongue lashing I'm bound to get, but he won't let him kill me. Can't and don't expect more.

My stomach plummets. The last real conversation I had with Teiran is another reason I want Ric to stick around. I'd needled him about having a crush on Vana Royd. That little slip of the tongue had shifted our strained relationship to another level of awkward. Reducing any conversation with him to a series of grunts and nastier than usual looks.

I don't know what got into me, or even why I'd lowered myself to the level of high school mean girl. Can't keep blaming it on my Talents emerging, or the stress of everything that's happened. I need to chill out and think before I open my mouth, instead of acting like a prepubescent school girl.

The stop and go action of the traffic lights, that keep popping up along highway 141 as the surrounding cities continue to expand, add to my agitation. I'm all for growth, but it's a highway for crying out loud, put in a stinking frontage road. The only thing they're good for is putting down the top on the car.

When I opened Fey Creations, my first real check went to having the manual top replaced for just this purpose. Nothing like that little rush when people stare in envy at your car, except the jaw dropping response as you lower the top at a stoplight. The downside? I miss my hair whipping in the wind. That could've been remedied if Var wouldn't have rejected my acceptance of becoming his Shadow.

I wonder why he didn't jump on the chance. Is he that secure about where he's stashed Einen? Then again, did he stash Einen somewhere, or is it all a bluff? Ric said he was banished, but what exactly does that mean? Did they put him in some magical prison? If that's the case, how was I able to visit? You'd think it would keep people out as well as in. If it weren't for this damn collar I'd attempt to find him again.

The exit for The Meadows looms in the windshield and my tummy does a little flip. I could easily continue my journey down the highway to the next town. Hel, if I stay on this road in three hours I'd be back in Sioux City, but then what? Go see The Sisters? Hide at Annya's? It's no use, Teiran and Ric would find me and bring me back, kicking and screaming to The Meadows. And the last thing I want is to endanger any of them with the mess I've got here. Taking a deep breath, I flip on the turn signal and glide the 'Stang onto the exit ramp, three hundred and ninety horses protesting all the way.

Edging closer to home, my pulse throbs in my ears. *Breathe, just breathe, Keely.* The closer I get, the more the more intense the pounding, until it encapsulates my skull. Mel's tea, I forgot to drink a cup before leaving this morning. Hel's Realm, that's all I need, the chain reaction of headache, errant Talents, death by collar.

Ric pulls in behind me and dismounts while I raise the top. He opens the garage door as I latch the top into place and motions me forward. Heart and head now keep time with the thump of the stereo. I reach over and turn the knob, slowly pulling into the blessed darkness of the garage.

"Until you turn off the engine and come outside, I cannot close the door."

His softly spoken words thunder in my pain addled brain. The urge to cover my ears is almost too much to resist. Nodding is out of the question, it takes all my willpower to climb out of the 'Stang without giving away my swift decent into the vortex of pain.

He closes the car door and I brace myself against the rear fender, knees buckling. Everyday white noise becomes a torrent of eardrum piecing hel and my stomach begins to revolt.

"Keely?"

The simple act of shaking my head fills my mouth with bile as I feel my way out into the blinding sunlight. Thank the gods for sunglasses, without them I'd be rendered incapable of the act of navigating even the shaded areas to my building.

"Keely?"

I feel his hand on my arm and bite my lower lip to keep from begging him to carry me the rest of the way. Once inside the cool near darkness the pain diminishes enough, I'm able to shuffle up the stairs, using the wall to keep upright. Gods, I hate headaches, especially the knee buckling, vomit inducing, I just want to curl up in the fetal position and die variety. The only thing worse is what's waiting for me on the other side of my apartment door.

Chapter 7

The eyes truly are windows and I can see the nearly white hot flame of Teiran's anger reflected as pale blue through my tinted lenses. Luckily his attention wavers to the man behind me and I'm able to slip past him into the kitchen.

"Where did you find her?"

"Lor-Mr. Royd's building."

With an inhuman swivel those flaming eyes are back on moi. Damn.

"What was she doing at *Lord* Royd's building?"

The question is for Ric, but his gaze is only for me, and I don't miss the little dig of emphasizing lord. Screw him, my head hurts way too much to deal with his temper tantrums. If this keeps up, I may have to dig out the pain pills.

Dropping my purse and keys on the table, I try to tune them out and search the fridge for a Pepper. The rhythm of pain accelerates as their voices raise. I don't give a tiny rat's ass what they're saying; I just want them to shut up. Almost more than I want to regain control over my life.

A hand closes around my forearm as I move toward the bathroom. I attempt to shake it off, knowing it belongs to Teiran without even looking.

"How did you evade me again?"

Ignoring the question, I continue on my path to the bathroom only to be jerked back. His grip tightens and I picture the imprints his fingers will leave.

"Get, your hand off me."

"I asked you a question now answer and take off those glasses."

The utter lack of civility amplifies my anger. I turn toward him, slowly removing my sunglasses and stare him down. "Get. Your. Hand. Off. Me."

He loosens the grip on my arm, but not his anger. A small smirk turns my lips when his Adam's apple rises and falls, but it's short lived. The collar begins a slow progression to the base of my throat as his hand drops. I raise my head, an empty attempt at bravado, secretly hoping he'll stop it before it detaches my head from my body. Without me having to ask.

His eyes narrow, the smirk I once wore now graces his face and it's my turn to swallow fear. I don't want to back down, don't want to beg him to stop it, but it looks like I've entered a pissing match I can't win.

"Stop acting like children." Ric's voice breaks the uncomfortable silence. "Teiran, halt the torque."

Teiran's smile widens, a small flicker of pleasure in his eyes before he reaches out and places his hand against my chest. The curve from thumb to forefinger resting on the shrinking band, stopping its progression just as it bites into my skin. Pulling his hand away, he raises it, making sure I see the red smear and probably the closest thing to a real smile—teeth and all—I've ever seen on Teiran's face.

My headache, forgotten during our little tiff, finds its way back as my own fingers touch the wetness along my throat. My anger follows close behind, the bastard got off on shedding my blood. Of course, he did, he's been saying how much he's wanted to kill me since we met. Why should it be a surprise the sight of my blood trips his trigger? Asshat.

Ric moves toward me, probably to inspect the damage and I wave him off before heading to the bathroom. I'll do the inspecting, thank you. Sure enough, a line of red rings my throat, slowly making its way downward in drips and smears. Strangely, the torque—as Ric called it—is clean. What did the damn thing do, drink my blood? Wouldn't put it past the evil, nasty thing.

I turn the water on full blast, hoping it will drown out the conversation in the next room. I care even less about what they're discussing than I did before. Grabbing a washcloth, I attempt to wipe away the remnants of my power play with Teiran. My anger builds as the blood continues to flow. The angrier I get, the more I scrub. The more I scrub, the more the blood flows. And so goes the vicious cycle, until my neck is stained red.

The color of my eyes wavers from charcoal to obsidian as I fight to hold my emotions in check. If this damn collar has acquired a taste for my blood, the last thing I need is to lose my cool. Taking a deep breath, I slowly let it out, grab a clean cloth, and attempt to gently clean up my blood coated neck.

Before the line of red can thicken, I make a gauze choker to stanch the flow, wrapping it until blood no longer seeps through. How is it, the smallest cuts bleed the most?

Gods, I hate Teiran right now and absolutely do not want to go back out there, but pride won't let me hide in the bathroom forever. Anger loosely covered, I head back to the living room, knowing full well the interrogation is about to begin.

Ric frowns, looking at the gauze decorating my neck. Teiran merely lifts his chin, waiting for me to say something. I don't take the bait, at least not verbally. Walking past him to the forgotten can of soda, I manage to *accidentally* rock him back on his heels with a full body brush.

"Excuse you."

A cough comes from Ric's direction, glad he finds this amusing. I might find it amusing too, if it was someone else fighting with Teiran, but not so much when it's me. Grabbing the can, I lean against the counter watching them watch me. As uncomfortable as it is, it's still better than what's about to come.

Teiran crosses his arms across the wide expanse of chest, legs slightly apart for maximum balance as if he expects me to push him again. And I just might if I don't like what comes out of his mouth.

"Care to explain yourself?"

"In what way?"

"What you were doing downtown."

"I image your buddy already told you."

"I wish to hear your explanation, not Alric's."

"Fine." I take a swig of carbonated caffeine, then set the can aside. "I went downtown to have coffee."

"You have coffee here."

"I wanted froufrou coffee."

"You could have gone across the street for *froufrou* coffee."

I should have stopped when his jaw began to twitch, but getting under Teiran's skin is one of the few slightly enjoyable things I still have control over. "I wanted Java Joe's froufrou coffee."

"Keely…" Ric shakes his head. "Remember our conversation?"

He's right, after the trouble I've inadvertently caused the least I owe Teiran is the truth. "I went to meet with Stasia Athory."

"What possessed you to meet with that woman, especially alone?"

"I wanted to know what she's up to and knew she wouldn't talk to me with you in tow."

"And did you find out, *what she's up to?*"

"In a nutshell? No good." My anger with Teiran and life in general is pushed aside by fear. "She wants my blood."

Chapter 8

"What could she want with your blood?" If I didn't know any better, I'd take Teiran's tone as sarcasm.

"Her latest anti-aging potion. She said I could give her tears if I'm not willing to part with the red stuff."

"And you wonder why you should not have met with that woman alone."

"Yeah, well, if I hadn't I wouldn't have found out she's willing to use another's body fluids if the deal with me doesn't pan out."

"Who might that be?"

"Um, your favorite person, next to me that is."

Teiran's brow nearly hits his hairline. "There is no possible way such a deal can be struck."

"She claims to have a key that will allow her to close the deal."

"There is no such thing."

"Yeah, that's what your partner and your boss said, but I'm not willing to take that chance."

"Really."

"Yes, really."

"I would have thought you would have jumped at the chance of releasing your lover."

Okay, fear hits the road and anger moves back in. "First, he's not my lover. Second, if he's as bad as you guys claim, you should be on board with finding out if she's bluffing, or if this *key* really exists."

"It does not exist."

I take a step forward and poke a finger against Teiran's chest. "You guys are way too confident in your *Mr.* Royd and whatever he's done with Einen. Try and be a little more realistic here, *nothing* is foolproof."

"Do not worry over what *Lord* Royd has done with your precious Einen. There is no possibility of *anyone* getting near him."

I may be dumb, but I'm not stupid, I know that *anyone* means me. The exaggerated pulse raging between my ears becomes a ball-peen hammer.

"This has nothing to do with me wanting to get near Einen and everything to do with a crazy bitch using En parts for her beauty products. I'm trying my best to be reasonable here. I've had enough of people wanting a part of me for some warped craft project."

"All the more reason for you to stop sneaking out on your own and obey the rules of your release. I should be with you at all times, then you would not become a *craft project*."

"Don't take this personally, but you're a...an asshat."

If I wasn't so pissed the utter confusion and dropped jaw would be hilarious. Ric's poor attempt at covering the humor he finds in my word choice tells me at least one of them has an inkling of what it means.

Confusion fades to restrained anger as Teiran glances from his friend to me. Maybe he's figured it out too, or at least that it was derogatory.

"Do not think I will allow you to make a fool of me thrice, my own conditions concerning your freedom shall be put into effect immediately."

"Oh, so now you're calling the shots?" I tap my fingers against the back of the chair next to me.

"Yes. You shall never again leave the premises without me. As a matter of fact, you shall only leave to go to your employment, unless previously discussed and agreed to by me."

Darkness hangs on the outer edges of my vision, a warning sign I choose to ignore. "Oh, hel no. I'll come and go as I see fit, with or without you. I'm a grown-ass-woman and I don't need you making decisions for me."

"You have not shown yourself to be a *grown-ass-woman*, you act and react like a child. From here on out you shall do as I say, when I say."

"I change my mind, you're not an asshat, you're a prick and please do take that personally."

Narrowed eyes blaze and fists form at his sides. Have I triggered an eruption?

I clench my teeth as a familiar itch builds under my skin. Light takes my sight, stabbing like a million tiny pin pricks as the shadows blanketing the corners of the room darken and stretch outward. Closing my eyes, I can see the brick wall holding back my Talents, shudder and warp. Nails bite into my palms, as I will the bricks back into place, the pain in my head intensifying. This isn't normal.

I may have skipped Mel's tea this morning, but that isn't what's going on here. It isn't just my anger triggering my Talents either. It's something more, something pushing its way in, not out.

"Keely, are you all right?" Ric's voice is garbled, tinny.

"Miss Fey?" I sense a hint of humanity in Teiran's tone; then again, I've been mistaken before. Makes me wish I could see his face, but my eyes are so dry I'm afraid my corneas will stick to my eyelids.

"Fine, I'm fine." My words coated with the film of my metaphysical wall, a tongue of sandpaper attempts to moisten equally dry lips to no avail.

"Your actions and appearance are anything but fine, Keely. Perhaps you should sit." I feel my head swivel back and forth, then up and down in the direction of Ric's voice.

Gingerly, I turn. Fingers reach for the chair I could have sworn was beside me and grasp empty air. I stumble, my midsection connecting with an object that slides. Probably the missing chair.

"Good gods, woman, open your eyes before you harm yourself."

"I do not think she can." The gentle pressure of Ric's hand on my arm—at least I think it's Ric's—steadies and guides me to a chair.

"Should we call a doctor?"

"I do not know. Keely, do you need a doctor?"

"No. No doctors. I'll be fine. Water. I'd like some water."

The clomping of feet. The creak of a cupboard. The clink of glass. Water as the tap is turned on. Every sound intensified tenfold. Everything hurts, but I can't stop concentrating on keeping my walls place. If I fail…I don't want to think about what might happen if I fail.

Someone grasps my hand, pressing my fingers around a glass and lifts it to my lips. Cool, wet hits my tongue and I gulp it down. Foolish, foolish girl water mixed with the dust—real or metaphysical—makes a sticky, chalky concoction that triggers a disastrous chain of events.

It coats the tongue. Gags the throat. Blocks the passage of air. Breaks the concentration. A ribbon of bricks unravels, falling inward. Grit fills my ears, muffling the voices of my self-proclaimed protectors. Protectors who have no power here, they cannot protect me from what lies beyond the haze.

Chapter 9

As the dust settles, a cloaked figure emerges. A glimmer of hope arises, could it be Einen? Fear quickly squelches that tiny flame as every sense screams death. Not the dead, but Death, with a capital D. Has the reaper come to claim the collar's offering?

Instinctively, my fingers reach for the nasty piece. Nope, still in place, well below the gauze-wrapped reminder of our last encounter. I turn, looking for escape, somewhere to hide. With none in sight, I reach for the next best thing. A weapon and there's a whole pile of them at my disposal. A brick in each hand, I face the cloaked figure making the painfully slow journey toward me.

"You're not taking me. I'm not ready to go." I let one of the bricks fly, pathetically it lands about six feet in front of me. Gods, I throw like a girl.

The figure wavers and before I can pick up another it appears again, barely a foot in front of me. I ready the other brick, but the forward motion of my arm is cut short and it tumbles from my hand. And running is not an option. My feet are super glued to the ground.

"Is this how you greet those who come to your aid, Schattenkind?"

"You."

"Yes, me." The hood lowers revealing a bisected beauty and beast. "Now explain yourself."

"I'm sorry, I didn't realize…I thought my time was up and I'm not ready to die."

Hollow and grating, exquisite and musical, Hel's laughter rolls over me in an odd combination of revulsion and pleasure. "Trust me, you will know when your time has come. I will send an engraved invitation."

That's a promise even scarier than not knowing. "What can I do for you?"

"As usual, it is not what you can do for me, but what I can do for you."

Here we go again, promises of help that never quite help. "I did what you said. I went to Var and accepted the job."

"And?"

"And he turned me down. I don't get it. He's the one who wanted me, not the other way around."

"How did you approach him?"

"I told him I wanted the job."

The one and only eyebrow she has rises.

"Okay, fine, I went in desperation. I'd just met with Stasia Athory, who propositioned me about her newest anti-aging cream. Something about the regenerative powers of my blood.

"Anyway, when I refused, she said she had another who would cooperate. I panicked and went to Var. I mean, what if she has some way to get to Einen and he's as bad as everyone says? What if she lets him out and he wreaks havoc on the world? It would be my fault." Amazing how good it feels to dump your trash at someone else's door.

"No wonder he *turned you down*. He wants you to come of your own volition. It does him no good if you are forced into his service under false pretenses."

"Yeah, but what if…"

"If ifs and buts were candy and nuts. None of that matters in the case of the Sun King, even if it were true that this Stasia Athory could get to Vereinen, he would never admit to it. You need to make him believe you truly want the position that you have no ulterior motives. As for this woman, you obviously fear, put her out of your mind until you are the Shadow. Only then can you deal with her."

"By then it might be too late."

"That is what I am counting on." Her laugh works my flesh like a cheese grater as she fades into the mist.

Annoyingly, incessant patting of my face and hand, pulls me from the grime coated recesses of my mind.

"Keely."

"Miss Fey."

Yanking my hand loose from one aggravating elf, I push the hand of the other away from my face. "I'm fine."

"You were hardly *fine*, you blacked out for several minutes." The concern on Teiran's face is something more at home on Ric's, and it sets my tummy a quiver.

"He is right. Perhaps we should call a doctor. This may be a lingering symptom from…"

"My incarceration?" I finish the sentence for him, it's evident he still feels responsible for my treatment. And truthfully he is, he's the one who brought me there, but I can't hold it against him. He was just doing his job. And telling them it had nothing to do with my jail time and everything to do with a goddess I owe a favor is not an option.

"I agree. We should call Dr. Herbert."

"Look, I'm just tired. We partied all night, then I got up early this morning. I'm running on like three, maybe four hours of sleep."

Teiran opens his mouth, then closes it and I have a pretty good idea of what he was going to say. 'Who's fault is that? Had you not run off to a secret meeting at a coffee shop you would have gotten plenty of sleep.' Probably not in those words, but he's right. Not that I'll ever admit it out loud.

"And maybe a little hungry, all I've had is coffee, beer and a few gator fingers."

His frown deepens and he turns on Ric. "You did not feed her?"

"I tried, but things were…complicated."

It's like watching a couple fight over an unfed pet and would be funny if I weren't the pet in question. Oh, hel, CC. "Hey, Teiran did you feed CC?"

"CC?"

"My cat."

"Please tell me that does not stand for Kitty with a C, Cat, or Cat Cat."

"It's short of Captain Curiosity, did you feed him?"

"A fitting name for a cat and yes, I fed your familiar. I believe he is in your bedroom doing one of the few things cats do best."

"Thanks." I ignore the cat verses dog animosity, calculating how much I have in my slush fund, pizza is probably the most affordable. Having eaten with him, I have a pretty good idea how much Teiran can eat, probably an extra-large on his own. Ric's another story, I've seen him nibble—hel, I've felt him nibble—but I've never seen him *eat*, as in real food, a full meal. "How about we order pizza?"

"I believe we should order more than one." Ric tips his head toward the door.

With the rap of an off kilter rhythm and turn of the knob, Rey's voice fills the apartment. "Everyone recovered from last night's festivities?"

Chapter 10

Rey waltzes into the kitchen, Nyssa in tow. "Oh, hey Ric didn't know you'd be here too."

"Keely and I had lunch and came back here to chat."

Nyssa's lips round into a silent oooo and Rey wiggles his brow at me.

Pervs, I mouth behind Ric's back. "We were just about to order pizza, care to join us?"

"What do ya think Nys? Shall we have pie with elves tonight?"

"As long as they don't get all esoteric on us and start playing flutes and harps."

"I believe you are thinking of the Celtic race." Disdain is visibly plastered across Teiran's face.

"It was a joke, Mr. Serious."

"I am glad you find them a joke also."

"Whoa, wait a minute, Teiran made a joke? And is that a smile? Keep it up. It gets easier. Not to mention, you're quite the hottie when you smile." She winks at him.

Ric kneels beside my chair as Rey rummages through the fridge muttering about beer and Nyssa continues to poke and prod at Teiran about smiling.

"Where did you go?" His voice soft, secretive.

"I don't know what you mean. I didn't go anywhere. I've been here the whole time."

"That was no simple blackout, what really happened?"

I lean toward Ric and lower my voice. I know Rey can probably hear us, but his foraging moves from fridge to cupboards, bringing him closer. And I'm in no mood to have an open discussion about my so-called blackout. "I told you, I'm tired and hungry. It's not like I have the power to time travel, or border hop."

He frowns and shakes his head. "You cannot expect help or trust if you do not reciprocate."

Tipping my head back, I stare at the ceiling and sigh. "Fine, I was attempting to strengthen my shields and it took all of my concentration. If my Talents decide to surface, I'm a dead woman. We've already proven that's a very real possibility and I don't want a repeat."

Tilting my head to the side, fingers lightly touching the gauze, I hope he takes the hint and drops the subject. Too late, I look up to see two suspicious sets of eyes on me.

"What's up with the nasty fashion statement?" Rey tips his head toward me, holding out a bag of chips to Nyssa who waves it away and walks over to me.

"I had a little mishap."

Ignoring my protesting slaps to her fingers, she unwinds my bandage, revealing the razor-thin cut encircling my throat. "Holy death by paper cut."

"What? Shaving?" Rey asks, around a mouthful of chips.

"Ha ha, no, with my control."

"Where was he?" He glares at Teiran.

"Close by, thank gods."

"Uh huh." Rey shovels a handful of chips into his mouth, doubt plainly displayed on his face.

"So, who's going to order the pizza?" I look around the room, hoping food is enough of a distraction to get off the subject of me and my *paper cut*.

Ric stands, pulling a cell from his pocket. "I assume you prefer Basement Brews, are there any requests as to toppings?"

"Keely hates cockroaches." Nyssa grins at the confusion on Ric's face.

"I'm not terribly fond of black olives, but I can pick them off if everyone else wants them."

He looks to the others. "Are there objections to leaving off the black olives on at least one of the pizzas?"

Rey and Nyssa shake their heads and Teiran shrugs.

I stand and grab the half a dozen empty growlers from the one cupboard Teiran didn't rearrange. "I'd suggest getting at least four extra-large pizzas and we can take these to be refilled. Whoever picks up dinner gets to choose what we're drinking tonight."

Rey raises his hand. "I'll do it."

"Oh no you won't, or at least not by yourself. We'll end up drinking some nasty hoppy creation."

"You can go with him, Nys and make sure he only gets one growler full." I turn Ric and Teiran. "Unless you guys like bitter, hoppy beers."

"It matters not what we drink."

"Now I know you're lying, Teiran." There is no way Mr. Culinary doesn't care what beverage we pair with dinner. "Why don't you go along and help choose."

He opens his mouth to protest then closes it. I so don't want to air our dirty laundry in front of Rey and Nys, who are watching the exchange like hawks.

"Fine, I shall accompany the Fox and Sprite across the street."

Wow, can he be any more subtle? He might as well have said, 'Don't try to leave while I'm gone.' I mean really, where the hel am I going to go? I'm not in the mood to repeat our discussion of my traveling habits. "Thank you."

He grabs my arm as I pass. "Where are you going?"

"Downstairs to grab some cash, so you can pay for dinner."

"There is no need. I will take care of the bill."

"Yeah, don't worry about it, Keely." Rey crumples the empty chip bag, tossing it in the trash. "We'll all pitch in, right Nys?"

"Sure."

"Whatever you guys want. Just no triple garlic, garlic bread with Dara's name on it, okay, Rey?"

"Oh, come on, it's funny."

"It was funny the first time."

"It's a tradition."

"Well, it's time to break the tradition."

"Whatever."

"The order will be ready in approximately thirty minutes."

"Thank you, Ric. Those three are going to pick it up, if you have any requests on the drink front let them know."

He glances from me to Teiran and back, a small smile turning his lips as he lowers his head. He's probably just as surprised as I am that my babysitter agreed without protest. Especially after the stink he made about me never leaving his side. And then it hits me like a shovel. I'm going to be alone in my apartment with Ric.

Chapter 11

Sweaty palms and topsy-turvy tummy ensue. Sure, I'd just had lunch with him, but that was in a restaurant, so technically we weren't alone, alone. As the unlikely trio head out the door, I nearly scream, 'Wait, Teiran needs to stay here,' but that would upset my tiny victory. Not to mention raise my blood pressure, I'm sure he's not done chastising me.

Ric turns to me as the door closes. "Now will you tell me what happened? I know you were not simply strengthening your shields. Your consciousness had fled; your body was an empty shell."

I shake my head, even if I wanted to discuss it, I don't know what to say.

"Keely, if there is to be any trust between us you must be truthful. Where did you go?" His brows pull together and looking down tells me why. My right hand covers the approximate area of my stitches hidden by the brace. "Is that where you were? She called you?"

Trying to shake my head again, it comes out as a strange circular nod.

Pulling a chair around, he sits, gently moving my hand away from the brace. "How often has she called?"

"A couple."

Slowly, he loosens the straps of the brace. I know he's trying to be gentle, but the grating sound of plastic fingers pulling away from the fuzzy base tingles along my spine and I wish he'd just rip them open.

"Where does she bring you?" Setting the cloth and plastic contraption on the table, he turns my wrist, exposing the scar.

"She says Niflheim."

The frown tugging at his lips grows. "We need to find a way to keep her from summoning you at will."

"Can we remove the mark? Like plastic surgery or something?"

"You could try, but I do not think it would do any good. What she has done goes deeper than a physical mark."

"So, like a spell?"

He nods. "Very much so."

"Is there something to counter act it? Another spell or charm I could wear?"

"I suppose it is possible, but I am not the one to ask."

"Then who?"

"Lord—*Mr.* Royd might—"

"Nope. No way. Not gonna happen. I'll find someone else."

"And how do you intend upon going about finding someone else?"

"I'll figure it out, but there is no way I'm going to him for this."

Thankfully, his jaw slams shut with the authoritative double rap on the door. It opens a crack and I sigh with relief, only one person in my life would be so hesitant to enter before full dark. The cavalry has arrived to save me from discussing dealings with *Lord* Royd.

"Keely? Are you home?"

"Hold on Dara, give me a second to close the drapes." Shaking his fingers loose from my wrist, I move to close the light blocking curtains. "Okay, come on in, it's safe."

Coinciding with the door swinging open there's a double thump followed by the rhythmic jingle of tags and stream of undecipherable cateese. I try and fool myself into believing I'm CC's number one, but Dara clearly outranks me. Kindred spirits? Respect? Knowing CC, it's the need to feel worshiped, he probably considers himself on the same level with Dara's cat goddess.

After a brief scratch behind the ears, she steps through the cat's figure eight movements and slides into the farthest chair from Ric. "Sword."

"Miss Kanika."

"Have you come to visit your dog?"

"No." He smiles. "Keely and I had lunch and I escorted her home."

She watches me from under enviable lashes.

"You're just in time. We sent the others to pick up pizza and beer." Somehow I feel the need to let her know we've had chaperons. No idea why, it's not like she's my mother. I shouldn't have to explain myself to anyone, but that look, it triggers the explain yourself gene.

Her upper lip twists. "Oh, lovely, garlic bread."

I shake my head. "Ric placed the order, just beer and pizza."

"Do you have an aversion to garlic bread, Miss Kanika?"

"No, I have an aversion to a fox who thinks the idea of it is amusing."

Ric chuckles. "He does push the boundaries, does he not?"

"Do you think it wise to be without your brace?" She looks from the itchy contraption to my uncovered wrist.

"It gets uncomfortable and it's not like I'm doing any heavy lifting."

"We were discussing the possibility of a charm or counter spell to dissuade *Her* from calling."

"She is summoning you?"

Gee, thanks for outing my secret before I'm ready. Damn nosy elf. "Yeah."

"Perhaps you have a suggestion, Miss Kanika."

Blood red claws click against the table. "I suppose cutting it out would be of no use."

"What the… I'm not some science experiment you can dissect." Like my arm, my little outburst is shoved under the table.

"No, just as I explained to Keely, such tactics would be of no use. She needs a charm or counter spell. I suggested she speak with Mr. Royd—"

"No. His interference is not what she needs."

"He may be able to—"

"No. There is enough of his influence in her life with you and the dog. The last thing she needs is the Sun King tampering with the mark. There has to be another way."

I grit my teeth, hoping Ric doesn't spill the beans about Royd offering me Einen's job. I need to be the one to tell her. After all, her goddess charged her to watch me, with a very real possibility of killing me if I step out of line. Someone else telling her would have me walking a very thin line, but combined with the mark and Hel using it to summon me…that combination may shove me over the line.

I understand why Ric thinks I should talk to Var, but I have to agree with Dara. I do not need his help with this. What if he decides it makes me a liability instead of an asset? Then it would just be a race to see who kills me first, Dara or Royd.

No matter how much I trust Dara, I'm leaning to the side of caution and figuring this out myself.

"Mel." I slap a hand against the table and they stop bickering mid-sentence, almost shocked to see me. About time they remember the object of their discussion is right here. "I'll go ask Mel. End of discussion."

Chapter 12

I stand in a large room, back against two massive doors. They won't open. I've already tried. The size lends itself to more of an auditorium or convention center, but there's nothing in it except a set of steps leading to a raised platform. On that platform sits what can only be described as a throne, and on that throne sits a woman in a long flowing white gown.

When I reach the halfway point the angelic garb morphs to brown leathers and shining, formfitting breast plate. Her hair, long intricate plaits decorated with feathers and jewels. One leg thrown over the arm of the throne, a sword dangling precariously from her fingertips. Her face wavers the closer I get. My vision blurring as I come to a stop at the foot of the first step.

The woman so comfortably lounging there is the most beautiful thing I've ever seen. Not beautiful. Perfect. No airbrushing or makeup tricks needed for this chick. I find myself wishing she at least had a zit in the middle of her forehead. No plastic surgery could produce this type of perfection. The symmetry of her features are exact, not a single imperfection, as if she'd been designed and made instead of born. A fashion doll come to life.

Her eyes are a strange swirl of summer. Sun, sky and cloud. Something tells me not to bother stretching the truth because they would see right through any lie. I know I've seen those eyes before, but can't place the when and where. The braids and trinkets fall away with the leathers, leaving her hair casually framing that gorgeous face and a cloak of feathers the body.

As she shifts upon the throne the mass of feathers parts and I can see the rest of her is just as flawless. Nothing too big or small. Perfectly proportioned. The only thing that rivals her perfection is an intricate netting of gold studded with amber, draped delicately across her shoulders and collarbone, dripping down across her bare breasts. This woman changes costumes more than Cher. Only someone this perfect can pull off this kind of confidence naked.

Neither of us speaks. Not because I don't want to, but because I can't get my mouth to work. I just stand here like a dolt. Then she smiles and the whole room tilts and spins. Warmth boils up inside me, something I've never felt before, at least not with a woman. That smile makes me seriously consider switching teams, or at least playing switch-hitter. The smile widens as she strokes the golden chains around her neck, stopping to twist an amber teardrop between her fingers.

Light flashes, filling me with need as I feel those fingers twist and tug. I find myself on the first step, then another. She tosses back that mane of wheat colored hair and laughs, before giving the chunk of amber another twist. I fall to my knees at the edge of the platform reaching out toward her. She lets the gem fall and smiles as she leans toward me, her hands cupping the sides of my face. Her breath a soft breeze as I close my eyes and tasting summer as her lips brush mine. When I open them, the elaborate chain and stone concoction is a single chunk of amber dangling from a chain and that beautiful laughing face becomes all too recognizable.

Vana Royd.

Laughter turns into feline howling and I wake in a sweaty, twisted pile of sheets, with twenty pounds of cat sitting on me. Crap. That's what I get for eating before bed, or maybe it was one too many beers. I've had some pretty messed up dreams, but that one takes the cake. What in Hel's Realm would trigger erotic dreams about a woman who's made my life a living hel? I know she hates everything about me and the feeling is mutual, but that dream. In that moment I felt... I don't know what I felt and I definitely don't want to analyze the why and how.

Untangling myself from the sheets, I scramble out of bed, grab my robe and head to the bathroom.

Water, the hotter the better, and soap. Not sure if it will erase the images and imagined reactions, but it's a start. If the loofah was made of steel wool, that might work. Eww, just eww. I scrub until greyish-white flesh becomes flushed-with-blood pink. Wish I could pull out my brain and scrub it too. Again, eww.

"Miss Fey."

"What the hel do you want?" Okay, maybe that was a little harsh, but oh well.

"You have a phone call."

"Take a freakin' message, I'll call 'em back later." It's not like he can't tell I'm busy.

Aw, crap, what if it was The Sisters? I can hear it now.

Why is there a man answering your phone, did he stay the night? Are you living in sin? Is it serious? When is the wedding?

So much for standing here until the water is cold. Hair haphazardly wrapped, still tying my robe, I rush into the living room. "Who was it?" Please, please, please don't let it have been The Sisters.

His slow head to toe gaze has me pulling at my robe, heat building in my stomach. With a casual flick of his head that doesn't jive with the intensity in his eyes, he motions to the phone. "Find out yourself."

I pick up the handset, the little green light

indicating someone on the other end. "Hello?"

"Teiran had told me you would be a while. I do hope you did not rush your shower just for me, Miss Fey." The deep, warmth of his voice wraps itself around me, turning my legs to jelly.

Shit. This is much worse than The Sisters. "No, Mr. Royd, I was finished." The sharp buzz of the intercom nearly causes me to drop the phone. "Can you hold a minute?"

"For you, I can hold an eternity."

Essh, what the hel? I hold the phone against my shoulder and press the intercom. "Yes?"

"Delivery for a Keely Fey."

Teiran pushes past me and out the door, before I can answer.

"Hold on a minute, someone will be right down." I take a deep breath, then lift the phone to my ear, trying to channel my polite business persona when all I want to do is hang up. So not in the mood for the king of manipulation. "Now, Mr. Royd, what can I do for you?"

"You can dine with me this evening."

"I, uh, I have plans, maybe some other time."

"Then change them, I will call for you at eight."

With a click I have silence that quickly turns to a sharp beep as what looks like a garden pushes its way through the half-open door. Teiran and half a dozen delivery flunkies begin populating every available flat surface with floral arrangements. My apartment looks like a cross between a funeral and a wedding gone bad by the time they're done and the smell is overpowering. Snagging the card from the largest, most ostentatious arrangement—a mean feat, considering the abundance of them—I immediately recognize the artfully scrawled hand writing. The last time I saw it was on the back of a business card.

Var Royd.

Chapter 13

"For crying out loud, what the hel am I supposed to do with all these?" I toss the envelope on the counter. Its contents can wait.

"Um, enjoy them?" The head flunky shrugs, pocketing the bills handed over by Teiran.

"Maybe you guys can take them back. Give them away on the street or something."

"No ma'am, we just deliver them to the address given. What you do with them after is your choice."

"You mean problem," I mutter, turning to look at the ridiculous display. "Who in their right mind sends," I give up counting after the third straight up dozen and sixth fancy arrangement, I don't have enough fingers, "this many flowers?"

"In this business, either a man in love or a man apologizing for something," says the delivery guy, holding onto his laughter until he's in the hall.

Crossing my arms, I look at Teiran. "Well?"

"Well, what?"

"What the hel am I going to do with all this?"

"I suggest you stop and smell the flowers." The evil glint in his big blues is enough to make me grind my teeth.

"The smell is enough to knock someone out and you can't move in here without knocking one of them over." My little tirade loosing traction as the towel slips on my head. "They've got to go, or I'm going to move them into the spare bedroom."

That gets me a raised brow. Yeah, I look intimidating in my raggedy-ass bathrobe and towel flopped over one eye. I vacate the dead wedding, muttering, "That's right jackass, your room."

Slamming the door, I slump against it, pulling the half kilter turban from my head and toss it on the bed. CC wakes long enough to do the stretch and yawn bit, sniff the towel and give me the stink eye. My waker of bad dreams deserves better, but it's been a bad, bad start of the day. First, a ridiculously disturbing dream, then a ridiculously annoying call and now a ridiculous display of the frivolous use of money.

Making matters worse, I haven't had my first cup of coffee and after my little shout and stomp I can't show my face for at least…what, fifteen, twenty minutes? Damn it.

Grabbing items from random draws and tossing them on the bed, my typical summer day off attire begins to take shape. Undies, shorts and a tank. Resentment and anger stir as I reach for a bra. Normally, I skip them when I don't plan on leaving the house, but with my roomie, I've been forced to wear them constantly.

Okay, maybe forced isn't the right word. Something tells me Teiran wouldn't complain if I let what little I have hang loose, but I feel funny without that extra layer in mixed company.

Lack of coffee, grumpy morning muttering continues down the hall to the bathroom. Luckily, fixing my hair consists of running my fingers through it until it looks somewhat presentable and the world will survive my bare face. Sunday is a makeup optional day.

I glare at the wrist brace on the vanity, knowing I should follow doctor's orders and the need to keep my damn scar covered, but it's ninety degrees in the shade. The last thing I'm looking forward to is a layer of sweat under that itchy, stiff thing. Screw it, if Teiran has a problem with me not wearing it, he'll have to get over it.

A nerve calming, mouthwatering scent wafts into the bathroom, nearly hidden by the overly perfumed scent of money wasted. Coffee. Teiran is getting to know my moods and habits a little too well. Not that I'm going to turn down a cup. He does make some of the best coffee outside of Midnite Expresso. Speaking of the devil, he stands in the doorway holding a steaming mug.

"I thought you could use this." He hands me the mug full to the brim, of caffeinated goodness, a luscious shade of caramel signaling the perfect blend of coffee and cream. "And I have started moving some of the floral exhibit to the salon."

My shoulders drop letting the weight of the world tumble away as I cradle my personal form of ambrosia. Inhaling the rich scent, I nod then take my first sip of the day. "Oh, sweet heavens on earth, how I love thee."

"Excuse me?" The look on his face tells me I was using my outside voice again and a painful flush rushes across my flesh.

"The coffee, I was talking about the coffee."

Relief I expected, but it's mingled with something else. A fleeting bit of disappointment? Rejection? For all I know it's disgust. That would be more in line with emotions concerning me in Teiran Rand's world.

Quickly, I take another sip. Anything to avoid whatever it was I saw in his eyes and bury my own subconscious response. Lucky for me, it's a pleasant anything.

"I am glad it is to your taste."

"It's perfect, the best I've had."

Little ridges crease his forehead.

"Seriously, you even have the cream to coffee ratio down."

One eyebrow rises higher.

"It's good. It's great. Stupendous even. Will you just take the damn compliment already?"

A corner of those stern lips curls ever so slightly. "I shall leave you to your stupendous coffee. I have more flowers to relocate to keep them from assaulting my sleeping quarters."

I follow him into the living room, enjoying the movement of denim across firm muscle a little too much for comfort. If it were a contest between the coffee, the July heat and that view, I don't know which would rank as hottest. He'd moved a third of the flowers of mass seduction to the salon, clearing the kitchen table and counters.

"That looks much better, not that I want to keep the rest, but I think you're in the clear of having them invade your private quarters. I'll find homes for the last of them tomorrow." I'll dump a few on Mel and Nys. I doubt Dara will allow them to breach her sanctuary. Maybe I can give them away to clients and take a few over to Midnite Expresso, doubt Candy will protest. And the local library. Maybe it will earn me some brownie points toward getting the director to find me some books on necromancy, without too many questions.

If one cup of caffeinated goodness can make the day a little brighter it's time to find out what two can do. Indirectly it can pull the rug out from under you, the unopened card lies not far from the coffee maker.

With a shaky hand, I refill my mug, ignoring the elaborate scrawl of my name to retrieve the cream from the fridge. Nothing good can come out of that envelope, but it begs to be opened. No matter how much I want to ignore it, it won't go away. Throwing it in the trash will probably come back to bite me in the ass. The urge to Irish up my coffee before opening it would be all too easy to give in to. I watch the thing, waiting for it to unleash its evil contents all over my day.

"Is something the matter, Miss Fey?"

The pull of that stupid envelope made me forget I'm not alone. Turning, I smile at Teiran. "Nope, just remembered I need to feed CC."

"Your cat has already been fed. I did so before you woke."

"Thanks."

He nods and begins moving the vases and containers blocking the view of the TV.

Setting the mug on the counter, I wipe my hands on my shorts before picking up the dreaded chunk of paper. Carefully, I slip a finger under the flap having no desire for a paper cut. A simple, yet elegant card, no flowery prose or silly sayings, only the unmistakable handwriting of Var Royd.

I look forward to our dinner date this evening.

This guy doesn't give up. If he wants to spend time with me, you'd think he would've accepted my agreement to take the job as shadow; at least both of us would have gotten something we wanted. I can't believe any of this is for any other reason than to keep me under his thumb and make me, as Hel said, come of my own volition. But this kind of smothering does nothing for me and I can only assume it's a clue as to what the future holds when I take that job. I have no doubt that I'll be trapped into it sooner or later, so I better set up some ground rules on our date tonight. If he thinks an entire flower shop and a fancy dinner are the way to control me, he's got another thing coming.

Chapter 14

Someone—probably Var's driver—hits the door buzzer with multiple nerve grating bursts, promptly at eight. I'm tempted to make him wait an extra fifteen or twenty minutes, throw him off schedule.

With someone as anal as Var, I'm sure there's a schedule for everything and everything is on a schedule. Pickup date at eight. Eight thirty arrive at restaurant. Have date in bed by ten.

A snort escapes and the lipstick bullet skips across my lower lip. Luckily, staying within the line, nothing worse than cleaning up a red lip color mishaps. Giving my lips a final sweep of color, I take a step back and survey the completed picture.

Black sequined tank, filmy hi-lo skirt and dainty sling back heels look more like club wear than date night.

Like I would know what to wear on date night. I haven't been on a date in, well…oh, hel, I can't remember the last *real* date I was on.

This isn't exactly the safest way to jump back in the game, date night with a man who both terrifies and fascinates me. From what everyone says, he should. Terrify me that is. A shiver runs the length of my spine and I shake it off as Teiran's reflection appears in the mirror.

"Lord Royd is waiting."

Gee, thanks Captain Obvious. Resisting the urge to say, so what, I shrug, toss the lipstick in my clutch and push past him.

"You look lovely." Stops me cold in my tracks. Did I just hear that correctly? Teiran Rand complemented me?

Slowly, I turn around and face his appraising gaze, that moves from the tips of my spiky hair to my glittery polished toes. "Um, thanks."

He lingers on my Viva Glam I coated lips, as if mesmerized by the words erupting from them. With a start he looks away, running a hand through his hair and clears his throat. "Best not keep Lord Royd waiting."

"No, can't have that." Not really sure why, but I'm slightly disappointed at the reminder. It's not like I have a thing for Teiran, but moments like this get the girly parts a tingling. Blame it on hormones. Yeah, hormones.

The driver stands poker straight, hands clasped in front of him until I reach mid-room. With the smooth reflexes of a cat, he opens the door, waiting for me as if I'm royalty. A girl could get used to this.

"Don't forget to feed CC, Teiran." I give him a lopsided smile before stepping over the threshold.

"It will be done." I hear as Var's flunky closes the door and motions toward the steps.

"Any idea where we're going for dinner, um… I'm sorry I don't know your name." Talk about rude. I should have asked sooner, it's not like he hasn't driven me around before.

"I am called James, Miss Fey."

"James?"

"Yes."

I pause as he opens the door. Tipping my head to one side, take in the downward tilt of his lips. "You don't sound terribly happy about it."

"My real name is Jeffery, but Mr. Royd seems to find saying 'Home, James' terribly amusing."

This just confirms my opinion of Var Royd and his self-centered life style. "Gotcha. Is it okay if I call you Jeffery?"

He smiles and tips the brim of his cap. "It would please me greatly. In answer to your question, Mr. Royd has made reservations at 801."

Holy buckets! He's going to drop a bundle on dinner. Hel, drinks are like twenty bucks a pop. I hesitate on the last step and the driver steps around me, opening the door. Is this going to be like the dating world of old? Where in return for dinner you…well, give a little to get a little, or in this case pay for the whole shebang? Gods, I hope not. I don't care how pretty my date is, or how swanky the restaurant is, I don't put out for food.

The car isn't the long, lean limo I'm used to seeing, but a sleek sedan. Jeffery opens the door and I slide inside, finding myself shoulder to shoulder with his lordship, looking every bit as smug and gorgeous as usual. I silently wish for the apartment sized interior of the limo. He's way too close for comfort.

"You look lovely, Keely."

Hmm, back on a first name basis, both a good and bad sign. Good in the sense he's not pissed off at me. Bad in the sense it shows he wants something. Yeah, I know, he wants me to become his shadow, but with dinner at 801 I'm wondering if there's something more he wants.

"Thank you. You don't look bad yourself." And he doesn't, not a hair out of place, a recent mani and not a speck of lint on his custom tailored suit. Like any lint would dare cling to the great and terrible Var Royd. He's pretty, but one shouldn't touch in fear of being burned.

Those signature sand and sea eyes—I've only seen the strange mix of blues and gold on one other person, his sister—stare intently at the brace around my left wrist. "How is your wrist, does it still pain you?"

"Now and then." I shift in my seat as he reaches out, cradling the metal and cloth encased limb in one hand as the other fingers the Velcro closures. Hel's Realm, if he takes it off and sees the mark

I'm done for. "The doctor said to keep it in the brace when I'm not doing physical therapy." I pull from his grasp, praying I don't come off as trying to hide something. Even if I am.

"And you are following her instructions, the physical therapy?"

"Yes, Teiran helps me."

Not a muscle moves, not even a faint twitch, but disapproval radiates. Wow, first he moves Teiran into my place and now he's not happy about him helping with my therapy? If it weren't so ridiculous I'd laugh. Then again, he was equally upset about my spending time with Ric. I find myself twirling the moonstone hanging from my collar. So much for absolute stillness, a tick, then another moves under the skin along his jaw. Again, laughter threatens, but I manage to keep it in line.

"I see."

"He's been very helpful. Thank you for suggesting I use him." Hel's Realm, what am I doing? I know better than to poke a bear.

Var gives me a brief nod, then glances out the window just in time to see one of The Meadows' more colorful inhabitants.

Flynn believes in free range chickens, as in no fences. Not a problem if you live outside the city limits, but Flynn and his pet chickens live on Main Street. City ordinances state all pets must be on a leash when outdoors. Even CC follows the rules, grudgingly of course, but he rarely ventures outside the building. After a lengthy battle with city hall and nearly bankrupting his gold pot, Flynn decided it was better not to buck the system. So, three times a day you get to see the flame-haired, bell-bottom wearing leprechaun walking three hens on leashes down Main Street.

My companion chuckles. "What a colorful little town you live in, Keely." The smile he flashes me could melt the polar caps.

"Yeah, it's interesting to say the least." Lately a little too interesting where my life is concerned.

Chapter 15

"Right this way Mr. Royd, your private room is ready."

Unholy turd balls, he's really flashing the cash tonight. Who gets a private room for dinner? Var Royd, that's who. If he's trying to impress me with his millions—What am I saying? It's probably billions or trillions—it's not working.

At least, not in the way he's probably hoping it will. All it's doing is making me wonder why he's spending it, when he could have accepted my initial yes to the job.

The host leads us to a table in the far corner of a room large enough to house a party. Var pulls out my chair, a gesture I appreciate, but would appreciate more from someone I actually like and trust.

"I hope you do not mind, I have pre-ordered our meal," he takes the seat across from me, "and wine."

A bottle toting waiter appears behind the host, lavishly showing the label to Var. He nods and the waiter proceeds to uncork and pour the wine.

"I hope all will be to your specifications, Mr.

Royd. Enjoy your evening. If there is anything else you require do not hesitate to ask."

"Thank you, Charles."

Var takes the offered glass, gives it a swirl and sniff before tasting. Good grief. If this is how the rich and famous waste valuable wine drinking time, I want no part of it, just give me a glass. He nods and the waiter finally offers me a glass with a bowl large enough to fit half a bottle, with only a finger's width inside. Carefully, I attempt to copy Var's scratch and sniff test before tasting. I don't have the heart to tell him, what is probably a two hundred dollar bottle isn't as tasty as my ten dollar bottle sitting at home.

"You do not like the wine."

"No, it's fine."

"Do not lie, if it is not to your taste, I can order something else."

"Seriously, it's fine. It's just been a while since I've had something this dry. I'm sure it will pair with the food perfectly. What did you order?" I'm placing bets on steak, what used to be my least favorite food, until Teiran cooked for me. I'm also betting it won't live up to the memory of that perfect meal.

His grin is wider than a child at a birthday party. "I have specially selected items with your favorite food in mind."

"Potato chips?"

The grin turns to a frown, until he realizes I'm joking. "No, but dualy noted. I seem to remember you having an affection for, what I distinctly remember you calling 'shrooms."

Red rushes toward my cheeks and I chuckle, remembering our meeting at Lorelei's party and the stuffed mushrooms bouncing off the deck of her boat. "Yes, I do enjoy 'shrooms."

The man has a mind like a steel trap. Gods forbid, I ever do anything worthy of his wrath, he'll never forget. Under the table I lay my hand over the mark hidden by the brace. For this alone, I could end up like Einen, or worse. No wonder Ric and Teiran walk on egg shells around him.

"Then you shall enjoy tonight's delicacies."

I nod, keeping my covered arm under the table, reaching for the wine glass with the other. Too dry or not, I need a drink. "I'm sure I will."

Small dinner salads are placed in front of us with silent efficiency and our glasses refilled to the prerequisite finger's width.

"A simple oil and balsamic dressing, I hope you approve."

"Wonderfully light and refreshing." What the hel am I supposed to say? I hate uncomfortable small talk. As long as the food is good and there's no nasty surprises, like escargot, I'll be fine with his choices.

The next course is steak as I expected. Filet

medallions to be exact, but I'm not bitching, I can handle a tiny chunk of steak when it's wearing a coat of lobster and 'shrooms. As if this isn't enough, I'm introduced to a lovely side of mushroom pan roast, basically 'shrooms with garlic and a fancy cheese I can't pronounce. And wine; let us not forget about the libations, a new bottle is opened, even though we haven't finished the first. This one, of course, is a better match for the meal. I don't even pretend to understand the fine art of pairing food and drink. I drink what I like, simple as that.

"Are you enjoying your meal?"

"Very much, you have wonderful taste in food."

His laughter lights the room and lifts the spirit, leaving behind a happiness like none I've felt. All my worries and cares have melted away and all I want to do is enjoy myself. He reaches across the table and refills my glass well over the prerequisite. "I am glad you approve."

"Mr. Royd, are trying to get me drunk?"

He laughs again, the room becomes brighter and that bubble of happiness rises higher. Crap, he's using some sort of Talent on me. A compulsion or something similar. I dig the nails of my maimed hand into my thigh and the room slowly returns to its normal mood lighting. Yep, the bastard is trying to manipulate me for some reason. What else is new?

"So, Mr. Royd—"

"Var," he corrects me, his tone a smooth as silk.

"Okay, Var, what made you decide to ask me out? Do you date all the help, or possible future help?"

"Are you always so direct?"

I shrug and reach for the wine. "Maybe it's all the wine."

The corners of his lips make the slow climb upward. "Then perhaps we should keep your wine glass full, and no, I do not make it a habit of dating the help. You are an exception."

I don't know if I should be scared that he didn't add *possible future* to that, or just take it as his usual arrogance. "Is that why you asked me to dinner? The possibility of my working for you?"

"With me, Keely, you would be working with me."

That sends a wave of cold over my exposed flesh, but I'm afraid to ask what it means.

"No, I asked you to dinner because I enjoy your company."

Somehow I doubt that. "Are my questions bothering you?"

"Not at all, ask whatever you wish, but I cannot promise I will answer."

"At all or just truthfully?"

A small twisted smile tells me more than words ever could, but what the hel, might as well give it a try.

"What are you? I know you're not an En and sure as hel, not an Un."

"As I told you before, I am but a man."

I want to scream bullshit, but it won't get me anywhere.

"Okay, if you won't answer that one, what do you know about necromancers?"

"What would make you ask me about necromancers?"

"I've got an inquiring mind. Do you know anything about them?"

"What do you know about them?"

"They have some power over the dead."

The wine in his glass goes round and round and I feel myself falling. Damn it, if this keeps up I'm going to have blood running down my leg before we leave. Best case scenario, I'll have tiny crescents decorating my thigh.

"Are you well, Keely?"

"Fine. Are you going to answer my question?" I fiddle with my glass, pretending to drink to keep up appearances. The last thing I need is alcohol dulling my senses when he's using Talents on me.

"Necromancers—true necromancers, not those who give themselves the title, but are little more dabblers in the dark arts—are a rare breed."

"And?"

"You are correct. They have power over the dead."

"Vereinen is a necromancer, isn't he? And so am I."

Storm clouds roll across the sunny blue of his eyes and all the warmth and joy he'd spread throughout the room is sucked away. "I think it is time I send you home."

Guess I found the question he won't answer at all or at least the subject he won't discuss. Einen or necromancy, wonder which shoved him over the edge.

Chapter 16

"James, see Miss Fey home." Var doesn't even look at me.

"Yes, sir." James…I mean Jeffery opens the door for me as Royd stalks off.

Ouch, I pissed him off enough he's going home to pout. "Jeffery, do you mind if I ride up front with you?"

"It is rather unconventional,"—he looks at his employer's fading form and gives me a small smile—"but I think we can make an exception, Miss Fey."

"Thanks, and call me Keely."

He shuts the door to the spacious back and opens the front. "As you wish, Keely."

With smooth efficiency he pulls out into the evening traffic.

"Think I pissed your boss off, hope he doesn't take it out on you."

"For all his eccentricities, Mr. Royd would never deal out punishment where it was not warranted. If you do not mind me asking, what could you have done to *piss him off?*"

I nearly giggle hearing that semi-cultured voice

speak the words, piss him off. "I asked him about necromancers."

With a flick of his head, Jeffery looks at me then back to the road. "Why on earth would you ask him about necromancers?" Even in the dim lighting I can see his skin lighten three shades as he thinks about what he said. "Oh."

"I'm sorry Jeffery. I didn't mean to scare you."

"You have not frightened me."

"I don't scare you? What I am, I mean?"

He shakes his head.

"You do know who and what I am, right?"

"Yes, but you do not frighten me."

"Oh, the collar."

"No, it has nothing to do with the collar. You do not seem the type to carry out the atrocities of the other shadow child."

"You knew Vereinen?"

"No, I have only heard tales."

"Like what?"

"Here is where I must put a stop to our conversation, Mr. Royd would not like me to speak on this subject, I am sorry."

"No worries, I understand and wouldn't want to put you in a difficult position."

"Thank you, Keely."

Silence fills the giant car, thick with questions and my over active imagination. I'd won brownie points with the staff by being nice, but not enough to get any real info. They're all too scared of their boss to discuss what I want to know. I sneak a glance at Jeffery and remember Frank's demeanor. Maybe scared isn't the word, it could be respect or loyalty. Maybe a healthy mix of all three. Doesn't really matter if it's one or all. Their reasons add up to a big fat no concerning my questions.

I have to admit Jeffery has won brownie points of his own for handling both the tank sized limo and this mid-sized sedan. Maybe it's the construction of the car, but his handling of the vehicle gives the illusion of floating above the pavement. And no one can question his safety skills, from blinker use to the constant checking of his mirrors.

"So, Jeffery, how long have you worked for Mr. Royd?"

"As of this summer, twenty years."

"Wow, twenty years. That's a long time in one job."

"And how long have you been doing hair?" There's a shrewdness to his question and the grin that follows.

"Okay, you got me. Have you always been a chauffeur?"

"In a way, before I became Mr. Royd's personal driver, I drove a taxi."

That explains his driving skills, but not the cultured tone. That must have come along with this job. "Then you know your way around the city."

"And the surrounding area."

"Bet you met lots of interesting people."

"I would have to guess as many as you meet."

"Touché again, but at least you didn't have to touch them."

"No, but I always had to keep one eye on the rear-view mirror, there was always a chance of someone becoming threatening."

"Never thought of it that way. I'll take dirty with a chance of lice, over someone pulling a gun on me."

I lean back in the plush seat as we exit the interstate and toward the highway that will take me home. Traffic is heavier than I expected, for a Sunday night, but Jeffery's mirror checking seems a bit beyond caution.

The set of his jaw and grip on the wheel as we coast toward the lights sends a flutter of dread through my stomach.

"Perhaps you would like to stop for coffee or a tour of the city, Miss Fey?" As the light switches to yellow, he pulls the car into the center lane that can turn either direction, ignoring the turn signal.

The lack of signal use and the dropping of my first name intensifies the bad vibe feeling. I glance in the passenger side mirror and watch a car attempt to squeeze in behind us, setting off a chorus of horns. "Whatever you think best, Jeffery."

"Hang on." He guns the engine, pulling quickly

to the left sending us through the intersection as the light turns red.

The momentum carries me to the side, my hip striking the door. A serenade of squealing tires and blaring horns fades behind us. I hope no one was hurt, but selfishly not caring enough to go back and find out.

"Are you all right?"

"I think my heart jumped ship, but other than that, I'm fine. Do you think that car was following us?"

"In my expert opinion?"

"Yes."

"I would bet my life."

"I guess the million dollar question is if they thought they were following your boss or knew it was me in the car."

He nods, weaving his way through the streets that will take us back to our intended destination.

"I suppose you'll have to tell your boss about this little detour."

"Of course, as you said we have no idea who they thought they were following."

Of course. I can hope and pray it was Var they were following, but with the way things have been going I'd rather not bet my life on that guess. Fear settles in with visions of Stasia Athory bleeding me dry. "I think I'll take that cup of coffee now, if you don't mind."

Chapter 17

Jeffery circles the block, paying close attention to the other cars on the street before pulling up in front of a well-lit Fey Creations. What the hel is going on in the salon at this hour on a Sunday?

I grab the door handle and smile at Jeffery. "I can handle the door, thanks for the ride and the coffee."

He smiles and nods. "The pleasure was all mine, Miss Fey."

I lean down and stick my head back inside. "It's Keely and I think it's about time you remind Mr. Royd that your name is Jeffery and not James."

Shaking his head he laughs. "Duly noted, and Keely," his expression becomes grave, "watch your back."

"Thanks, Jeffery." I shut the door and tap the top of the car.

The only reasons the salon would be lit up like this is a special client or group hair night. Considering it's been a while since we've had one, I'm betting on the latter. Time to find out who decided to have a hair party and not invite me.

Before I can dig my keys out of the shallow

clutch, a four-foot-something sprite with foils in her hair opens the door.

"Group hair night?"

She nods with a grin. "Yep, I've decided to add some lavender highlights."

"Lavender, interesting choice."

"I thought so. Teiran picked out the color."

"Teiran? As in Mr. Super Stuffy, Teiran?"

"Yep."

I hustle through the reception area to find Teiran in Rey's chair, having his ends trimmed, while Dara lounges nearby laughing.

What the hel happened while I was gone? Even CC is enjoying the party, stretched across Dara's vanity.

"Who decided to have a party and not invite me?"

Rey shrugs. "You already had plans. A date if I'm not mistaken, at least that's what Teiran told us."

"So? It's not like I was going to be gone all night."

A round of laughter fills the room, with the exception of Teiran.

"Get your minds out of the gutter, it was just dinner."

"Nothing is ever *just* dinner."

"Says the man who flips through girlfriends faster than I can wrap a perm."

"That's not saying much with that thing on your wrist."

Nyssa flops down in my chair. "Where did his lordship take you?"

"801."

"No way!"

"Way."

"That place costs an arm and a leg just to walk into."

"Wouldn't know, he pre-ordered our meal, so I didn't see a menu."

"Well, if you want your mind blown, look it up online."

"The prices are not that bad." Dara looks up from filing her nails.

"What? You've been there?" Nyssa twirls the chair to face her.

Dara shrugs. "A time or two. The food is more than passable."

"Girls, girls, all this talk about food is making me hungry." Rey waves his comb at us. "Somebody open a bag of chips while I blow Teiran."

Another burst of laughter as Teiran leaps up, the cape catching on the chair, yanking him backward.

Nyssa stands and leads him back to the chair. "He means blow dry, silly. Rey doesn't swing that way."

"Sorry, I couldn't resist, but I'm the other

stereotype. The one that got into the hair business to meet the ladies."

"Too bad most of the ladies he meets have blue hair and carry tissues up their sleeves."

"Not fair crazy cat lady."

Dara shrugs. "The truth hurts."

"Enough you guys, I want to hear about Keely's date."

"Nothing to tell, Nys."

"Yeah, right the richest guy in the greater Des Moines area asks you out and there's nothing to tell."

"Seriously, we had dinner, chatted, I pissed him off and he ordered Jeff to take me home."

"Jeff?" Teiran pushes Rey's dryer away from his ear.

"Jeffery, his driver. You many know him as James."

Teiran nods. "Yes, James."

"His real name is Jeffery. Var thinks it's funny to say *home James*."

"Hashtag, rich people problems."

"It will be hashtag dead nixie, if you say that one more time." I'd hug Dara, if she'd let me. Nyssa latches onto some of the most annoying trends.

Nyssa sticks her tongue out at Dara. "What did you eat?"

"Filet medallions covered in lobster and mushrooms with a side of mushrooms smothered with some fancy cheese that I can't pronounce. And wine…lots of wine, a different bottle with each course. Heck we didn't even finish a bottle before a new one arrived."

"What a waste."

"Alcohol abuse."

"I know, right?" I glance over to the bottles of wine and beer on the back-bar behind the shampoo bowls. "Looks like you guys have been making up for it."

"Can't have hair night without a little incentive." Rey pulls the cape off Teiran. "All done and virtually painless."

"What do I owe you?"

"Nothing, it's hair night and you've been adopted into our little group for the night. Besides, you bought the beer."

I've got to say it's nice to see everyone getting along so well. Strange, but nice for a change. "Well, sorry to say, I'm not sticking around for the unveiling of Nys' new 'do. I've got to get into something comfortable and scrape off my war paint."

Nyssa's lower lip protrudes. "Awe, come back down after you change. I want you to see it."

"It's been a long and trying night. I'll see it tomorrow."

"But you didn't tell us how you pissed him off." Her disappointment over me seeing her new

I remember how beautiful she was when I touched her. "What they say, it's true?"

Her one and only brow rises, the plump, pink side of her mouth curving upward in a wouldn't-you-like-to-know smile. Yeah, she caught my meaning.

"You and Einen?" It's not just a twinge of jealousy that stabs my heart, more like a dagger.

She tips her head to one side, shrugging. It's easy to see, I'm not going to get a straight answer, but she's enjoying my discomfort and the dagger twists. It's not like he cheated on me with her, I wasn't even a thought when they knew each other.

Let's face it, I have no right or reason to feel this way, we're not a couple. Sure, I had warm fuzzies for him when I was a kid. A childish crush that disappeared when he did, but now he's back.

I really need to get my crap sorted out, but not with a goddess audience. Heck, I don't even know if the rumors are true, or she's just baiting me for shits and giggles.

"Are you willing to help me?"

"Child, there is proof that you already know how to use your Talents."

She waves a hand and like curtains parting, the scene of a tormented Collector kneeling on the ground, hovers between us.

Closer inspection reveals the chief tormentor standing behind him to be Jenny. Her pale blue lips move, but I'm unable to hear the words. His terror glazed eyes are enough to send chills along my spine. When she lowers the length of rope stretched between her hands over his head and around his neck, I have to look away.

Hel waves her hand again and the reminder of my atrocities disappears from sight. But it's too late. The images are burned into my subconscious, left to stew until I close my eyes tonight and every night from now until eternity.

"That's not fair, it was self-defense."

"Who are you trying to convince? Me or yourself? You did what was needed. I have seen into his soul, Stanley would have done far worse had he been allowed to continue. He is now paying for his crimes."

"And I'm paying for mine."

I stand perfectly still as she reaches out, lifting the stone attached to the collar. "Unjustly." She lets go, the stone hitting my breastbone with a thump.

Shaking my head, I take a step back. "No, I had no right to take a life, especially the way I did."

"And you think the world would have been a better place with Stanley's survival and your termination?"

"Probably not, but it still didn't give me the right to take Stanley's life." My tongue stumbles over his name; it's difficult to think of him as anything but The Collector. Giving him a name has made the load of guilt I carry heavier.

"My dear girl, you need to stop rejecting who and what you are. They are called Talents for a reason and you have a formidable one."

"Yeah, one that everyone is terrified of, even me."

"As they should be, and you as well."

"I don't want everyone scared of me. I don't want to be scared of what I can do. I just want to go back to what I was."

Her laughter grates against my skin. "What? A simple hairdresser? Why would you want that when you can be so much more?"

"I wasn't just a simple hairdresser. I'm good at what I do. I have my own business, a successful business. People respected and liked me."

"Is that what this is all about? The approval of the masses?" She shakes her head. "It does not matter that they *like* you, only that they respect you and with a Talent like yours you will have that in droves."

"Respect is something that needs to be earned by actions. Good ones, honorable ones, not brought on by fear."

"Respect is respect, something you will learn in time. And a little fear is a good thing."

"A little maybe, but the kind I induce…that's far from little."

"I said a little fear was a good thing, a lot of

fear is a great thing." With a chilling smile she steps back, letting the mist engulf her.

Familiar surroundings meet my open eyes. Farewell Niflheim, hello apartment. "Damn it."

I know I owe the woman a favor, but this is getting ridiculous. She yanks my chain whenever she feels like it, telling me she's wants to help me, but nothing ever gets resolved. I don't get the help I need and I still don't know what she wants.

"Wise up, Keely. She wants a playmate, or better yet a plaything, and you're it." Sighing, I sit up, tossing the covers to the side. Plaything or playmate. Neither is appealing. Nor is the flower shop stench that hits me when I open the door.

Chapter 19

More damn flowers. Lucky for Var Royd, they don't block my coffeemaker. Lucky for me, Teiran made coffee.

"I see we've been invaded by the floral shop again." I give the envelope with the familiar scrawl of my name a one finger push. It teeters on the edge of the sink, the disposal, so close and so tempting.

"Yes, I am running out of places to dispose of them. Your workplace is nearly as full as your living space."

"We'll take a load to Mel's, I need to pick up supplies and I'll take some across the street to Midnight Expresso."

"I have already visited with the barista, she has agreed to you decorating her tables, but we are not to *dump* them on her counter."

"Understood." Glaring at the overabundance of perfumed flora I can understand her reluctance to have interfering with customer interaction. "Maybe I can take some over to the library."

He nods, intently perusing the daily paper.

The library might kill two birds with one stone, if I can somehow not have Teiran hanging over my shoulder "How about if, after I'm done with my coffee, you take some over to Candy and I'll take a load over to the library?"

He lowers the paper and turns, giving me *the look*. "You would not by chance be using this as a ruse to slip away again?"

"Not at all, I have too many things to do before work to have time to *slip away*. I'm trying to save a little time." Attempting to appear casual is harder than it sounds when you've got ulterior motives.

He tips his head to one side, a brow shooting skyward.

"Seriously, I don't want to get you in any more trouble than I already have, we'll be less than a block away from each other. If it makes you feel better I'll stay at the library until you come get me."

"Agreed, you stay at the library until I retrieve you."

If I thought acting nonchalant was bad, holding back elation has it beat tenfold. Quick way to deflate that little bubble of elation? Look over at an envelope holding what can only be more complications. I refill my cup, glaring at the envelope, hoping it will burst into flames. No such luck. May as well get it over with, the worst thing that can be inside is a note letting me know Teiran and Ric ratted me out about the mark and I'm a dead woman.

Slipping my finger under the flap I carefully

open it, revealing a crisp white note card, with pristine handwriting. *Forgive me.* Wow, short and to the shocking point. He is the last person I would have expected an apology from, leaves me wondering how many people *have* gotten an apology from Var Royd. Wonder what I'm supposed to forgive him for, the rudeness of his departure, or being chased by thugs wanting a piece of him? I'm still clinging to the hope that whoever followed us last night was after him and not me.

I read it again the thought of him having to apologize to me, or anyone for that matter, brings a smile to my face. May have to frame this, just for that purpose. Too bad it doesn't have his signature. Sliding it back into the envelope, I pop it on the fridge with a heavy duty magnet. Leaning against the counter, I finish my coffee, unable to take my eyes from the envelope. Yep, definitely need to get a frame and find the perfect spot to hang this treasure.

⟨⟨⟨⟨⟨⟨⟨⟨⟨⟨⟩⟩⟩⟩⟩⟩⟩⟩⟩⟩

Our library is run by Mrs. Books from Jamaica. No, not the island. Jamaica, Iowa. Made famous by tourists taking their pictures in front of the *Welcome To Jamaica* sign in the middle of winter, dressed in their best tropical shirts and shorts. I get it, I do, but it doesn't mean I'll be donning my summer attire and joining in. The average Iowa winter requires all body parts be covered.

"Hello, Mrs. Books." I take my time enunciating her name so I don't slip and say Brooks. I think her name is Brooks and she changed it up when she took the job, probably one of the many reasons she isn't found of me. Seriously, how convenient is it that the librarian's name is Books?

"If you are here to cause trouble, you can leave now, Miss Fey. I will suffer none of your mischief." Her snooty tone and steely eyed accusations are almost enough to make me want to turn tail and run.

"No, no trouble, Mrs. Books. I'd like to make a donation of sorts." I tip my head down toward the box I struggle to keep upright.

"Donation? What kind of donation?" She grabs the edge of the box as I lower it, nearly upsetting the delicate balance, but I manage to keep gravity from winning.

"I have a friend who's generosity is a bit overzealous and I was wondering if you'd like some of these floral arrangements for the library."

She lifts her chubby little chin, yet still attempts to peer down her nose at me, her gaze ending up on my brace covered arm. "That have something to do with that whole Collector business you were messed up with?"

"Nothing so glamorous."

Eyes narrowed, she waits for further explanation. An explanation I'm not willing or able to give, not if I want to keep a modicum of privacy. Whatever I tell her will be blown out of proportion, leaving me with having broken my arm either battling the bad guy or fighting off the good guys. With the way she seems to be leaning today, probably the latter.

"I tripped and fell. Now I'm stuck with the brace for a while." Only time will tell how she spins the tale of Klutzy Keely.

Clearly, disappointed at being bilked out of fodder for gossip, she frowns and looks at the box. "I suppose it wouldn't hurt for you to leave them on the desk and a few of the tables, but if they get in my way I will dispose of them." The lower lip of her frown juts forward.

"Of course, I wouldn't want you or your patrons to be inconvenienced."

"Don't make a mess," she waves a finger at my midsection, "I have work to do." With a huff she spins on her sturdy shoes and heads to the off-limits section behind the desk.

As I place the flowers in various places, I check to see if we are alone. Seeing as the woman already dislikes me, I may as well put it to the test and see how much. "Mrs. Books, do you have any books or information on necromancers?"

"Fiction or non-fiction?"

I force a big smile and nonchalant tone. "Non, please."

"What would you want with a filthy subject like necromancy?"

Her eyes grow wide as I come around one of the shelves. She takes a step back, careful to stay behind the sanctuary of her desk.

"I'm just curious, a friend brought up the subject and I want to learn more."

"What kind of friend would bring up such a topic?"

"It was something he saw in a movie and we want to see if they got it right."

Her eyes narrow behind the Mrs. Claus spectacles. "You should know better than to believe anything you see in movies."

"Exactly, and we didn't want to look it up on the Internet."

"Of course not, that is last place to find accurate information."

"Everyone with a brain knows books are the only way to do *accurate* research."

She gives me a nod, physically relaxing. I'd hit the sweet spot of every old school book lover.

"I'll see what I can find and call you."

"Thank you, Mrs. Books." Yay for me finishing my delicate conversation as Teiran walks through the door.

"Hello, is there anything I can help you find, sir?"

"He's with me." I quickly step between them.

"Is this the friend you were discussing—"

"No, no this is another friend. Thank you for your help, Mrs. Books, I'll be looking forward to your call." I grab Teiran and hustle him toward the door away from her inquisitive nature. He glares at me as we hit the sweltering pavement outside.

"What are you up to?"

"What makes you think I'm *up to* anything?" The furrows along his brow deepen.

"I was just having her find me a couple of books. I needed some new reading material. Come on, I need to get to Witchy Weeds and pick up supplies." I leave him standing there contemplating my truth telling skills and head back to the shop. Knowing full well, like a dutiful dog, he'll follow.

Chapter 20

Witchy Weeds, a place of peace, relaxation and no judgment. My happy place. It's like going home, without the three hour drive. And a lot of animal attention. Mel's pack rushes to meet me as I pull in the drive, jumping, barking and chasing the car up to the shop. Two fluffy geese waddle out from the garden area, wings spread, sounding the alarm honk. With all this, who needs a doorbell?

Teiran manages to real in his machismo enough that the dogs aren't cowering when his boots hit the dirt, but the geese waddle-run off when he fully emerges from the car.

I've learned over time it's easier to open the trunk now than to wait till my arms are full of product. So what if I pick up a little extra country dust, it's a small price to pay.

The tiny bell above the door jingles and half a dozen cats scatter, a couple between my feet outside, others into the corners, behind shelves, or the front counter.

"About time you pick up your order, it's taking up space on my floor."

"Whatever, it's not like you have any other

customers." I dump a box of floral arrangements on her counter, followed by the one Teiran holds.

Mel laughs. "Yeah, right." She glances at the boxes. "What the heck is this? Trying to butter me up?"

"Yep, pretty flowers for a pretty lady."

Her brows nearly hit the ceiling.

"Don't ask, just enjoy."

"Still have the babysitter, I see."

"Today, he's going to play the part of muscle and haul all these boxes to the car."

Without a word, he starts grabbing boxes and takes them to the car.

"See?"

"Wow, where can I get one of those?"

"Doubt you'd be willing to pay the price."

Her forehead creases and lips turn downward. "You're probably right. So, what's new?"

"Well, I had dinner with Var Royd last night."

"You what?" The elevated pitch of her voice tweaks my ears, like nails on a chalkboard.

"You heard me. Dinner, Var Royd."

"What would possess you to have dinner with that man?"

"Expensive meal at 801?"

"I guess that is a plus, but seriously, what were you thinking?"

"You try telling him no, the word doesn't work, I've tried."

"You really need to stay away from that man."

"That's what everyone keeps saying, but no one will tell me why."

"He's too powerful and unpredictable, that's why."

"According to some, he's also the only reason I'm still alive and not locked up in the C.U."

"And I'm sure you've figured out he does nothing without a reason that benefits him."

I nod, dragging a toe along the floor. It's time for a change in conversation before I let the reason slip. "You were right. Stasia Athory is using En… fluids, for lack of a better term, in her serums."

Mel's eyes narrow and she shakes her head, letting me know she knows what I'm doing, but is willing to let it go. For now. "You know this for sure?"

"Yep, got it straight from the horse's mouth."

She leans forward, elbows on the counter. "She just volunteered up the info, or what?"

"She offered me, payment for my blood."

"What? You've got to be kidding."

"Nope, said she does it all the time and if I don't want to give her the red stuff, she'll take tears. She seems to think my blood will make the ultimate anti-wrinkle cream. Oh, you think that's good, get this. She says she has a get out of jail free card for Einen if I don't help her."

"No effin way. That's not possible."

I clutch the edge of the counter and lean toward her. "What if it is? She needs to be stopped."

"Is that why you had dinner with dipshit?"

"He already told me it's impossible and if I'm afraid of Stasia forcing me to donate, to use the *tool* he gave me."

We both look back at Teiran working his way through the pile of boxes.

"Well, on this I agree with him. Let the Shield do what he does best. There's nothing we can do about her, unless we can prove she's taking what she needs without consent."

"Yeah, I know."

"How's the arm doing?"

"Yeah…about that, I need a little help with something."

She laughs. "When don't you?"

"This is, well, it's…here, I'll just show you." Grabbing the cloth tabs I give three quick pulls and slip the protective barrier off. I flip my arm, palm side up showing off my scar in all its helish glory.

"What the…"

"Yeah, everyone's sentiments exactly."

"How the hel—" she slaps her hand over her mouth.

"Did this happen?" I finish for her. "You already know the story of how The Collector kidnapped me and then I killed him."

She nods, slowly lowering her hand.

"Well, this happened between those events. Long story short, somehow I ended up in Hel's throne room. Her healer mended my wrist and this is what I was left with. I just thought it was an ugly scar, but Teiran said it was Hel's mark."

"I suppose he ran off and told his boss."

"No, for some reason he hasn't told him."

"Good, keep it that way." She gingerly takes hold of my wrist and gives it a closer look. "There's nothing I can do about this, only she can break the bond."

"Kinda figured as much, but I was hoping you could come up with a charm or something to keep her from calling me to her."

"Damn, she's using it to pull your subconscious to her?"

"Yeah, when I'm sleeping."

She sighs, shoving my brace toward me. "Keep it covered and I'll see what I can do, but I'm not making any promises."

"Thanks."

"No promises."

"Understood. What do I owe you?"

Chuckling, she slides a sales slip toward me. "For your supplies, this. For trying to keep your ass out of trouble, my sanity back."

"Let's start with the supplies," I fill out the check and hand it to her, "the rest I can't make any promises on, but I'm trying."

Mel sticks the check in the drawer and comes around the counter. "Sounds like a puppy party outside."

Turning toward the open door, letting in the sound of happy barks and yips, I see the pile of boxes has disappeared. Damn, maybe having him around isn't so bad. Between hauling boxes and cleaning the apartment—minus the rearranging of my things—he's been pretty useful.

I follow Mel outside to a sight that no one would believe, at least not without a picture. Mel snaps a couple of covert phone shots of Teiran on all fours playing with her mutts.

"Better email me a copy."

Any red-blooded, animal loving, woman would be melting right about now. Just as the moment couldn't get any more heartwarming, the most skittish, anxiety ridden, anti-social of Mel's pack crawls up onto Teiran's lap as he sits back and tosses a stick for the others to chase.

"Holy crap."

"I can't believe it."

"He must have spelled my dogs."

"Maybe it's because he is one."

She shrugs, snapping off the world bending picture. "Gotta have proof, no one will believe this."

"No kiddin'."

She palms the phone, slipping it behind her back, as he turns toward us. Gently lifting the small dog from his lap, he stands, brushing loose ground clutter from his jeans. "Are you finished?"

"Yep. Thanks for doing all the heavy lifting."

He nods to Mel and heads to the car.

"Rut ro, I think I'm in trouble."

"How can you tell with that one?"

"Trust me, I've been around him long enough to tell." I can tell already, this isn't going to be a pleasant ride home.

"I'll call you if I figure something out for your little problem."

"Thanks."

Before I get the key in the ignition, he starts. "Why did you not tell me about the car following you last night?"

Shrugging, I pull out onto the gravel. "Guess I didn't think it was important enough."

"Not important? Someone follows you and you do not think it important? What if it had been someone wishing you harm? You seem to forget you have no way of defending yourself without the certainty of death."

"Yeah, yeah, yeah, the collar. I get it, but who said they were following me specifically? I was in Royd's car, maybe it was him they were after."

"Either way you were in danger. Had it been Lord Royd they were after and they found you instead, do you think they would have let you live?"

I shrug. "Maybe if they didn't know who I am."

His laughter turns July to January. "Do you really believe no one knows who and what you are?"

"Uns?" I hide a shiver with another shrug, but make the mistake of looking over at him. There's no hiding the fear, the cold ruthlessness of his expression induces.

Chilly silence is a passenger on the long stretch of main street and into the garage. If the slam of the car door is any indication of how the rest of the day will go, I'm screwed.

Chapter 21

Flipping through the appointment book brings a smile to my face, until I realize why business has gone from non-existent, to a trickle and now a flood. The flood is brought on by Var Royd. He's made good on his word by suggesting employees utilize our salon.

Rey leans over my shoulder, looking at the closely timed appointments. "Damn, I have a cut during every shampoo set. Hope they aren't demanding, most of my regulars don't need much dryer time."

"Yeah, we're really crunched."

"You going to be able to keep up?" He touches my brace.

"I have no choice." I flip through to the next week and the week after, no break in sight. How many employees does he have?

Rey moves my hand and flips back to today. "Did you see this?" He points to my eight thirty.

"You've got to be shitting me."

"Nope, it's right there in pencil."

"Maybe I should erase it." I flip my pencil, hovering the eraser over Var Royd's name.

Patting my shoulder, he laughs. "If only it was that easy, but I'm glad it's you and not me. I'll take my crammed cuts and shampoo sets over that any day."

"Gee, thanks, you're such a thoughtful and caring friend."

"I'd trade you one of my blue hairs for this one." He flips the page and my shoulders droop as his finger underlines Stasia Athory. At least she only wants a blowout, probably afraid I'd shave her head if she asked for a cut.

The wig will be a must for tomorrow night. May as well mess with her a little and let the bitch wonder if it's my Talents or her magic potion. Maybe I can hide the collar and move Ric's pendant to a longer chain.

"This is going to be the best week ever."

"It will be if everyone is in a tipping mood." Giving my shoulder a squeeze, he heads off to the cutting floor.

Laying my head on my crossed arms I start laughing. When I was a kid, I couldn't wait to grow up and have an exciting life. Now that I have an exciting life—albeit not the type of excitement I'd dreamed of—I'd give anything to go back to boring and average.

I want to go back to worrying about things like how am I going to pay my bills, or what to wear Saturday on night. Worrying about someone trying to kill me for what I am, or use me because of what I am is exhausting. The extra bonus of trying to find out what I am, when everyone who claims to know won't share is a kick to the head.

An invite to a pity party dangles in front of me, but I'll have to decline, there's no time in my über exciting life. It's five to seven, people are already gathering outside the door and the phone is ringing off the hook.

I really need to get off my butt and hire a new receptionist. With this scheduling overload it's going to become unmanageable. There's no way we can keep running for the phone and give our clients the attention they deserve.

"The mob has arrived, everyone to their battle stations." I grab the phone tossing Nyssa my keys as she passes.

"Fey Creations, how may I help you? I'm sorry, but we are booked until mid-August." It's easier to deal with someone getting upset on the phone than in person. I don't take getting hung up on personally.

"We're going to have to turn on the answering service at this rate."

"Yeah." I catch a glimpse of Teiran standing off to the side. "Go ahead and start shampooing and I'll see if I can get someone to help out with that."

She nods, grabbing Rey's first client as I motion Teiran over. Almost reluctantly he approaches, eying the waiting room as if some unknown threat will pop up.

"Do you think you could change the settings on our answering service?"

"It is not a difficult task, why?"

"Usually it's only on when we're closed, but with the deluge of appointments and no receptionist, we don't have time to answer the phone every two seconds. If you could change the settings to be on all the time, we can call clients back when we have a break. I'd really appreciate it, Teiran. The instructions are in the top drawer of the desk." I don't bother waiting for a formal answer; instead motion for my first client to follow me back to the cutting room.

With cuts every half hour, there's no way Nys can keep up, we'll all have to do some shampooing tonight. Rey is the one who will need her services most, with Dara a close second. They're both double booked with cuts between chemical services and shampoo sets. I on the other hand am going to have to figure out how to shampoo, cut and style with a brace on, there's no way I can take it off with that thing on my wrist.

"Sorry, Sara," I mumble after smacking her in the head for the third time.

"Are you sure you're okay to cut my hair? I mean, if that thing is going to get in the way..."

"It's going to be fine." I know it's not concern

over my comfort, but worry over the outcome of her cut that she's questioning. Brace or no brace, I'm capable of giving a decent cut. It just might take me a little longer than usual, setting me behind schedule, leading to irritated clients. Last thing I need to do is get rattled enough to fall off my game.

Putting my shears into the holder on my belt, I tousle her hair with my right hand, checking the movement. "Go ahead, run your fingers through it, see how it feels to you."

She pulls it in every direction and smiles. "It feels short enough. Can I see what it looks like dry?"

"No one walks out wet, if I can help it, I need to see how it lays and acts. Give it one last check." I grab the dryer, testing my grip before holding it near her head. Concussion by dryer wasn't a service listed under her appointment. I'll save it for my eight thirty as an extra added bonus.

I click the dryer off and give her hair a few swishes with my fingers. The cute shag frames her face beautifully. I don't even need to take an iron to her.

"Amazing." She shakes her head, the hair falling right back into place. "I can't believe this is my hair. I should have come here sooner."

"I'm glad you like it." I pull off the cape. "Meet you up front."

Rounding the corner, I stopped dead in my

tracks by the last thing I expected to see. Teiran Rand sits behind the desk reassuring patrons that their stylist will be with them shortly and running the credit card of Rey's client. He glances my direction and nods to Sara. "I will be with you in just a moment. Keely, your next appointment is here."

I stand there gaping for a moment, then shake my head, the rocks up there rattling into some semblance of reason. "Th…thank you, Teiran." Turning to my next cut, I smile. "Give me a second to clean up Mary then come on back."

What the hel is going on with Teiran? He's being so helpful. Have I warped into some bizzaro world? With a quick, but thorough use of the vacuum I remove the hair from my station. Mary rounds the corner, fanning herself as I'm tossing the bag of hair into the receptacle for later disposal.

"Where did you find that receptionist? Please tell me he's not a temp."

"Teiran's a friend." I wrap the cape around her neck, something about her smile makes me want to pull tighter, but I remind myself she's joking. Lousy subject, but still joking. Mary's been a steady client for years, minus the short time during The Collector fiasco.

"A friend? What kind of friend?" She giggles. "One with benefits?"

"Hardly."

She rolls her eyes at me from the shampoo bowl. "Puhllease, just looking at him is a benefit"

"Trust me; there are very few benefits to being Teiran Rand's friend."

She sits up, knocking the hand holding the hose and water sprays everywhere. "Did you say Teiran Rand?"

"Yes." I hand a wet and very pale Mary a towel. "Sorry about that."

She turns and whispers, "Seriously? The Teiran Rand, as in works for Var Royd, Teiran Rand?"

I nod, gently easing her back down.

"Well, shit."

Even though she doesn't know it, her words pretty much sum up the entire situation.

Chapter 22

Over the dryers and chatter, I hear the unmistakable voice of my eight thirty. My stomach drops. I'm a good fifteen minutes behind, thanks to this damn brace.

Catching Nyssa's eye, I nod in the direction of reception. She nods in return, lifting the dryer hood off of Mrs. Clark for Rey. Yay, for silent communication, I don't have to shampoo Var. The less I have to touch him the better. Although, the thought of *accidentally* spraying him with the hose is mighty tempting. Hel, I'd like to hold the hose over his face.

Nancy's reflection returns my smile, oblivious to the reason behind my amusement. Considering her allegiance to the man, something she's been overly vocal about, I'm glad she can't read my mind.

She's not the first of his female employees crushing on him, nor will she be the last. I get it. He's rich, gorgeous and single. Too bad they don't know what a self-centered jackass he is, or maybe they do and think they can change him. I wish them all the best of luck with the impossible endeavor of getting him to notice them as more than worker bees. Heck, he probably doesn't even know they exist at all.

I, on the other hand, wish he'd forget my existence. His unwanted attentions and flirtations in an attempt to make me want him and in turn want the job are ridiculous. I know he doesn't want me for anything more than to become the third leg of his power base, the spy to Teiran and Ric's protector and enforcer. As if spying isn't bad enough, it's the part he hasn't told me—the part Ric eluded to—that bothers me. Einen wasn't just a spy.

His deep, sensual voice has the hair on the back of my neck standing at attention. Nancy is rewarded with a face full of hair spray for turning unexpectedly toward the shampoo bowls. I don't bother apologizing, as she gags and pushes away the can that obscures her view.

Her now shellacked smile wide and fingers wiggling to match the giggled, "Hello, Mr. Royd!"

He returns an indulgent smile and nondescript greeting as Nyssa wraps the cape around his neck.

"Nancy. Nancy from accounting."

"Ah, yes, Nancy. Your hair looks magnificent, Nancy." His gaze settles on me and I feel the excited little puppy under my hand slump.

Come tomorrow I will be public enemy number one around the water cooler. The hatred in the mirror as I finish fluffing her hair is almost laughable. If only she and the other members of the *I heart Var Royd* fan club knew how much I don't want to be a part of their little group. I don't bother asking her how she likes it, just help her to untangle herself from my cape and let her stalk off to reception. Let Teiran deal with her, I have neither time nor patience.

Nyssa takes her time shampooing Var, her usual flirtations and chattiness exaggerated, as I clean up my station. I'm tempted to run to the back for a quick slurp of soda, but the sooner I get him done and out of my chair the better. After he's out of the salon I can take all the breaks I need. She towels him off and sends him over at my cue, following close behind. I'm not sure if she thinks I need help, or if she's just enjoying the view as he walks. Can't blame her. I've seen the view and it's a pretty package, too bad what's inside sucks.

I turn the chair toward him, blatantly stepping back behind it as he leans toward me. What the hel? Did he think he was going to kiss me? No way, no how, especially not in my salon in front of clients. "If you'll have a seat, Mr. Royd."

His admonishing smile is aggravating to say the least. "And good evening, to you too, Keely."

He gracefully takes the chair and I grab the back of the cape, pulling it none too gently over the chair. "Yes, Nyssa?"

"You've had several calls inquiring about hair

growth service. I've told them you're booked, but they didn't sound too happy about it."

"There's not much I can do about it," frowning at Var in the mirror. "You'll just have to keep telling them I'm booked and hope they don't come in when I'm not busy."

She nods a slow smile growing as she turns away from the mirror. I want to give her some sign of appreciation for trying, but it would defeat her effort.

"You have to turn away clients because of the business I have sent?"

"No, Mr. Royd, I have to turn away clients because I can't use my Talent to perform the required services."

The corners of his mouth slowly rise. "There is a way to remedy this problem."

"I know and I've tried, but you turned me down." I add a silent, asshat, but I think he knows, or at least guesses as his smile widens.

"As I told you before, you must want the job, not need it for silly purposes."

"I don't find needing my Talents to perform my job a silly purpose." Clutching my shears at my side, a familiar itch creeps along my arms. The desire to push them into the base of his scull begins to play out in my head, until I catch sight of Teiran standing to the back of the room. I'd be dead before the first drop of blood hit the floor.

Taking a deep breath I take a step to the side, grab a comb and center myself behind the chair. "How would you like your hair cut?"

"Are you still angry about last night?"

"No, I never was."

"Then why all the animosity, Miss Fey?"

"We are busy and I have other appointments."

"Surely, that is no reason to be so angry. Having a full appointment book should make you happy."

I clench my jaw and begin pumping the chair upward. Once the chair is high enough, I lean in so my mouth is level with his ear. "I. Am. Not. Angry."

Looking into the mirror, I catch and hold his gaze. The smile on his face hints at pleasure, the very last thing I want to give him. Glancing at my own reflection, I see the darkening of my eyes. Not yet the endless black of a full manifestation, but well on their way. Shadows flicker and fade in the corners of the room. Under my vanity. Awaiting my call. All that power, waiting to do my bidding. Too bad the collar reminds me of my fate if I reach out and grasp it, that and Teiran Rand taking a step forward. With a deep breath I push the bricks back into place. Caging the temptation.

"Although your anger is still very apparent, you are becoming more adept at controlling your Talents."

Again, I lean in and whisper, this time letting

my lips brush the outer edge of his ear, "How would you like your hair cut?"

Those sand and sea eyes remain cold and calculating as he flashes me his pearly whites. "A trim. Clean up the neckline and around my ears, please."

Chapter 23

This has to go down as the worst night in history. I'm tired, I'm sore and I've had enough of Var Royd and his employees to last a lifetime. We all have. Rey's mantra of the night says it all, *doesn't matter how big the tip is, it's not worth this headache.*

I swear Dara was making a grocery list out of her share of the Royd empire. Not even Chatty Cathy, Nyssa wanted to stand around and shoot the breeze once the last person left. We all stumbled through basic clean up, grunted our goodbyes and they headed out, leaving me to lock up.

Staggering up the stairs, I wonder if I can persuade Teiran to skip the physical therapy. I'm not in the mood to fight about skipping it.

Truthfully, I'm not in the mood for anything but my bed. His takeover of the front desk was a huge help and I owe him at the very least a thank you, but that can wait too. I also owe him for not taking me down when Var bated me into losing my control. Maybe he's starting to trust me? Nah, he probably figured the collar would stop me before anything serious happened. And it stopped me cold, just like this locked door.

Strange, I don't remember locking it before work and Teiran doesn't lock it when he's here. That can only mean one thing. I jam the key into the locks giving them a gleeful twist and swing the door into a dark room.

"Teiran?" I nearly do the Snoopy Dance.

Flipping on the light, I make a beeline for the bedrooms.

I tap on the closed door, no answer. "Teiran?" Excitement bubbles as I give the knob a twist and poke my head inside. The dimly lit room is empty. I punch the air and do a little dance. Maybe this night isn't so bad after all. I'm alone. All alone for the first time in weeks.

"Looking for something?"

That jump of ecstasy turns to a leap of fear and giggles to a shriek. "Hel's Realm, Teiran, you scared the shit out of me. And yes, I was looking for you."

"Well, you found me."

"So I see." Pushing my hand against his chest, I stalk past him, heart still racing. "The place was locked and dark when I came up, I was just wondering where you were."

"I was out."

"And now you're back." I plop down on the couch long enough to slip off my heels.

My poor aching feet protest the walk to the kitchen, but I suddenly feel the need to grab a soda. And possibly some aspirin as the rest of my body catches up to the burning throb radiating upward. Setting a can of Dr. Pepper on the table, I loosen the straps holding the brace and it follows. Pressure removed, my wrist makes the aches and pains of the rest of my body seem like a tickle.

Rolling the cold can along the length of my forearm, it's back to the couch. Biting back groans of pain, I lower myself, letting my head fall back and close my eyes.

Cushions depress next to me and the can is taken away, opened and returned. Slowly, I lift my head and take a sip as a large oblong pill is pressed into my hand. My aversion to pain pills is quickly forgotten as I toss it back. I don't care if it makes me loopy, just as long as it takes away the pain.

"You over did it tonight."

"You can say that again."

"You over did it tonight."

A small tremor of fear weaves its way up my spine. Flashes of The Collector masquerading as Rey. I swivel my head to the side, making sure Teiran Rand still sits beside me and not some replication. He's smiling. Teiran Rand made a joke and now he's smiling. Either I'm dreaming, The Collector has returned, or that pill is working its nasty magic faster than it should.

His smile fades and creases appear across his brow. Concern? Closing my eyes, I shake my head and pain rolls over me like a truck. Not the pill and

I'm in too much pain to be asleep. When I open them, I'm faced with the patented blank stare. Yeah, that's the Teiran I know. So no Collector.

"Very funny."

"It was meant to be."

"It was, it really was, you just took me off guard."

"How so?" He gently picks up my aching arm and begins massaging.

"You don't normally joke. For a minute I thought…"

"You thought what?"

"Don't worry about it, it's silly."

"Please, tell me."

His fingers feel so good and the pill is taking effect. "I had a little flashback of when The Collector impersonated Rey, the night he abducted me."

"Forgive me, I did not mean to revive such memories."

"It's okay. I like it when you joke. I also like it when you touch me."

His eyes widen and he places my arm in my lap.

Unholy crap, I said that with my outside voice. "I'm sorry, It's the pill and I'm tired. Seriously, pain meds make me say stupid shit."

"I understand," he says, even though it's clear from his expression he doesn't. Mr. Cool, Calm and Collected would never let stupid shit fall from between those perfect lips.

"Perhaps it is time for you to retire for the night." Standing he holds out his hand.

If I take that hand, I run the risk of saying or doing something else stupid. I take the safest option, holding out my soda, careful not to let my fingers brush his. "You're probably right."

Setting the can on the couch side table, he waits for me to stand and make my way toward the bedroom. Bedroom, maybe I should invite him in. Damn pill. Thank the gods I only took one. I stagger walk down the hall on pins and needles, not just from the lack of circulation in my feet, but those metaphorically raised by my drug induced chatter.

The living room light flicks off and I place my palm against the wall, continuing the mile long journey in the dark. The dark, where all things better left unseen happen. Shaking my head, I reach my bedroom. Extending my arm around the wall, I flip on the light. I'm greeted with a yowling yawn and exaggerated stretch from ears to tail.

"Hey, CC, I forgot to feed you."

"He will be fine. I took care of his evening meal."

I can almost feel his breath on my bare neck and lean backward. Hands grasp my shoulders, righting me. "Thank you."

"Let us get you into bed." He guides me toward the bed and a myriad of dirty thoughts surface.

"I need to change and should take a shower." The residual hair from tonight's cuts pokes and itches.

"The shower can wait until tomorrow, when you are coherent."

"You could help me." Once again with the stupid, it's like a bad joke. You might be high on painkillers if sexual innuendos are your standard answer.

He turns me toward him, pressing down on my shoulders until I'm sitting on the edge of the bed, staring up at him. Devouring every last luscious, icy inch. Suddenly I'm very warm, the only answer in my drug addled brain is to remove my clothing and press his hard cold body against mine. I pull off my shirt and toss it aside. Reaching out, I grab his, pulling it loose from his body plastering jeans. My free hand slips under the securely buttoned cotton, his stomach muscles rippling under my touch.

With something that sounds remarkably like a sigh of exasperation crossed with a growl, he removes my hands and steps out of reach, flicking off the light as he backs out of the room. "Goodnight, Miss Fey."

Chapter 24

Amber eyes hover above. Fingers tangle in every shade of blond imaginable. The taste of honey on lips and tongue. Sun-kissed flesh and the heat of a summer day. Ric, the light at the end of the tunnel.

Flesh cools as the sun sets. Sapphire seduction beneath black lashes. Skin, starlight pale and bright. Captivating, frostbitten kisses. Teiran, the darkness in the deepest recesses.

Silvered moonlight made flesh and blood. Pale eyes darkening with desire and power. Hands and body that know me better than I know myself. The piece of me I didn't know was missing. Vereinen, the perfect combination of light and dark.

Undeniable attraction and unattainable beauty. Power radiates from every perfectly carved inch, flowing over my skin with a branding heat. Warm breath against my ear. Promises of immeasurable pleasure. If I submit. If I say the words.

I want to answer. I want to repeat the words.

A nip of the lobe and more promised delights. All I have to do is say the words. Admit what we both already know. A trail is traced from breasts to belly button. A shifting of bodies and I gaze into sand and sea eyes as he lifts his face from my belly. The arrogant twist of his mouth. The knowing gleam in his eyes. The possessive grip of his hands on my hips.

"Say the words, Keely. I belong to…"

"No one. I. Belong. To. No. One." Bolting upright, clutching sweaty sheets around my shaking body, I gasp for air.

The door slams against the wall, a muscular silhouette framed in the doorway. Teiran moves with the unexpected speed and grace of a much leaner, smaller form. He checks every corner, the closet, even behind the drapes and under the bed. "What happened?"

"Nothing. It was nothing."

"You cried out, was there an intruder?"

"It was just a dream."

His eyes narrow in the dim afternoon light. "Just a dream made you cry out with fear? Just a dream has caused you to shake and hide beneath the covers?"

"Fine, a nightmare, then." I take a deep breath, thrusting the sheet away. His ridiculous questioning driving away the fear.

"Was it her?" He nods toward my wrist.

"No."

"Then what would cause such terror?"

"I don't remember." Like I'm going to tell him my boogie man is his boss. He'd tell Var

I'm having dreams about him. That would be the kicker, wouldn't it? Mr. Inflated Ego would twist it into something other than a nightmare. Probably an erotic dream, one where I'm his latest favorite sex toy. Residuals of the dream float to the surface, images of lips and hands and the sensations. Suppressing a shudder, I finish kicking the sheets away, avoiding the large lump at the foot of the bed resembling a sleeping cat. I prod the blankets with my toe, no movement, too soft. Where is CC? Usually, he plays the part of alarm clock from dreadful dreams. I'm feeling a bit abandoned here.

"If you are looking for your cat, he is in the kitchen."

"Um, thanks?"

"For?"

"Feeding him, I guess."

He nods. "That cat wails louder than any beast should, food is the only way to get it to stop."

Hiding a smirk, I slide to the edge of the bed and stand. Looks like CC is growing on him. "And thanks for coming to my rescue. Even if it was just a stupid dream."

"A dream that you will not divulge."

"Seriously, I can't remember."

"You shouted I belong to no one."

"I did?" Wonder how long I can keep up the ignorant act.

"Yes, you did. Do the words mean anything to you?"

"Probably the pain pills. I almost always have nightmares if I have to take pain pills. That's why I hate taking them, that and they make me say and do stupid things." Heat rises in my cheeks as he tilts his head to one side, slowly taking in my attire. Hel's Realm, I'm still in yesterday's work clothes, well, minus shirt and shoes. Painkiller induced foolishness floods the brain and my stomach drops. Standing here in my favorite demi-cup and slacks is an obvious answer to foggy questions. Taking advantage of his averted eyes, I grab yesterday's shirt and pull it over my head as I push past him. "Is that coffee I smell?"

Hightailing it to the kitchen, the little voices in my head wonder if it was an attempt at respecting my privacy or something else that made him look away. Something like embarrassment. For me, that is, he has nothing to be embarrassed about. Had I actually told him I like it when he touches me? Sighing I grab a cup, hoping my hands steady soon. If this is any indication of how my day is going to be, I better crawl back into bed.

I turn, gasping in pain and shock as coffee sloshes over the cup and down the front of me. "Damn it, Teiran don't sneak up on me like that."

"Did you forget you are not alone?"

"No," I set the cup down, grabbing a towel, "I

just didn't expect you to be standing right behind me. How the hel do you do that?"

"Do what? Walk?"

"Walk without making any noise." I give up wiping my shirt, it needs washed anyway, and drop the towel. Giving the floor a quick foot mop, before snagging it with my toes and lift it so I don't have to bend-over.

"Years of practice. I might ask you the same question."

"I make all kinds of noise when I walk."

"True, but you seem to have very dexterous toes."

"That? That's based purely on laziness." I shrug, moving toward the bathroom to dispose of the towel. "Why bend-over when I don't have to."

"Lord Royd called while you were asleep."

It's all I can do to keep my lips sealed around the *so what* dancing on the tip of my tongue as I round the corner back into the living area. "I'm sure he left a message."

"Yes."

"Well?" I take the refilled cup he offers. "What did he want?"

His expression darkens, teetering on anger. Whatever it is, it can't be good, at least from Teiran's perspective and it has me between worried and delighted. Anything Teiran is unhappy about could swing either way.

Being ordered to work with me would put a bur

in his back-pocket, but it could also mean he's been relieved of duty. Which could mean I'm getting a new babysitter. If it's Ric, I'm in luck, but with what little luck I have lately, it will be someone like Vana. The possibilities are endless when it comes to the whims of Var Royd.

"He wants me to remove your collar."

"What? Did I hear you right?" I struggle to push down the desire to jump for joy and chant, *no collar, no collar*. This is like the best thing ever.

"Yes, he wants me to remove your collar so that you may resume practicing services requiring your Talent."

"Oh. That's great." I know I sound a little ungrateful, but how can I not be disappointed that it's only for work? "I can start booking hair growth and skin manipulation appointments." Most of the clients who abandoned me are starting to call again, fickle populace. Especially, when it comes to the beauty world, but I've got bills to pay and their money spends just fine. "So, does this start tonight?"

"Do you have any appointments requiring your Talent?"

I shake my head. "No, but you could let me practice growing mine back. I'm a little rusty."

He frowns, but steps forward until we are toe to toe. My lips part, tongue darting out to wet them as he raises his hands and places them around my neck a hair's breadth from touching me. As his head lowers, mine tips back, our eyes now locked in what could be considered a lover's pose.

"I shall not remove it for this experiment, but I will stop it from…hurting you, while you regrow your hair."

Trying to hide my disappointment is futile and triggers the faintest upward movement of his lips. With his recent attempts at being civil, friendly even, I'd forgotten that deep down he would rather I didn't exist. But I have to trust him in this moment. He could easily strangle me or pull away as I call on my Talents, just as easily as I could conjure up shadows to pull him into oblivion. Looks like this experiment is a two way street in the land of trust and I want to prove—no, need to prove—I'm trustworthy.

Taking a deep breath, I lift my head a little higher. "Understood."

He stares into my eyes, his own narrowing, as if looking for some sign that I'm tricking him. I must have passed the test, his hands rest on my shoulders, fingers spanning the collar. "You may begin."

Closing my eyes, I reach down into my core and grasp my Talents. A wonderful, cool breeze blows through my mind, welcoming me. Embracing me. I've forgotten how good it feels to use them. I picture the hundreds of thousands of follicles covering my head. I picture the hair they hold. I picture that hair growing and coax it into action. Down past my ears. Below my jaw. Brushing my shoulders. The middle of my back. Ending at my waist. Slowly, I open my eyes and smile. The reaction on his face is all I need to know I succeeded.

Chapter 25

"Holy shit, you've got hair."

I laugh still riding the high of using my Talents. "Yep. Long beautiful hair."

"Shining, gleaming, streaming, flaxen, waxen."

"It looks amazing." Nyssa runs her fingers through my waist length curls.

"Thanks. I can't take all the credit though," I nod in Teiran's direction, "he had a hand in helping me out."

Rey leans in close. "What made him change his mind?"

"Var ordered him to remove my collar so I can do my job."

"He took it off so you could grow yours?"

"Not exactly, he touched it so I could practice." Rey snorts. "Dude has trust issues."

"Yeah, but can you blame him?"

"Guess not, you could have gone all Schattenkind on his ass for making you wait this long."

"True." Not even the mention of my supposed evil side can dampen my spirits. Getting to use my Talents felt so good, almost better than sex good.

Looking at the appointment book I'm reminded of the one thing that can ruin the night. I have to admit feeling slightly relieved my seven canceled, so I'm not running behind for my seven thirty, Stasia Athory. I'd love to go all Schattenkind on her ass.

"What's the plan for tonight?" asks Nyssa, leaning against the desk. "Think Teiran will watch the front desk again?"

"Maybe if you ask him, he seems to have a soft spot for annoying nix—oof." Rey rubs his solar plexus. "Damn girl, take it easy, I'm still sore from last night."

"That's not what she said."

"Okay you two, enough horsing around. Doors open in fifteen and we better be ready, tonight looks busier than last night. Nys, why don't you go ask Teiran if he'll watch the desk again, please?"

"Guess she can't read." Rey nods toward the slender girl beating frantically on the door. "Should I let her in?"

I glance at the clock and nod. "Might as well, she can wait in here as easily as she can in her car, I guess."

He flips the lock and holds the door open enough for her to enter. A golden ponytail, set high on her head, brushes him as she ducks under his arm.

"You must be Rey. I'm Winola, Win for short." She gives his hand a hearty shake then nods toward the door. "You may want to re-lock that."

It's probably the first time I've seen Rey completely speechless, it leaves me wishing for a camera to capture the utter confusion on his face. When she makes a beeline toward the desk, hand extended toward me, I'm feeling confident he's wishing the same thing.

"Miss Fey, I presume. I'm Winola Mallory and I've been sent to fill in as your receptionist." Her bright pink smile complements her fair complexion, highlighted by a smattering of freckles. Giving the appearance of gold dust sprinkled across her nose and the tops of her cheeks.

I take her hand, looking into large sky-blue eyes that resonate friendliness and competence. "I wasn't expecting anyone, hadn't even advertised the position yet."

"Mr. Royd sent me." She sets her bag under the desk, adjusts the chair and proceeds to arrange the appointment book, pencils and phone within reach of her small frame.

"I see."

"Hi, Teiran." She smiles, obviously thrilled to see a familiar face coming around the dividing wall.

Of course, my new receptionist would know my babysitter; they work for the same pain in my ass. What I didn't expect was a squealing whirlwind of blonde and black hugs and giggles.

Rey leans down, as Win and Nyssa hug it

out, and whispers, "Think they know each other?"

"Nah, they've been paid to act out a random fantasy of yours."

Laughing, he pats me on the back. "I wish." Glancing at the clock he sighs. "As much as I'm enjoying the show, we've got two minutes till the horde descends."

His words speak volumes, volumes of people lining up outside the door. It's too late to worry about whether my new receptionist is qualified, can handle the mob, or screw me over like the last one. Inadvertent or not, Jenny's part in The Collector's plan was still a betrayal. "Battle stations everyone."

Rey hustles to the cutting room floor, with Nyssa close behind. Winola straightens her business casual attire and heads to the door. Flipping the lock, she opens the door and steps to the side. "Welcome to Fey Creations salon, please approach the desk in an orderly fashion. Once you are signed in, please take a seat and your stylist will be with you shortly."

A million things run through my head that I should have told her before we opened. Like how much time is needed per service isn't a set rule, more of a guideline, depending on the stylist and the client. Teiran grabs my hand before I can broach the subject, pulling me to the back room.

"Hey, I need to explain time allotments."

"Do not worry about Win. She is more than

capable of handling the job. If she has questions she will ask."

"You know her better than I do, but if she screws up; it's you I'll be yelling at."

His brows shoot upward. "As if I expect any less, now come if you want your collar removed."

How the hel do I argue with that?

Shutting the door behind us, he stands in front of me, reluctance written all over him. In truth, I don't have any appointments tonight that require my Talents, so it makes me wonder why he's taking it off. "Um, Teiran?"

"Yes." His hands hover over my shoulders.

"Why are you taking it off tonight? I thought Var said only when I need my Talents and I don't need them."

"Your first client of the night is Stasia Athory."

"So?"

It's apparent that straight-laced and stoic, Teiran Rand is spending too much time with me and my crew when he rolls his eyes. "Are you an idiot, woman?"

"I like to think not, but there are times when I wonder. Like now, what's the big deal with Stasia and my collar being off?"

"If she thinks you are in control of your Talents, she will be less likely to manipulate you."

"One little flaw in that plan, the next time she sees me I have it on. What then?"

He pinches the bridge of his nose between thumb and forefinger.

"I was nice of you to try and help me, but sorry, your plan sucks. There is no easy out for this. She's not going to just disappear if I don't have it on. I get it, Teiran, you're an action guy and you want to fix things, but this isn't the way."

"This is what I get for spending so much time with you and your friends."

I laugh, reaching out to give his arm a squeeze. "Guess there might be a heart in that big ol' chest of yours after all."

"And a brain in that small head of yours."

"I have my moments," my hand lingers on his arm, "and so do you." His smile is all it takes, my hand travels up his arm, pulling him closer. The heels aren't quite tall enough and I find myself on tip-toe as I lean in toward those generous lips. Three authoritative raps against the break room door before it opens gives us enough time to stumble away from each other.

"Miss Fey, your appointment is here." Win looks from me to Teiran and back, my flaming cheeks speaking multitudes.

I can only hope her pretense at blandness means she'll ignore anything she thought she saw. The last thing I need is a spy for Var Royd telling tales. Gods only know what he'd do with this information. After seeing his displeasure concerning Ric's present, I can only guess how a kiss from Teiran would cause him to react.

Say the words, Keely. I belong to…

Shaking off the memory of the dream, I smile at Win. "Thanks, I'll be right out."

"I'll let her know." She backs out of the room, but the closing door doesn't hide the frown she shoots Teiran.

"Sorry, I didn't mean—"

He places a finger over my mouth. "I shall stay at the back of the room, watching."

I nod, wondering if he cut me off because he trusts Win, or wants to pretend it never happened. A part of me wants to believe it was some romantic, you have nothing to apologize for gesture, but I'm betting he's already forgotten.

Chapter 26

One of the most difficult things about the service industry is keeping your personal feelings out of the workplace. Seeing my new archenemy sitting in reception, poker-straight back, legs crossed, one red-soled shoe bouncing impatiently as she flips through a magazine, pushes that to the limit. Smoothing my expression to banal disinterest, I take a deep breath and step into view.

"Stasia, I'm ready for you."

I know she heard me, but she takes her time responding. Slowly lifting her gaze from the ancient fashion rag—I really need to re-up my subscriptions—deer in the headlights eyes, her mouth a perfectly shaped O of surprise.

Good grief, I really hate dealing with women sometimes. Too many games. Stupid, bitchy games. Well, she's on my turf now and she'll play by my rules. As she stands I turn and head back to my station. It's not like she'll get lost on the way if I don't wait for her. I can hope, but it's not likely.

A cat, a big cat stalking its prey comes to mind as she slinks toward my chair. Grabbing the cape from the back of my chair I wait for her to sit down, a ceremony all of its own. With only Rey and Teiran on the floor you'd think she'd give the high-class seductress act a break.

I sweep my cape over the showy presentation of her legs, tempted to tighten the neck closure as far as it will go, settling for just tight enough to let her know who's boss.

The twitch of her jaw and rustle of plastic fabric almost brings a smile to my face, but I bite the inside of my cheek. Just like she fights the urge to ask me to loosen the cape.

I can't decide if the French twist is a blessing or a curse as I pull pins. A blessing that removing them gives Nyssa time to finish Rey's client. A curse if I have to attempt to replicate it, with the brace it will be difficult at best. On the shiny side, I'll get to smack her a few times with a justifiable excuse.

"A twist again?" I brush the lacquer from her hair. Hel's Realm, what does she use for hair spray? Spray adhesive? It's stiffer than anything I've ever worked with.

"I'm not sure what I want. Perhaps something similar to yours, although mine is nowhere the length of yours. It's lovely tonight. Who made your wig, or are those extensions?"

A wig joke, awesome. That familiar itch creeps along my skin, the first warning sign. "Actually, I was born with this." I run a hand through my hair at the scalp and smile, loving the minute it dawns on her that it really is my hair.

"Have you been using my serum?" Her voice raises on *my serum*.

"Nope, this was me." I lay my hands on her shoulders and lean in, letting her get a good look at my eyes in the mirror as they darken. "All me. Now if you'll go over to the shampoo bowls, Nyssa is ready for you."

I give her a little shove forward. I may not have been one of the mean girls in school, but I had plenty of experience at their hands. A little may have rubbed off. As she totters off to pester Nyssa, I make a quick getaway to the back room. I just need a couple of minutes to breath. Alone. I'm coming perilously close to acting unprofessionally and even closer to losing my head. Literally.

Grabbing the counter, eyes closed, I take deep breath after breath. Mentally tightening the blockade I've built around my Talents, forcing them back. As much as I'd like to obliterate her, it's not worth dying for. A hand drops onto the back of my neck, fingers spanning the shrinking collar. Once it flows back to normal, Teiran removes his hand and I turn to face him.

"Thanks."

"Do not allow her to manipulate you into something you may regret."

"I'm trying not to, but everything about her gets on my last nerve. It's not just what she wants from me. It's the whole package. I dislike women like that."

"Women like what?"

"Women who blatantly use their beauty and sexuality to get what they want. Promising everything, yet giving nothing in return. Women who know they're beautiful and think the world owes them, or use it as a reason to be nasty."

The low rumble of laughter tweaks my buttons.

"What are you laughing at?"

"You, for believing all women do not do this, you included."

"I don't throw myself out there as eye candy, writing checks with my body that will bounce if someone tries to cash them. I certainly don't believe anyone owes me anything, nor am I mean because I'm slightly above average in the looks department."

"All I am saying is that everyone uses something to manipulate things to their advantage. You have an understanding of hers; use this to your advantage."

Rubbing my temples, I sag against the counter. He's got a point. "You're right."

The door swings open and a wide eyed Nyssa enters. The pallor of her face alarming. It takes a lot to rattle Nyssa, but it's obvious Stasia Athory has found the breaking point. "Keely, I'm done with Crazy Bitch, your turn."

"What did she do?"

She shakes her head. "Don't worry about it now, just get her out of here."

"None of you are to be alone with her ever again." Teiran stands in the doorway, waiting for me to follow.

"I'll get her out of here as soon as possible, Nys."

"I'll be fine, I just need a moment."

I nod, knowing the exact feeling after dealing with Crazy Bitch. I push past Teiran, trying like hel to keep the reins on my anger. You can mess with me all you want, but don't fuck with my friends.

A hand clamps on my shoulder, stopping me mid-step. I feel his breath against my ear. "Keep your anger in check, she wants you angry. Somehow it serves her purpose."

"Noted." Taking a deep breath, I plaster a smile on my face as I approach the bitch in my chair.

"Your shampoo girl is delightful." The smile on Stasia's face contradicts the calculating glint in her eyes.

"She's very good at her job. Have you decided how you would like your hair styled?"

She waves a hand dismissively. "Do what you think will look best."

The noise of the dryer keeps her chatter to a minimum, giving me lots of time to think. Think about what would look best on her. A buzz would be the cut of choice, but since it's just a style I settle for blowing her hair forward so it sticks against those perfectly made up lips. Think about how many others she's probably blackmailed or tricked into giving up their blood, sweat and tears. Think about how she keeps giving both Rey and Teiran covert looks and what the thoughts are behind those looks. Think about how I'd like to hand her and her nasty potions over to the shadows. But most of all I think about keeping my anger in check, especially when I trade the dryer for a hot iron.

"Have you given any thought to my business proposition?"

There it is, the one thing I've been trying not to think about. "No."

"No, you haven't thought about it?"

"No, I'm not giving you my blood."

"Tears would do, although it will take more of them."

"Sweat and urine would probably do it too, but the answer is still no."

Her laughter may sound musical and sweet to others, but it's like nails on a chalkboard to my ears. "Yes, perspiration and skin oils are acceptable, but harder to obtain than tears. Urine…urine is unacceptable, even if it were not disgusting, it contains other unwanted variables."

As if the rest of the choices aren't disgusting. Grabbing the stiffest hold spray on my vanity, I begin manipulating her hair into place. "Look

Stasia, I'm not going to give you any body fluids for any price, so drop it."

"Not even to get the collar removed? Yes, I see it peeking out from your blouse and I know they will not be removing it the near future."

"And you think you can get rid of it for me."

"I know I can. It will take some work, but I can get rid of him," she nods to Teiran's refection, standing at the back of the room, "and the collar."

"It's still a no." Setting the hair spray down, I remove the cape, waiting for her to take the hint and leave.

Standing, she grabs my hand mirror from the vanity and checks her style from every angle. "You really are as talented as they say."

"I'm glad you like it, Win is waiting for you in reception." I take the mirror from her outstretched hand.

Stepping into my personal space, she places a finger on the collar. "Do not waste your Talents on those who would harness them for their own purposes." Leaning in, her breath caresses my ear. "I'll be in touch."

Chapter 27

"What a bitch." I hear from the corner where Nyssa and Win are huddled in animated conversation. It doesn't take a rocket scientist to know who they're discussing.

Rey looks up from his nightly clean up. "Who's a bitch?"

Okay, it doesn't take a *female* rocket scientist. A male, on the other hand, is blinded by her glossy exterior.

"I believe they are speaking of Stasia Athory." Teiran hands me my keys, having locked the door after the last client.

I stand corrected, not all males. Then again, Teiran doesn't seem to have an ounce of Rey's womanizing ways in him. It does make me wonder if he even thinks about dating, or if his devotion to his dream girl, Vana Royd, has spoiled him.

Not that I should care, just hate the idea of him wasting his time on the other bitch in my life. Call it a gut feeling, but something tells me she'd consider dating him a step down. His feelings about me aside, he doesn't deserve the treatment he gets from the Royd twins.

"What did the *bitch* do?" Leave it to Dara to ask the question we're all dying to hear the answer to. It's not like I don't have an inkling what the answer is when I know what Stasia wants from me.

"She offered to 'buy' my body fluids," says Nyssa, accenting buy with finger quotes as she drops into the shampoo bowl chair next to Win.

"Wait a minute, did I hear you right?" Spinning his chair to face her, Rey sits down.

Leaning against her vanity, Dara looks from Nyssa to me, a silent question simmering below the surface.

Damn, she knows I was offered the same deal. Her gaze shifts to Teiran standing sentinel beside my vanity, then back to me. Double damn, she knows I told him. The scar on my wrist itches, reminding me of the last betrayal she felt I inflicted. Am I in 'take her out' territory?

"Yeah, you heard right."

"Why'd she want your body fluids?"

"She wants to put them in her newest moisturizer. *It would make it extremely hydrating.*" She shudders and Win reaches over and squeezes her hand.

"How much did she offer?" Rey swivels the chair back and forth with one foot, grin growing.

"I didn't ask, just told her no and deposited her in Keely's chair. It was just too weird, who asks for body fluids? Eww."

"Wonder if she has a use for any of my body fluids."

"Gross." Nyssa tosses a towel at Rey as she and Win giggle.

Dara stares accusingly in my direction and I fight the urge to wipe the sweat doting my upper lip. Time to fess up, but I'd rather not do it with Win here. There's no need to air my dirty laundry in front of a stranger. It'll be hard enough with those I know. Friend of Nyssa's or not, she's still a stranger to me and I don't need her running back to Var Royd with any info that I don't want shared. Not that he doesn't already know this secret. Hel's Realm, another reason for Dara to be pissed at me.

"You okay, Keely? You look a little paler than usual."

"Fine, Rey, just a little tired."

His eyes flick from me to Dara and back. "If you say so."

"I do."

With a shrug, he slides forward in his chair and stands. I know he's not buying it, but I'm not saying another word on the subject, until we are minus one temporary receptionist.

With measured steps, I walk over and holding out my hand. "I wanted to thank you for coming down and helping us out tonight, Win."

With a bright, angelic smile, she takes my hand, pumping it with more strength than expected. "It was my pleasure. I'll be here tomorrow at a quarter till."

"Quarter to seven?"

"Unless you need me earlier."

"You're coming back?" I loosen my grip, but she doesn't take the hint.

"Yes, I've been contracted to fill-in until you find a replacement."

Finally, I manage to slip my hand from her over enthusiastic hold. Sliding it in my back pocket does the double duty of keeping it out of her reach and wiping off the nervous sweat condensing on my palm. "Contracted?"

"I'm a temp, that's how I met Mr. Royd. I fill in for Celia when needed."

Unholy shit, he just keeps doing things to make me feel indebted. "Ah, well, thanks for your help. I'll see you at quarter to seven tomorrow."

Ignoring the stares and silent accusations shot my way; I maneuver Win toward the front door, Nyssa practically stepping on my heels. Only after they say their good-byes and the door clicks shut behind Win, do I remember to breathe. But with the looks I'm getting from my entourage, maybe I should have held it a little longer. Like until I passed out.

Flicking off the switch to the outdoor lights and reception, I move past them without a word, flipping the switch to the cutting room on my way to the break room. The clickety-clack of Nyssa's kitten heels followed up with the lighter tap of Rey's loafers and determined stride of Dara's boots echoes behind me. Without a doubt, I know Teiran's nearly silent step can't be far behind.

Heading to the fridge, I ignore the line of ducklings filing in behind me and reach for a soda, hoping to hold back the desert encroaching on my throat. I'd give just about anything for a little liquid courage right now, but this will have to do. Sitting, as much as my feet would love it, is not an option. I need to stay upright, show a little confidence. Rey and Nyssa I'm not as worried about, but I can't let Dara have the authoritative stance. Bracing myself against the counter, I wait for the onslaught of questions and accusations.

Teiran pushes past Dara's form leaning against the door frame, coming to stand near me. Spinning a chair, Rey straddles it, arms braced on the back, watching every move. Silence hangs thicker than hair gel in the room. Hoisting herself onto the counter next to me, Nyssa finally breaks the silence.

"Did she ask you too?"

I nod with a grimace.

"What was she going to make out of yours?"

"Anti-aging serum."

"Guess that makes sense. What did you tell her?"

Tipping my head to one side, I turn toward

her. "Seriously? You actually think I'd take her up on her offer?"

She shrugs. "No, but having you say it is better than listening to crickets chirp in here."

"What was her offer?" There's a dangerous edge to Dara's soft tone. It's almost worse than if she'd yelled at me.

I take a sip of my soda, contemplating what will get me in the least amount of trouble. Dara may not approve of my half of the deal, but I highly doubt Teiran will be a fan. Not that I blame him, since getting rid of him is the bonus prize. The only way to do that is to do what he offered to do to me. Remove him permanently from this world. Call me unimaginative, but the only thing I can come up with is the truth.

"In exchange for some of my blood, she'll get rid of this," I flick the collar, then nod in Teiran's direction, "and him."

Teiran stiffens, jaw twitching, blue flames dancing behind hooded lids.

"No way." Nyssa and Rey echo.

"Yes, way."

"She can do that?" Rey heads to the fridge, pulls out five bottles of beer and starts handing them out.

"She says she can." I shake my head when he offers one to me.

Surprisingly, Teiran takes one. He seems to

be assimilating into our little group. Even Dara recognizes he's not going anywhere and no longer addresses him as Dog, instead using his title, Shield. In turn, he's dropped Vampire for First Arrow. A mutual respect thing? Tolerance on my behalf? Whatever it is, it makes life easier.

"Not possible."

"Which part?"

"I am the only one able to remove your collar and we both know I will never do so without orders from Lord Royd."

"What if she just killed you? Would that cut the tie between us so it could be removed?"

He takes a long pull from his bottle, studying me. Probably gauging my intent, was it innocent curiosity or should he be watching his back? "If I were removed before it is, you would die."

"Seriously?"

Dara nods. "It is a safety mechanism to keep the collared from trying to kill their keepers."

"Unholy shit, by putting the two of us together, Royd has played right into her hands."

Mr. Over-Confident shakes his head. "Stasia Athory is hardly a threat to me or Lord Royd. Besides, we were thrown together long before she entered the picture."

"Don't you think you're being a little short sighted?"

"No, he is correct," says Dara. "I believe the

Sun King assigned him to you for a reason and by ignoring the problem of Stasia he is achieving his desire."

I roll my eyes at Dara. "Besides his desire to keep me in line?"

"His ultimate desire is that you learn to trust each other and work together."

Chapter 28

Dara's right, she just doesn't know how right. I haven't said a word about the proposal of becoming the Shadow to Ric's Sword and Teiran's Shield. Bunching the sheet in my fist, I raise it to my mouth, wondering if it will muffle a scream. Maybe a pillow would be a better choice. Frickin' Var Royd. Everyone keeps telling me to stay away from him, but it's damn near impossible when he keeps inserting himself in every aspect of my life. You can't make someone trust someone they inherently don't. A part of me trusts Teiran. I have to. He, on the other hand, has made it clear he doesn't trust me and never will because of Vereinen.

Oh, Einen, what did you do? Are the things they say true? Are you evil incarnate? Did you conspire with Hel to take down Royd? Why am I paying for something I know nothing about?

This is absolutely, totally ridiculous. I need to get to sleep. Questions with no answers and the sister of the mother of all headaches are going to keep me up all damn day. I'm going to be worthless at work tonight. A cup of Mel's tea might help, that is if I can get my sorry ass out of bed. Sitting on the edge of the bed, I lower my pounding head to my knees. It hurts so bad I want to cry. Not the silly little tears that are leaking down my cheeks, but a full-blown sobfest. If it keeps up, I'm going to be hugging the toilet. More likely the trash can next to my nightstand. There is no way I'll make it to the bathroom.

Grasping around in the dark—there is no way I'm turning on the lights—I manage to grab the can and pull it onto the bed next to me as I slide back into the pile of pillows. If my head is going to explode, I wish it would do it already. The sister of the mother of all headaches is working on an upgrade. Even the gentle pressure of CC's paws against the mattress, makes me want to scream.

They say petting cats can relax you; at this point I'm willing to try anything. I manage to bop him on the nose, before finally making contact with his back to lightly stroke his silky fur. "I'm sorry bud, be thankful it was my good hand." This elicits a grunt as he leans in toward my hand.

My body cradled in pillows, an arm lazily draped around the trashcan, I concentrate on deep breaths and petting the cat. The headache may not be gone, but it's lessened enough, I can close my eyes without the room spinning. I must have dozed off at one point as a little wet nose nudges my hand to continue, but the combination seems to be helping.

The room may not be spinning behind my eyelids, but it's grown foggy. Waves of mist swirl around my ankles and calves, tendrils reaching up to tickle my thighs. Shit. I'm no longer in my bed. Damn it, I'm in Niflheim again, wonder what Hel wants this time. I search the bleak landscape for the two faced goddess, but there's no sign of her. There's no sign of anything, living or dead. How the heck did I end up here if she didn't call me?

Something slides across my upper arm. I swat at the air, spinning around, but there's no one there. Light pressure, like a finger, runs the length of my spine, sending me prancing across the mist covered ground. Distorted laughter rumbles in my head.

"So you think scaring the crap out of me is funny?"

My hair lifts in the light breeze that swirls around me.

"Who the hel are you? What do you want?"

Feather light, the invisible fingers stroke my cheek. Jerking my head away, I take a step back. There's something very personal about that touch. Something familiar.

"Show yourself."

Sadness, longing, hang in the air. Tangible and thick like the mist and then it's gone.

"Who are you?"

"I know it's been a while, but I would expect one to remember their BFF." Bright red hair shines like a beacon in the fog and mist of this dark, dank world. Running toward each other, we end in a head-on hug collision.

"You brought me here?"

"I didn't bring you anywhere. I'm up here," Annya taps my temple, "in your dream."

"Ah." I step out of the hug zone. "Dream walking again, huh?"

"Yeah and I've got to say, this a pretty gloomy place to dream about."

"It's Nif—nothing, probably remnants from the scary movie we watched the other night."

Red brows pinch together and her pink pout becomes a pinched line. Totally not buying my explanation.

"So what's with the dream walk?"

"Can you think of a better way to get a hold of you? You don't answer the phone, or call back if I leave a message, heck you don't even answer your email."

She's right, I've been pretty lousy at getting back to people, but in my defense, I've been busy. "Sorry about that, it's been kind of crazy around here."

"At least call The Sis—What the hel?" The smattering of ginger freckles across her nose stand out, against quickly paling skin.

Ah, shit. My fingers instinctively fly to the collar. Busted. One of the many things I'd been trying to keep from those back home has now been outed.

"Tell me that's not what I think it is."

"Um, a moonstone?" I twiddle with the pendant, grinning like an idiot.

Annya steps into my personal space. Anger turns her whiskey colored eyes a red that nearly matches her hair. "It's a collar. What have you done?"

Ah, crap. Second time in twenty-four hours I've had to answer questions I'd rather not. "I don't suppose you know what schattenkind means."

"Shadow child. Why?"

"Did your mom ever talk about what it is? Maybe mention, Vereinen?"

"I remember her mentioning something about him, but she never really went into details. On occasion I'd hear her mumble it when you were around. What's this got to do with why you have a collar on?"

"Long story short, I'm what can happen when a liosâlfar and a döckâlfar get it on."

"Your parents were both elves?"

I nod.

"That means your grandmother isn't…"

"Yep."

"Wow. Still, what's that got to do with the collar?"

Grimacing, I take a deep breath. "Seems The

Sisters attempted to block my Talents when I was a kid."

"But—"

Ignoring her, I keep rambling. May as well get it all out at once. "The block wore off and they came out to play. These new and improved Talents give me power over shadows and the dead. I'm a necromancer, or so I'm told. Anyway, if you remember that crap with The Collector, he kidnapped me." I hold up a finger every time she opens her mouth. "And I killed him, but turning the dead loose on him. That's how I ended up with this lovely, fashion accessory."

"Unholy shit," she whispers. "That's a lot to take in, in the short span of a dream."

"Yeah, now you know why I've been so busy. Killing people and all, fills up your time."

"Do The Sisters know?"

"I'm sure in their own freaky way they do; they probably just don't remember it when they're in the real world."

"Unholy shit."

"So, still friends, or have I scared you enough to drop me like a hot potato?"

"Of course we're still friends…I just need time to process everything you've told me."

"Just spill it, you need to run home and ask your mom about schattenkind."

"Well, yeah, I want to know everything."

"Then I'll get a dear Jane letter in the mail and you'll change your phone number."

She frowns at me. "Will you just let me think this through? Maybe I can come up with something to help you get that thing off."

"Um, didn't you hear me? I. Killed. Someone."

"It was self-defense, right? And hadn't he killed others?"

I nod.

"Then he freakin' deserved it. Just give me some time, you're waking up anyway."

"Just don't tell The Sisters."

"That's your job, Scrawny."

She hugs me, which is all the reassurance I need. Through thick and thin, she's still my BFF.

I wake cuddling a trashcan under one arm and a cat under the other, but it's okay. Somehow, seeing Annya and dumping the load I've been carrying has made everything okay. Even Teiran standing over me scowling doesn't bring me down.

"Good morning." I smile up at him.

His scowl deepens and my smile disappears as he raises his hand. "The book you wanted from the library is in." He drops it on my midsection and I curl up and around it, gasping for air as the door slams behind him.

Chapter 29

"I don't see what the big deal is; I ordered a book from the library. It's not like you had to go get it, I would have gone."

"It is not that I had to retrieve your book, it is the book itself that is the problem." Teiran's frown deepens.

I already knew that, but playing dumb blonde sounds like a safe bet. With any luck, it'll wear him down—like it does Ric—and he'll give up shouting and go back to brooding. "What? You don't like books?"

He pinches the bridge of his nose between forefinger and thumb. "It is the subject matter, I am opposed to, not books in general. What would make you want such a book?"

Sighing, I flop onto the couch. "I want to understand what I am."

"You believe that book will tell you what you are?"

"It can't hurt. No one else will explain it to me." I throw in a little pouting, not a difficult task with the mood I'm in. "Besides, it's none of your business what I read."

Teiran finally stops pacing, anger barely concealed. The coffee table is going to make a lousy barricade if he loses control. "You are my responsibility. Everything you do is my business by proxy. If you step out of bounds, it falls upon me to correct the situation."

Or take the blame. He doesn't say it out loud, but it's hanging there between us. I've gotten him in enough trouble already. Do I feel bad about getting him in trouble? Yeah, I do, but it doesn't mean I'm not going to buck the system every now and then.

My finger traces the title on the book's cover. Necromancy In The Modern Age. The modern age of what? Part of me expected a leather bound tome, old and cracked, or even covered in skin—à la Evil Dead—with raised lettering, nearly worn smooth and brittle pages fading from yellow to a darker tan. Instead, I'm holding a dog-eared paperback that could be picked up at any chain bookstore.

"I suppose you want me to return it unopened."

"That would be preferred, but I know you will ignore my desires."

If only Teiran knew how wrong he is with that statement. Raising my eyes from the book, I take my time meeting his gaze, objectifying every inch of him. Not only do I not ignore his desires, some I've even contemplated helping him out with. Excluding the desire to kill me, of course.

He flinches, breaking eye contact under my scrutiny and turns away.

"Read the damned thing, but do it quickly and do not repeat out loud anything you read."

Read it quickly? That's not going to happen. I don't have that kind of time. "Why shouldn't I read it out loud? It's not like it's the Necronomicon." I can't help but giggle.

Teiran spins on me, eyes blazing. "Do not laugh, for every myth, or work of fiction, there is a seed of truth."

"Seriously, this thing looks like a joke." Flipping through the pages, I shake my head.

"Do not judge a book by its cover."

The eye roll isn't the slightest bit involuntary. "Come on, you don't really believe there are ancient secrets of the dead in here." I stop on a random page, scanning the text. "And with such power can one achieve control of—"

He rushes me, using the table as a springboard, and snatches the book from my hands. "I said do not read it aloud. What part of your hearing is impaired, or is it your ability to comprehend?"

"There is nothing wrong with my hearing and I comprehend just fine. You're being ridiculous. Reading that out loud won't conjure any demons."

"Did your guardians not teach you anything about the power of words?"

I'm on my feet, tempted to use the coffee table

to snatch the book he holds over his head. "Yeah, yeah, yeah, words have power, but you have to place intent behind them."

"Sometimes the intent is unconscious." His finger makes contact with my temple. I weave to avoid a second tap, but the tight space lands me back onto the couch.

"What? You think I have some subconscious desire to release demons on the world?" Once the words are out, I realize how stupid that sounds. Who's the one who unconsciously released shadow creatures on her friends? Um, yeah, that would be me.

"I do not know if it is a desire as much as your innate nature."

"Gee, thanks." I know he's only stating fact, but it doesn't sting any less. Maybe a little more than if the words were said just to be cruel. I could brush that off as a typical Teiran reaction.

Sitting on the table, our knees touching, he lays the book to the side and stares at me. "From what I have learned in our time together, I do not believe you would intentionally hurt anyone. But that does not change what you are, what you are capable of, or the uncontrolled power inside of you. It will eventually drive you mad, like the other. If it were up to me, I would spare the woman I have come to know from that fate."

There are no words to fill my gaping mouth.

Has Teiran, in his gruff, matter-of-fact way, just told me he *likes* me?

Rising to his feet, he slides the book on the table until it sits directly in front of me. "Do what you will with this, but keep my words in mind and do not forget whose mark you carry."

Glancing from me to the book, he heads down the hall to his room.

Ah, crap, I'd forgotten about my open invitation to hel. Will reading a book about dealing with the dead offend Hel? She's not exactly found of the hold I have over her subjects, proven by her irritation at her healer's reaction to me. Maybe I should just leave well enough alone, listen to Teiran's advice and not read the book.

I slide to the edge of the couch, arms resting on my knees, fingers dangling above the book. It's just a book. Probably doesn't have the answers I need anyway. The pages flutter as I draw my finger up the side, coming to rest on the cover. I slide it back and forth. What if Teiran is right and there is an ounce of truth cloaked in crap? It teeters on the edge of the table and topples to the floor, begging to be picked up.

I silence it.

Chapter 30

Lack of sleep does not do a body good. It was a night of read, skim, repeat. Shampoo, rinse, repeat. And read, skim, repeat.

Necromancy In The Modern Age reads like a primer for Uns wanting to dabble in the *dark arts*. As expected, most of it bullshit, like silly rites paying homage to the darker powers. I have doubts that anything between the covers would actually work, but some people will try anything for a chance at attaining power. I managed to glean the names of a couple of supposed true necromancers, so it wasn't a total loss.

Work was a whole other fiasco. Another night, filled with His Lordship's employees. Overtly vain women, prattling on about a new spa in the East Village with the most miraculous products. Some suggesting I carry the line, others questioned the difference between my facials and Stasia's. Then to add insult to injury, arguing the cost of her topical treatments were more cost effective than my Talent driven methods. I don't know if it was cattiness that drove them, or they really believed what they said. Either way, by the end of the night

I couldn't care less. It almost made going back to reading that ridiculous book pleasurable. Almost.

Hovering over my third cup of Mel's tea, nursing the worst kind of book hangover, the last thing I want to hear is the obnoxious ring of the phone. Luckily, my personal assistant is here. Unluckily, he hands it to me.

"Lord Royd."

Another thing I don't want to hear, the seductive tones of a master manipulator. "What?" I say into the handset.

"And here I thought you would be happy to hear from me."

"You thought wrong. What do you want Var?"

"You to join me for a light meal before your salon opens."

"Not interested and I have a headache."

Laughter trickles through the receiver, gliding along my body in a pleasurable wave. "And next you will tell me you are washing your hair."

"Well, yeah, I've got to do that too, but what I said is true. I do have a headache."

"Have you eaten today?"

"Seriously, Var, I don't feel like having dinner. I just want to crawl back into bed until I have to get ready for work."

"You need to eat; perhaps it will help ease your pain." His words may be innocuous, but the husky tone of his voice screams, 'I'll join you in bed.' Sending me reeling back to the dream of him using his male wiles to get me to say the words. Words that would trade my freedom for a moment of pleasure.

"I'll grab some toast, before I take a nap. But there is something you can do for me."

"Whatever your heart desires."

Yeah, right, like he'd actually take the collar off permanently. Not without signing off on my soul. "Stop sending flowers."

"You dislike like flowers?"

"I like flowers just fine, but there are too many. I've exhausted the list of places to dump them and had to resort to leaving them on the sidewalk outside. Not to mention, the intense scent does nothing for a headache."

"I will have them disposed of while we are at dinner."

The click, on the other end, keeps me from disputing his no argument tone. He'll do anything to get his way, won't he?

❦❦❦❦❦

Teiran's signature triple rap cuts through the blessed silence and my head answers in kind. I pull the sheet over my head as I hear the door crack open, maybe if I pretend to be asleep, he'll go away.

Triple tap, only louder. "Lord Royd is here."

"Tell him to go away. I don't want to go to dinner."

"He is in the living room." He closes the door on our pseudo conversation.

Damn it, I may not be able to get away with ignoring him, but I'm not going to dinner. Pushing the sheet away, I gingerly turn and swing my legs over the edge of the bed. Head throbbing with every movement. Reaching for the trash can, I bang my hand against the corner of the nightstand. Biting my lip to hold back the high-pitched whine, I pull it against my chest. My stomach rolls and I quickly change my mind, grab the can and hold it between my knees. Nothing comes up—three cups of tea don't amount to much, in the way of stomach contents—but I have it just in case. Hel's Realm, it hasn't hurt this bad in a long time. There is no way I'll be able to handle dinner, even the thought of food triggers my gag reflex.

A much softer, almost seductive slide of knuckles on the door, gives me a tiny warning before it's opened. "Keely?"

"Go away; I don't want to go to dinner." My voice is ragged whisper, words interspersed with choking back the bile threatening to make an appearance.

Lowering my head, I rest it on the rim of the can clutched to my midsection. Super sensitive ears pick up two sets of elephant sized steps, following

Var into my room. Can't they just be quiet if they're not going to go away?

"How long has she been like this?"

"Since she awoke."

"Have you called a doctor?" Ric leans down, his hand brushing my forehead. "She is burning up." He removes the trash can from my death grip and lowers me back onto the bed, tucking the sheet up around me.

"No doctors," I mumble, "just a headache. Go away, so I can sleep it off before work."

"Teiran, contact Winola, have her call and cancel Miss Fey's appointments for the evening."

Teiran pulls a cell from his pocket and backs out of the room.

"No, I—'

"You are in no condition to work. Alric, make sure Miss Fey stays in bed and keep me updated on her condition."

Yay, I get two babysitters, but I'm not bitching. It could be worse; he could have dismissed them and stayed by himself. Nah, that would never happen. He might have to dump my trashcan. The thought squeezes a giggle from me, ending in a moan of movement activated pain.

"Miss Fey?"

"Aspirin. Water."

He snaps his fingers in Ric's direction. Poor Ric, always the lackey. I'd feel sorrier for him, if it weren't a situation of his own making. Var looms over my bed, taking a step back when I reach up to rub my temples. Any other guy trying to endear himself to a girl would take advantage of the situation, nursing her back to health. But there's a can't-get-away-fast-enough vibe hanging between us. Is he afraid I'm contagious? It's just a headache, for crying out loud.

Ric returns and I take the glass, frowning when he drops one of the prescription painkillers in my hand, instead of aspirin. "This will be far more effective than aspirin."

"Far more effective at knocking me for a loop."

He grins and lifts my hand toward my mouth. "You want the pain to go away, right?"

"Right." Grimacing, I pop it into my mouth, hoping the horse pill doesn't stick on the way down. The bitterness on my tongue is enough to make me want to gag and the water does little to wash it away.

"Sleep tight," he whispers, taking the empty glass.

"Don't let the shadows bite," I whisper back.

Elevens appear between his brows. "What made you say that?"

"I don't know. It just came out." I really don't know where it came from; it tumbled into my head and out of my mouth.

His frown eases, but something tells me, the

man standing in the doorway wouldn't be too happy about what I said. Ric gives my hand a squeeze as he stands, the concern painting his face erasing before he turns toward his boss.

"She should sleep the night through with the pain-relievers Doctor Herbert prescribed."

"Why did she not take them earlier?" His pretty face twisting in irritation. Probably because his plans to take me to dinner were canceled because I didn't want to take a pill.

"She would rather suffer in pain, than say or do foolish things." This from the returned Teiran, who knows all too well, how foolish I can be under the influence.

"Watch over her, make sure she takes the pills if needed and keep me apprised of the situation." With that Var spins on his heel and stalks out of the room, leaving behind a mixture of relief and irritation from my nursing staff.

The pounding in my skull begins to feel like a friendly tap as they turn to hazy silhouettes and I close my eyes. The shuffle of their steps and closing of the door, sets free a sigh of release. Yes, I'm a lightweight, but the pills shouldn't be working this fast, even on an empty stomach. Maybe it's the reprieve from dealing with clients who don't want to be in my chair, or dodging another dinner with Var. There's no time to over think it, exhaustion washes over me, carrying me off to sleep.

Chapter 31

Sleep-sanded eyes peel themselves open, attempting to read the glowing red numbers on the clock. Shaking the fog from my brain, four o'clock comes into focus. Hel's Realm, have I slept twelve or twenty-four hours?

Heavy limbs struggle, finally freeing me from the tangle of damp sheets. It's not often I wish for central air, but this is one of those times. When you can smell yourself, you know it's time for a shower. With their heightened senses, my babysitters are probably out there gagging right now.

I make the slow progression from bed to standing with little bodily resistance. Except for being a little foggy around the edges, I'm feeling much better. Guess sleep is all I needed. Sleep with a side of mother's little helper, or in my case painkillers. At least Ric didn't give me two, that would have knocked me out for a week.

Retrieving a fresh pair of shorts and a tee, I grab the door knob, intending to head to the shower. Instead, I end up face to chest with one of my sitters.

"You are awake." The deep rumble of Teiran's

voice gives me another reason to sweat. One my body isn't opposed to, traitorous thing flagrantly responds.

"That or I'm sleepwalking." I give him a push. Not the wisest thing, considering his proximity alone makes me tingle. "Out of the way, I need a shower."

"There is coffee when you are ready." He steps aside, enough to let me slip past, but not without touching.

I hustle my ass into the bathroom, leaning against the closed door. What the hel was that about? Does he like half-awake, sweaty chicks? There's a cure for that. Stripping down, I step into the shower, shivering under the cold spray. Letting it take away the stank and remnants of sleep. As the water warms, bits and pieces of what I thought a dreamless sleep float to the surface.

Einen, I know it was him, had invaded in my dreams. Looking back, it feels so real, not dream-like at all. And not just a silent presence, he was trying to tell me something.

Massaging shampoo into my scalp, I struggle to remember what he said. Had the pills allowed him to communicate with me, or was it a drug induced hallucination? Do I dare remove a block or two of my shields to see if I can recover the memory?

My fingers brush the collar. Still intact below my collarbone, where it belongs. If I start playing with my Talents over something that may or may not have been a visit, it might rebel. And then it won't matter. Screw it; I'm not in the mood to find out the hard way. With the pain in my head gone, I really don't want to lose it over a possibility.

Water off and common sense on, I dry and dress, securing my hair with a jaw clamp. Gods, it's nice to have hair again, real hair, my hair. Not something I have to worry about putting on before I leave the house. It's amazing how vanity can make or break your day.

With a clean body and clothes, I can now smell the scent of Teiran's fabulous coffee making skills. It pulls me toward the kitchen, salivating all the way. Has it been that long since I've fed the addiction? I'm greeted with a mug, filled with caramel colored liquid. Perfect.

"How are you feeling?" Speaking of perfect, Ric's dazzling smile could brighten the gloomiest of days.

"Much better. Thank you for making me take that pill."

"It seemed a better choice than simple aspirin."

"It was." Turning to Teiran, I raise my mug. "And thank you for feeding my addiction."

No smile, not that that's a surprise, but his expression lacks the usual chilly disdain of everything I say or do.

"Did I interrupt something important?"

The look cast between them screams, 'Yes,' but Ric shakes his head. "Not at all, but it does concern you."

"Really." Setting my coffee on the table, I slid into a chair.

Frosty stillness glides over Teiran's expression and Ric frowns. "We agreed it is best to tell her."

"Tell me what?"

"We feel it is time you know who you are dealing with, perhaps then you will show the proper respect." Teiran's superior attitude has returned. Wonder what triggered that, I thought we were finally getting along.

"Um, okay." Turning to Ric, I wait for him to explain.

"Did your guardians teach you anything of your âlfar heritage?"

I shake my head. "Not really, the only thing they told me was that I'm a half-breed. Which you guys disproved."

He nods, frowning. "It would have been so much easier had they explained."

"True, but there are a lot of explanations that would've made life easier."

While Ric looks contrite, Teiran manages to give the impression I should be kept in the dark.

"Have you heard the name Ingvar?"

It rings a bell and I try to make sense of it in my jumbled brain. Where had I heard it? Studying

Ric's questioning gaze it dawns on me. "You said it once."

His brow raises.

"When you were trying to explain about Einen being crazy."

A grunt comes from my left and I shoot Teiran a nasty look, before turning back to Ric. "Want to explain why the name is important?"

"The man you know as Var Royd is Lord Ingvar. The Sun King. King of the âlfar."

The blood drains from my brain to my feet and I grab my coffee, chugging it as if it were a stiff shot. Var is my king? No wonder he treats everyone like they are beneath him. Nothing but tools at his disposal.

"The God Frey, in human guise," retorts Teiran.

Unholy crap! On shaky legs, I head to the coffee pot and refill my cup. Pondering the ramifications of my insolence, I grab the cream from the fridge. As white swirls through brown to make caramel, laughter hits me, but I choke it back.

Turning to my companions, I lean against the counter and study them. They don't get it, not that I can blame them. Neither seems too hip on slang.

"So you're telling me Var is short for Ingvar and that he's the god Frey?"

"Yes." Ric smiles, probably glad I'm taking this so well.

"And he could choose any name he wanted in

this human form?" Laughter is harder to hold back.

"Of course. What are you getting at, Keely?"

"Why, of all the names he could have chosen, did he pick Royd?"

Ric shrugs.

"Does he know what it means?"

"From the forest or dwells in the forest, from what I understand."

"Maybe, but that's not what people think of when they hear it, now days it's slang for something else. In truth, it fits him perfectly."

"I have a feeling I will regret asking this, slang for what?"

By now I'm laughing so hard tears roll down my cheeks. "A major pain in the ass."

His face scrunches, somewhere between confusion and understanding.

"Hemorrhoids. Don't you guys keep up with the times?"

"We have more important things to keep up with than slang terminology." Teiran's face twists like he's been sucking lemons.

Ric rubs the back of his neck. "Much of pop culture and slang sips by, but now that you mention it, I have heard this before."

I know I should quit while I'm ahead, but I can't leave well enough alone. "The only way to make this more perfect is if he had chosen Hemi as his first name."

Resting his elbows on the table, Ric lowers his head onto steepled fingers. His shoulders trembling with what I guess to be suppressed laughter. Teiran on the other hand is an icy brick of disapproval and revulsion, not a trace of humor. Wonder if I should tell him how his precious Lord Ingvar thinks of him. Teiran the Tool. Nah, no matter how much he pisses me off, he doesn't deserve that.

"Is that how you found me? Var's godly powers?"

"No," Ric shrugs off the laughter, but not the twinkle in his eyes. "We were tracking The Collector. He is what led us to you."

"I don't believe you. Hem—" I almost slip on the name, but the look on Teiran's face stops me in my tracks. "He owns the loan on my building. You all knew who and what I was long before The Collector came into the picture."

His head drops, breaking eye contact. "No, he purchased your loan after we figured out who you were."

"And when did you figure that out?"

"At my hair appointment."

My Talents went haywire when I touched him, growing his buzz cut into the lovely shoulder length locks he has now. That's what tipped them off as to what I am.

"We knew you existed, but not where to find you, your guardians can be very secretive."

"No shit." I love The Sisters dearly, but they've kept too much from me, including my true Talents. I would've been better prepared if I'd known what to expect. But now I know they were hiding me from two threats. Vereinen and a god.

Chapter 32

Crossing my arms, I pace back and forth as the conga line of my coworkers files into the apartment. "All right, why didn't any of you tell me?"

"You're supposed to greet us with a kiss on the cheek and an after work martini. And ask, 'how was work, honey,' before you hit us with the hard questions."

I turn to Rey. "Did you know?"

"Darlin', I know lots of things, except what you're talking about."

"How about you?" I lean down, until Nyssa and I are almost nose to nose. Her mouth gapes, violet eyes wide, questioning, with a touch of fear.

A hand on my shoulder spins me around, to face the one person I *know*, knows. "What are you babbling about?"

"Like you don't know."

"In truth we do not. We have had a long night, stop with these silly female games and enlighten us." Dara's grip tightens, nails biting into my shoulder.

She's right, I'm playing a game I detest and didn't even realize. Hanging my head, I take a deep breath. "You're right, I'm sorry."

"Now," she releases her grip, "Tell us what has you so upset."

Rey leads Nyssa to the couch, draping himself on the arm next to her. Dara takes the other end, scooping up CC and placing him on her lap.

"I can only guess whatever has you upset, has something to do with these two." She glances from Teiran to Ric, sitting in the armchairs across from them. Two warring camps with a tenuous truce, neither side looking happy with my outburst.

Well, I hate to break it to them, but I'm not happy either. Their lies and omissions have left me in the middle, not that I want to pick a side. I'd rather go back to twelve hour workdays, twice a month Saturday night dancing and drinking ritual, and being in control of my life. As it is, I'm floundering in a game I know nothing about.

Standing in the center of the group, I look down the line, knowing I have my work cut out for me as my eyes rest on Dara. Everything from the curled position to the gentle stroking of my traitorous cat, says she's not budging. She won't tell me crap, at least not in front of everyone else. It is possible that Rey has no idea. He's never been one to worry about politics or anything that doesn't affect him personally. Nyssa, on the other hand, has the ability to appear clueless if it benefits her. Usually, she saves it for the male persuasion, but she's not above manipulating females to her advantage. Of the three of them, I'd place bets that Dara and Nyssa know what and who Var is.

"So how many of you know who Var Royd really is?"

Rey's face scrunches. "Besides a the richest pain in the ass in Iowa?"

"Yeah, besides that."

Nyssa looks from Dara to Ric and Teiran. If she doesn't know, she has an idea.

Fingers gliding through CC's fur, Dara stares at me. "What do you know?"

"I know he picked a dumb-assed name."

She tips her head in agreement. "Go on."

"I know he's far more than he claims."

"Such as?"

"Oh, come off it, Dara. Why didn't you tell me who he is?"

"Would you have believed me?"

Sighing, I shake my head. "I don't know."

"Somebody wanna fill me in on what's going on?"

"I'm sorry, Rey. You truly are the only one who doesn't know who he is, aren't you?"

"I know he's a powerful son of a bitch who can squish me like a bug if he wants to, or have his henchmen do the job, to keep his hands clean." He nods in Ric and Teiran's direction. "No offense, guys."

"None taken," says Ric, "you are correct."

He nods, attention falling on Nyssa. "You know, don't you?"

"I wasn't sure, but now…" She shrugs.

"You going to tell me?"

"Maybe Keely should and then we'd both know for sure."

All the eyes in the room are on me, some unhappy, slightly angry, others full of curiosity. Whatever comes out of my mouth will be treated like gospel.

"Come on, Keely, stop the suspense. Tell me what everyone else seems to already know, I hate being the only one on the gossip train who doesn't."

"Var Royd is the god Frey."

Rey's jaw hits the floor. Nyssa nods, her suspicions answered. Dara continues to pet the cat, her eyes studying my every movement.

"Wow, a god and he picked a name like Royd? I can forgive the poor sap saddled with a name like that, but he chose it, damn." Rey shakes his head, laughing. "Someone should have warned him."

I burst out laughing, should've known Rey would pick up on that. "I know, right?"

Behind me, I hear Ric and Teiran shift in their chairs, an uncomfortable, nervous noise. I would love to continue making fun of their boss's name choice, but the twinge of pain in my wrist reminds me they've committed the ultimate betrayal in the name of protecting me. They haven't told him about the mark. Speaking of, why didn't Hel tell me who I was dealing with? Another part of a game where everyone knows the rules but me ?

It's becoming clearer that I'm just another *tool* in the arsenal of an ongoing war.

Chapter 33

I've been granted a much needed lazy day, dozing on the couch, watching old movies, before I have to go to work.

After all the chatter about Var's true identity, the headache returned. A dull reminder at the base of my skull, instead of the icepick of doom between the eyes. I can live with that, I don't want to, but I can.

Teiran took off to return the library book and pick up more tea from Mel, leaving Ric to watch over me. Neither have reported an update on my condition to their lord and master, yet.

My bet is on Teiran cracking first. Ric seems happy to avoid his duties, even going as far as to shut off his cell, claiming it would be rude to leave it on during a movie.

Ric cringes as they roll through clips of an upcoming movie monster marathon. I can't imagine what it's going to be like when Halloween hits. Both he and Teiran probably avoid T.V. entirely, not that either of them seem to watch more than the news. Considering it's my favorite time of year for T.V. they'll be out of luck, if they're still around.

What am I saying? Of course they'll be around, in what capacity is another story. If I become Var's third wheel, we'll be partners. If I don't, they'll still be my jailers, babysitters, whatever they want to call themselves.

There's only one other option. I tell Var about Hel's mark and the favor I owe her, but I'm not sure even death will release me from my problems. I'd just end up one of Hel's minions.

The trailer for a nineteen seventies vampire film catches my attention—one I've never seen if you can believe it—and Ric reaches for the remote, but I hold tight. "Hey, I want to see this."

"Why would you want to see this ridiculous fluff?" He slides forward, attempting to block my view.

I lean to the side, dodging his movements. "I've never seen, let alone heard of this flick before and I love seventies horror movies." I don't bother adding that his agitation is another driving factor.

He hangs his head as the announcer touts the depravities of Countess Dracula. How the beautiful, Elisabeth discovers the wonders of bathing in blood.

Suddenly, I lose my desire to watch the movie and hit the up arrow on the remote. This is hitting a little too close to home.

"I thought you wished to watch that?"

"Changed my mind."

Tipping his head to one side, he studies me. "Are you feeling unwell?"

I shake my head. "That whole bathing in blood thing may sound ludicrous to the average person, but now that I know what Stasia Athory puts in her lotions…it kinda creeps me out."

"I understand, those images bring—"

Teiran enters, bag in hand and marches to the kitchen, without so much as a hello. The tea kettle is placed on the stove and the rustle of paper and cellophane tells me he's brewing up a batch of Mel's nasty bitter tea.

"Don't forget to put honey in it."

"No honey, you will drink this straight."

"Oh, come on."

"She ordered it to be drunk straight, no additives."

"Why?"

He turns and glares at me. "Because that is what she said, so that is what you will do."

"Fine." Arms crossed, I lean back into my corner of the couch.

"Do not pout, it does not become you. The witch said that this was a different mix and I was to see that you drink it straight, nothing added."

Crap, something new. Like the last batch wasn't bad enough. "Whatever."

Teiran turns to Ric. "Do you see what I must endure?"

I roll my eyes, waving a hand at him. "Ric, you were saying something before we were so rudely interrupted."

"I was?"

He can fake it all he wants, but he's not getting out of explaining what he was talking about, I know it had something to do with the movie trailer and Stasia Athory. "Yep, you were saying you understood how I felt about the movie comparison to what's going on with Stasia, something about the images."

Abandoning his post at the stove, Teiran takes one of the chairs across from us. "What movie? What images?"

"There was a movie trailer for Countess Dracula, when they got to the part about her bathing in blood; it reminded me of Stasia's concoctions."

His gaze moves from me to Ric. "What images did this movie trailer invoke?"

There's a touch of concern mingled with a bit of suspicion in his expression, but his tone is neutral. Maybe he's worried it has something to do with Ric's vamp side.

Sighing, Ric leans back until his head is resting against the couch and stares at the ceiling. Have I picked an old scab? It wasn't my intent to hurt him, but it would be just like me to open my yap and insert my foot.

"I'm sorry, Ric, I should have left it alone."

He reaches out and pats my hand, never taking his eyes from the pale beige of my ceiling. "You have nothing to be sorry about; it is I who needs to apologize."

"What do you have to apologize about? That you don't like tacky, seventies horror flicks?"

This draws out a tight smile, but he shakes his head. "No, I do not, but that is not the reason I feel the need to apologize." He sits up straight, looking from me to Teiran and back. "I know Stasia Athory, who she is."

"Um, yeah, we kinda already established that, I'd even go as far as to say you two were...more than friends."

"Yes, we were, until I found out who she is."

Teiran and I exchange a glance, both a little confused as to where this is going.

"She is Elizabeth Bathory's bastard daughter."

As if on cue the tea kettle's whistle rips through the silence. None of us moves, then all of us move at once. Teiran, beating me to the kitchen, waves me back to my seat. Should have known he wouldn't trust me to make my own tea.

"Elizabeth Bathory? As in Countess Dracula?" A morbid part of me, deep within, shivers in expectation.

He nods. "Yes, although, I would guess the movie to be a sanitized version of the Blood Countess."

Teiran hands me the tea, standing over me until I take the first sip. I choke and sputter, eyes watering. "Good gods, this is horrible. Is she trying to kill or cure me with this stuff?"

"Drink it all."

I stick my tongue out at his back when he turns toward his vacated spot. Ric gives me a smile and nods toward the mug. "Do as he says, it is for your own good."

"Blah, blah, blah." Taking another sip, I make it my mission to down it before it cools. Mel's medicinals have a tendency to taste worse the cooler they get. It's hot, not scalding, but hot enough to make chugging it uncomfortable. So I settle for large gulps between questions.

"The Blood Countess wasn't an En, was she?"

"No, but Stasia's father is a lidérc."

"What the hel is a lidérc?"

"A demon," answers Teiran, glaring at Ric. "What would make you have relations with this woman?"

Unholy crap, I don't want to picture it, but it invades the subconscious like a hungry parasite. Ric and Elizabeth Bathory's daughter, having—as Teiran put it—relations, eww, just eww.

"It was a time when it did not matter." Sadness, regret and a touch of anger color his tone. "I was just as much a monster as her mother."

Teiran slouches in the chair, eyes averted. Their

silence is damn near solid enough to touch. So much grief…and fear. Something I never expected to feel from either of them and by association it scares me.

Chapter 34

I'd been screaming for answers and now that I have some, I don't know what to do with them. It's a lot of weirdness to process. Sometimes answers aren't really answers at all, but new questions.

Var Royd is a god and Stasia Athory is the daughter of the infamous Hungarian Blood Countess. Their chosen names suck if you ask me, one's a pain in the ass and the other has no imagination. They both want me for their own reasons. One for a new and improved version of her mother's sick beauty regimen. The other to strengthen his power base, as if a god doesn't have enough power. Speaking of gods, might as well toss Hel, and the favor I owe her, into the mix.

The only thing I want to be wanted for is my ability behind the chair. Nothing beats the rush I get when a client is happy with my work. Well, almost nothing, there is the rush I get while using my newly acquired Talents. But instead of basking in the afterglow of a job well done, I end up doing the walk of shame.

Having the full use of my Talents may not be the best answer, but wearing this collar limits me in multiple ways when dealing with psychos and power hungry gods. I'm tired of relying on everyone else for answers and protection. The trick is to make Var Royd believe I want the position of Shadow and don't have any ulterior motives.

Teiran and Ric sit in silence and as much as I'd like to know more, I respect Ric's right to privacy. Both of them have been slowly opening up to me and I don't want to screw that up. I need them to trust me for this to work; Var isn't the only one I have to fool in this charade.

My stomach drops watching them, it will be harder to fool them than Var. I actually have come to like them, so my little half-truth is going to suck. From the bits and pieces I've gathered, they are as much victims of the Royd twins as I am. And poor Teiran shares in the double whammy of being indebted to Hel in some way. Perhaps, at some point, I can convince them this is a bunch of bull. So what if they're gods, none of us should have to put up with their self-serving crap. We aren't tools to be used, then left out to rust.

My tea has gone as colder than the mood in the room. There's no way I'm finishing the last of the sludge at the bottom of the cup. Uncurling myself from the couch, I plan on heading to the kitchen to dump the offending dregs. Something outside the window catches my eye, something that looks vaguely familiar. I can't be sure until I get a better look. Stepping over Teiran's extended legs; I cross the room, staying to the edge of the window. Slowly moving the outer edge of the sheer, I peek around the frame.

"Um, Teiran?"

"Yes?"

"It may have been dark, but I can damn near swear that's the car that was following us Sunday night."

Both of them come to the window, not bothering to sneak like fraidy cat me, standing blatantly in the center. "Which car?" they ask in unison.

"The black one."

Teiran tilts his head to one side. "Which black car?"

Leaning in a little further, I poke the curtain. "That one, the sedan with the tinted windows, in front of Midnight Expresso."

Ric frowns as they exchange a glance, both nodding. Like they've just exchanged some secret code, Teiran heads to the door.

I take a step toward him and Ric grabs my arm. "What the hel? You can't seriously be going out there, what if they're dangerous?"

"Thank you for your concern, but what better way to find out their intentions than to ask?" A treacherous smile creeps along his lips and I suppress a shudder as he steps out the door. I almost feel sorry for whoever is in the car. Then I remember they're following me, so screw it, let Teiran do his worst.

I step back in front of the window to watch and Ric wraps his arm around me. The car doors swing open when Teiran reaches the centerline and two familiar black suited figures climb out to meet him. Aw crap. The tracker and berserker—I'd unaffectionately nicknamed Frick and Frack, because I couldn't remember their names—who'd taken me downtown for questioning in The Collector case. I thought I'd seen the last of them when he disappeared. What the hel are they doing following me? I haven't done anything to garner the interest of the Numinous Task Force. Have I?

I sneak a glance at Ric, but he's too busy watching Teiran and the agents. With the way he's squinting, I wonder if he can read lips. But now is not exactly the appropriate time to ask.

The berserker—aka Frack—looks up and smiles hungrily at my window as if he saw me step behind Ric. That asshat had it out for me from the moment we laid eyes on each other and it scares the living daylights out of me. If he knows I have this collar on, I'm toast. The tracker—aka Frick—lifts his nose as if scenting my location and I take another step away from the window. Where Frack's need to physically hurt me scares me, Frick's uncanny ability to find me terrifies me. There is no getting away from a tracker. Except death. And I'm not ready to go there yet.

Peeking over Ric's shoulder, I suck in a deep breath as they climb back into the car, releasing it once they pull away. Teiran glances up at the window and nods. Ric returns the gesture, then turns to me.

"Seems your friends have left."

"Wonder why they showed up in the first place."

"We shall have to wait for Teiran to return for the answer."

Glancing down at the street, he's already disappeared. The wait won't be very long.

Or so I thought. Just when I've rinsed the mug three times and paced from kitchen to living room and back at least a dozen times—much to Ric's amusement—there's a knock at the door. Ric opens it and Teiran steps inside. My mouth opens to holler at him for taking his sweet time, but how can I be mad at a man holding three to go cups from Midnight Expresso.

"One of those better be holding a white chocolate mocha."

There's a hint of a smile as he sets the cups on the kitchen table, turning one so my name is visible. "I thought you deserved a treat."

Suspicious? Yeah, this is more along the lines of something Ric would do, not Teiran.

Do I really deserve a treat, or is this to soften the blow of the bomb he's about to drop? Who cares, I've never met a white chocolate mocha I didn't like. Grabbing the cup I take a seat at the table, sniffing the lovely sweetness before I take a sip. The heavenly creaminess almost makes me forget the subject at hand.

"So, did you find out what Frick and Frack wanted?"

"Frick and Frack?" asks Teiran, his puzzled look mirroring Ric's.

"Yeah, that's what I nicknamed them when they took me downtown." I almost laugh at their growing confusion. "They are the agents who questioned me in The Collector case."

"Ah, that explains a lot."

"What do you mean? Is that why they showed up?"

"They still do not believe you had nothing to do with those incidents."

I shrug. "It's not like I can come out and say, 'Hey, I killed him, it's over.' They wouldn't believe me anyway."

"No," says Ric. "No, you cannot."

"So if they want to waste time following me around, there's nothing I can do."

"As long as there is nothing else to allude to those crimes, you should have nothing to worry about."

"Exactly," I say, feeling a little better about the situation.

Teiran frowns at both of us. "Unless someone decides to help them along."

"Who would do that? It's not like what I did is common knowledge."

"Take a moment to ponder your question, who has something to gain by discrediting you?"

Both Ric and I answer in unison. "Stasia Athory."

Chapter 35

"That bitch would probably go to the ends of the earth to get what she wants. In all seriousness, I don't understand why she hasn't just killed me."

"If you are alive, she has a continuous supply, if you are dead that supply will dry up, along with her profits." Ric fiddles with his cup, sliding the paper sleeve up and down. "There are only two of you and one is unreachable."

"So bleed me slowly and charge more." I hate to say it, but it makes perfect sense. "Guess I'm lucky she hasn't kidnapped and locked me away."

"As long as I live that cannot happen." There is nothing romantic or even friendly to Teiran's tone. He's just stating a fact.

"I know. The bond through the collar. And if she kills you, I die. A no win situation. The only way around it would be if she kidnapped both of us." I glare at both of them. "Don't laugh, it's a possibility."

"No, no it is not."

"Listen, you may think you're the Big Bad Wolf, but he wasn't invincible and neither are you." Great, more laughter. If this wasn't a genuine concern, I might be able to enjoy the delightful tone, but it is and I'm not.

"I thank you for your concern, but Stasia Athory taking me against my will is the least of my worries."

"Whatever."

"And if she did somehow succeed, I would not stay captive long."

"So silver wouldn't detain you like normal werewolves?"

"I am not a werewolf. I am one of Hel's Hounds." All traces of levity vanish. Like a door slamming shut, his tone ends the discussion. "I think it is time you rest before work."

Snagging the paper cup, I head toward my room. Fine, if that's the way he's going to be, but he's out of luck if he thinks I'm leaving my coffee behind. Giving the door a kick, I plop down on the bed. Greeted by what can only be cursing in cateese.

"Sorry, bud, didn't mean to disturb your napping." I reach over and scratch CC behind the ears. "Ever get the feeling no one listens, or if they do, they don't respect what you say?"

My answer is a giant yawn and a paw planted on my thigh, that nearly brings me to tears. Blinking them back, I take a large swig of my coffee and it does nothing to cheer me up. I'm not sure if they're tears of anger, fear, or childish pouting. Probably a combination of all of the above. Maybe Teiran's right; I do need a nap before work. Setting the paper cup aside, I snuggle down into the bed, motioning CC to join me.

I really don't understand why Teiran thinks he's above being kidnapped. Sure, he's strong and can turn into a ginormous puppy with teeth the length of my forearm, but that doesn't mean there isn't something to contain him. I'm betting they could take him down with tranquilizer darts. No one is invincible, no one. Look at Einen. With all the talk of him being a badass and them not knowing how to handle him, they still managed to contain him. And what about Var? He's a god and still has body guards. If you ask me, that says he's not invincible.

Speaking of which, I wonder how he's getting along with both of them here with me. It's nice having the eye candy around and the extra sense of security, but I'd still like a little alone time. I need a little alone time, real alone time. The kind where you can dance naked through the house without worrying about having a roommate catch you. Probably another reason I'm weepy, lack of alone time. Having CC along for the ride doesn't count. He's essential to my mental well-being and keeps me in line.

I close my eyes and pretend the apartment is empty. It's just me and CC, like old times. The olden days, before newly acquired Talents, gods, psychos and babysitting roommates. No matter how I fight it, the apartment slips away to the land of fog and mist.

"Greetings Schattenkind."

Yeah, the gravel on glass voice confirms it. I'm in Niflheim. Hel has called me again, wonder what she wants this time. "Hel."

"You do not seem happy to see me."

"I was trying to take a nap before I have to go to work." Smooth, I know, but it's not like I can rip into her for cluttering up my alone time. "What can I do for you?"

I bite the inside of my cheek, holding back the shudder her laughter raises along my spine.

"So agreeable and always wanting to please me."

"Yeah, that's me, always trying to please others." Checking myself before I punctuate the sarcasm with an eye roll.

Her chastising tsk-tsk sounds like a wounded cricket. "Temper, temper."

"Sorry." The not hangs between us, a knife she could easily use to slice me to shreds. I've really got to watch my mouth, or better yet, keep it closed.

I fight to stand my ground as she steps closer and not flinch when she places her flesh covered hand on my cheek. "What troubles you?"

Her hand isn't supposed to be warm. She's

death, for crying out loud. Nor should her tone project that she gives a tiny rat's ass about me. Tears well in my eyes and I close them, shaking my head. "Just tired."

"No," she grips my chin, tipping my head back, moving it side to side, "there is more to it than that."

I can't deal with her in my personal space or the feigned kindness any longer. Seriously, I'm not stupid or gullible enough to believe she cares. It's an act. The same act Var pulls to get me to do what he wants. Guess it's true, you catch more flies with honey, or in this case, idiots with bullshit.

Stepping back out of reach, I take a deep breath and let it out, focusing on anything but her face. "Look, I'm tired of all the games; can we just get down to business? What do you want from me?"

"The kitten has grown claws."

I shake my head.

"Be careful who you sharpen them on."

"I'm not sharpening anything on anyone. I'm just tired of everyone manipulating me for they own goals and not letting me in on that goal."

Her laughter is harsh, grating on the nerves. "You want to know our goals. Has the Sun King not told you why he needs his power base restored?"

I shake my head. "You know he hasn't."

"But you know his true nature."

"Yeah, he's the god Frey, yada, yada, yada.

Stupid name choice, yada, yada, yada. Major pain in my ass, yada, yada, yada."

"And yet, he has not revealed why he needs you to replace Vereinen."

"Because he's a control freak and needs minions to do his dirty work."

"That would be part of the equation. He needs his base restored so he can attain his lost power."

"Huh?"

"With the ever changing views in religion followers wax and wane and with that, power waxes and wanes."

"So you're telling me that he needs us to prove his prowess and gain back his lost followers?"

Tilting her head to one side, she shrugs. "I am sure there are other motives, but essentially, yes."

"And you? Are you using me to gain followers?"

Again with the nails on chalkboard laughter. "Death never loses followers."

"So let me guess, you need me to keep him from regaining his status."

Half sweet smile, half lipless grimace, all that's missing is 'good girl' and a pat on the head. "Do you think it a coincidence, one of my hounds shadows you?"

"No, it was by design, by both of you. Your hound. His shield. Do you guys do this on purpose? Splitting people's loyalties? Well, Teiran's, not mine, I hold no loyalties to any of you. I want no part of the great pissing match between you and Lord Ingvar."

Fucking gods and their infighting, they're just as petty as the rest of us. They've done nothing, but mess up lives, it's no wonder they've lost followers.

Damp air chills, lifting every little hair to attention. I can literally see her jaw clench through decayed flesh, vacant teeth and rotted nubs never quite touch. Scraggly bits of grey hair mingling with pale blonde, halo her head in a wild, teased mass. I swear she purposely focuses her empty socket on me, giving me the heebie-jeebies. I've pissed her off and before the thought of consequences comes to fruition; an invisible fist punches my chest, sending me tumbling.

Chapter 36

The contents of my stomach rise as I fall through the absence of light. I should have thought twice about pissing off Hel.

Of course, she'd never kill me, that isn't her style. What good would my death do her in her fight with Royd?

She'd much rather teach me a lesson for my impudence. As punishment, the bitch pushed me into The Between. She may not want me dead, but she—like Royd—wants me broken and anything can happen in The Between.

My punishment doesn't stop there. Heat builds along my wrist, white-hot streaks of light radiate outward from the scar, further blinding me to my surroundings. Primal survival instincts outweigh common sense, much like my last visit to The Between. The near perfect crushing of reality. A mental breakdown that left me a jabbering fool arguing with herself.

Pain—far worse than the time I grabbed the wrong end of my curling iron—burns away any chance of cognizant thought and fear steps in to play with the primitive bits of the brain.

My horrifying, gut-wrenching decent is stopped by something surprisingly soft. Voices swirl around me, calling a name. Familiarity tugs at my mind, but my companions, pain and fear, keep me from remembering. Kicking, slapping, scratching, I thrash against grasping, unseen hands.

"Keely, wake up."

The hands become incessant trying to restrain me.

"You are safe in your bed, you little fool."

The fight against the unknown switches to breathing, as oxygen becomes a commodity. My hands search the softness beneath me. At least I'll die in my own bed. I roll to the side as the bed gives under added weight and a light pressure touches my throat and collarbone, easing the intake of air. Allowing the deafening screams to return.

"Hush, your caterwauling."

I know that voice. Cold anger. Teiran.

"Her arm, there is something wrong with her arm."

And this one too. Concern. Ric.

One set of hands continues to restrain me. Another set undoes the closures on the brace. Stars dance behind my lids as it's peeled from my arm and air hits my naked flesh. I sob against what can only be Teiran's cool chest as he pulls me into his arms, keeping one hand in constant contact with the collar.

My wrist is flipped upward and Ric whispers, "Good gods."

I manage to hold back the screams, but not the sobs it hurts too much. I bury my face, not wanting to see if it looks like it feels. Raw and exposed, flesh blistered, or completely gone.

"Hel did this." Teiran's voice rumbles against my ear and he tightens his hold.

I nod. Tears and gods know what else, soaking the smooth cotton of his tee-shirt.

"We need to call a healer."

I shake my head and Teiran answers for me. "No one can know of this, if it were to get out that she is marked by Hel and under her control, Lord Royd would put an end to her."

Those words force me to open my eyes and make sure this is real and not some demented illusion created by my own mind.

What I see and feel almost scares me more than a breach in my own psyche and I look away before he notices. Teiran actually cares what happens to me. You'd think I'd be happy about it, but I'm not sure if it's because of the link through the collar or with our connection through Hel.

If we are to be friends, or possible future coworkers, it has to be because he likes me for me and vice versa. Not because of circumstances placed on us by gods. It's not fair or natural.

"We cannot heal her, " says Ric, his concern

growing. This is as close to panic I've ever heard him, it must be as bad as it feels.

"No, but perhaps her friend the witch can be of use, until then, I can dull the pain."

Ric places my arm into Teiran's hand and the white-hot pain begins to subside into calming coolness, leaving behind a dull throb. As I sigh in relief, he lowers my arm into my lap and slowly removes his hand.

Ric leaves to call Witchy Weeds and I try to untangle myself from Teiran's hold. "Thank you. I think you can let go now, the collar is under control."

He hesitates on the back of my neck. I'm not sure if he's worried about the collar or wants a reason to keep touching me. Truth be told, I don't want him to stop, but now that the pain is under control I need to remove myself from his lap. This sudden realization that he cares will make life more difficult for both of us, I'd almost rather go back to believing he hates me.

My forgotten, feline friend's nose, sends the throbbing pain into overdrive. "Damn, CC." I yank my wrist away, glaring at the cat, but my anger quickly dissipates. This is the first look at what Hel has done to me. I expected torn flesh and exposed muscle, figuring most of my skin was stuck to the brace during removal, but I'm surprised. The scar is colorless and swollen to the point of distortion, leaving the surrounding flesh an angry red, but intact.

"What did she do to me?"

"She used her mark to demonstrate her power over you, by causing pain. What did you say to her that would invoke such anger?"

I run what I can remember of our meeting through my head. "She explained why Var needed me. I asked why she needed me. She told me that it wasn't a coincidence that you were my babysitter. I told her I was tired of the games—aw, crap, I basically told her to get bent."

"She told you I was not a coincidence?"

Turning to face him, I nod. "Yeah, I think she had some influence in sticking you with me."

"That is not possible."

"Then I guess she lied. Would you mind doing that thing with my arm again? It really hurts." I hold it out to him. Without even flinching, he places a hand on it and the area immediately cools and calms.

"I was given the job of watching over you by Lord and Lady Royd."

I flinch at the mention of Vana Royd, the original mean girl. Teiran's secret crush. Twin of Var, the god Frey, making her the goddess Freya. Which explains a lot about her presence in my dream the other day. The sooner we get off this topic the better. "Look, I don't know if she had a hand in sticking you with me or not, I'm just repeating what was said."

"What were her exact words?" He's not angry, yet, but on the verge.

"Something about, if I thought it was a coincident that *her hound* shadowed me."

I can practically see the wheels turning in his head, but I don't think his irritation is pointed in my direction. For once.

"Mistress Beinwell is on her way." Ric's return is a blessed distraction from Teiran's questioning. "She has something she thinks may answer our problem."

There was no doubt in my mind that Mel would have something in her cabinet of curiosities to cure my ills, I just wish she had something to keep it from happening again. Besides me learning to keep my mouth shut.

Chapter 37

"What in hel have you done to yourself now?" asks Mel.

"Hel is the keyword here, I opened my mouth and crap came out."

Mel's head drops, chin touching her chest. She sighs before she lifts her head, eyes boring into me. "Please lie to me and say you did not piss off Hel."

I'm a lousy liar and she knows it, lowering my head I shrug.

"Show me the damage."

Holding out my arm, I bite back the urge to squeal as her fingers press into the tender flesh. Turning my arm back and forth, she studies the damage, making an annoying little tsk-tsk noise.

"She did a doozy on you, didn't she? But it doesn't look like you pissed her off enough to give you more than a warning shot."

"This is just a warning shot?"

"Uh huh, had she really wanted you maimed, she would have done more than just rewire your nerve endings."

"What does that mean?"

"It means that scar tissue doesn't have nerve

endings. If I'm right, she upped the ante on her control over you. Now, not only can she call you through the mark, she can send currents of energy through the tissue."

"She can do that? Rewire basically brain-dead tissue?"

"Yep."

"Crap."

"Crap is right, if she did what I think she did, she can cause you pain any time she wants. If you step out of line. Zap. If she's bored. Zap."

"So you're telling me she can zap me just for shits and giggles."

"Yep."

"What do I do now?"

"Try learning to keep your mouth shut."

I flip both middle fingers into the air, in answer to the male snortfest behind me. "Not helping guys. There has to be something I can do to protect myself against her call and now zaps."

"I've been working on that. I'm not sure if it will work, but if you're willing to wear it we'll find out." She pulls something wrapped in cloth from her patchwork bag and hands it to me. "It's kind of big, kind of bold. I'm not sure how you'll explain having to wear it day and night."

Ric and Teiran move to stand on either side as I unwrap what looks like a medieval bracer made of metal.

"If you make me a duplicate, I can get a red, white, and blue swimsuit and play Wonder Woman."

"Too big for that and I wouldn't try suggest using it to stop bullets."

"What is it made of?"

"It's a combination of metals."

"Like?"

"Platinum."

"So I'm holding the world's most expensive bracelet." I weigh the thing in my hand, not as heavy as I expected considering what it's made of, surprisingly light, in fact and flexible.

"Not exactly, there's more to it than that."

"Are you going to make me drag it out of you, or is it some super-secret design?"

"Well, it is a secret I'm sworn to, but I can give you the basics. There's also aluminum and lead in the mix."

"Lead? Aluminum? Are you crazy?"

"You seem to forget you're not human, lead and aluminum won't bother you one bit. Besides, the inside is coated in platinum."

"Are you going to tell me why those metals?"

She shrugs. "Just think of it as protection and in true Wonder Woman form a way to reflect magic."

"Ookaay, how about where you got it? I'm guessing you didn't take up metallurgy, or alchemy since I saw you last."

She draws her fingers across her lips.

"Fine, I get it, but at least tell me if I'm going to have to sell my car or my business to pay for this thing."

"How about you work on not pissing off gods."

Sighing, I shake my head. "Can't make any promises."

"As expected, I suppose you better try it on and see if it fits."

Not finding a clasp or any opening besides the top and bottom, I try sliding it over my hand, but no go. "It's too small."

"No, it's spelled."

I place the bracer in her open hand and she reaches out, pulling a hair from my head.

"Ouch."

"After everything you've been though, you'd think losing a single hair would tickle." She lays the hair across the sleek metal, pressing it in place with her thumb. "Öffnen."

Great, more German.

She motions for me to hold out my arm, then slides it over my hand and into place, where it shrinks to fit. "If you want it off, you repeat the word. Go ahead, give it a try."

I grasp it toward the middle and repeat, "Ofnen." Frowning I give it a tug and try again, still nothing.

All three of them are snickering.

"Fine, laugh at the German language challenged."

Mel shakes her head. "Sorry, kid, can't help it, but I think you have plenty of help. I have to head out, but one more thing. Only you can make it open, no thinking you'll get one of them to help. Heck, after that little trial, I can't even help."

"There's no other way to get it off, except taking on a second language?"

"I didn't say that, but I don't think you'll like the alternative."

"And that is?"

She makes a chopping motion with one hand over the wrist of her other.

"Uh, yeah, you're right. I don't like that alternative."

"See ya later kid. Boys, make her keep practicing that word." She continues to laugh and repeat my interpretation of the magic word as she closes the door behind her.

"So who has the patience to help me work on my German?" I glance at the clock. "Looks like we'll have to hold off until after work."

"Are you sure you are up to work this evening?" Ric tilts his head to one side and studies me.

"Can't skip out on work two days in a row."

"I believe you are the boss and that entitles you to *skip out* any time you wish."

"Alric is correct, you should not be attending

work. You should be resting." Teiran's crossed arm, stance echoes Ric's.

"If I don't work, I don't eat and neither does the cat. You guys can tell him he's not getting fed because I decided to rest instead of going to work."

"Money is not an issue, neither you, nor your cat will go hungry because you put your health before your job."

"Money may not be an issue for you two, but it is for me."

Teiran gives Ric a look that says, I'll have more than a verbal argument on my hands if I persist, and heads to the door. "You are not going to work." His words as final as the door slamming behind him.

"I am sorry, but I agree with him. You were just physically attacked by a goddess and you must learn to pronounce öffnen. That alone should take up most of your evening."

Staring at my latest adornment with a frown, it's not all I need to figure out. "I also need to decide how to explain this thing. I can't suddenly have a favorite bracelet that I refuse to be without."

"No, no you cannot."

"Fine, if I'm not working tonight, you two are helping me to come up with a cover story. Speaking of cover stories, don't you have to check in with your boss?"

Ric's pretty face twists. "Thank you for reminding me. I'll be just a moment."

"Don't forget to let Teiran and I in on the story so we can back you up, if asked."

He nods, stepping into the hall as he pulls out his cell.

What a night. Attacked by a goddess. Another new piece of jewelry, that I didn't get to pick out. And finding out Ric, Teiran and I are doing exactly what Dara said Var Royd wanted. Trusting each other.

Chapter 38

The phone rings and I let the machine answer. Surrounded by laughter a single word is audible, "Fleas?"

It's almost enough to make me want to march downstairs and throttle Rey. There's not much I can do about it now, considering, *I'm supposed to be sick*, but later we'll see what the fox says when I get even.

"What did you tell them?" I ask Teiran as he enters with Ric close behind.

"That you had contacted a bug. Why?"

I play the message and watch his jaw twitch. I wonder if he knows Rey well enough to take it, as it's mean to be, a sexual innuendo and not a slam on his cleanliness. I'm not sure if Ric finds it amusing or insulting as he heads to the kitchen and my coffee pot. Still fuming, Teiran follows, grabbing three mugs from his neatly organized coffee area.

That's one of the reasons enjoy about having him around. The house is always clean. With one exception, the sanctuary of my bedroom. It's the only room he doesn't enter unless he feels it's absolutely necessary. Can't blame him, weird things tend to happen in there, between us.

I settle into a chair at the table waiting for my newly appointed guardians of the caffeine to join me.

"So what am I going to tell everyone when they ask if I'm going into battle?" I turn my wrist back and forth, catching my reflection in the mirrored surface. A little distorted, but not bad considering I've literally been to hel and back.

Both of them look a little more than confused. I have the bracelet; it serves a purpose why should I need to elaborate? Typical male, non-fashion conscious attitudes.

"Look, guys, this is a unusual accessory and it'll draw attention. There will be questions. I need to figure out how to handle them. Especially since I'll be wearing this every day, from here to eternity."

Again with the blank looks. Why do I even bother?

"You could say it was a gift and you wear it out of respect. The less that is known about it the better."

Technically, Ric's right, it is a gift, since Mel wouldn't let me know what it's worth. She'll take it out of my hide later, in some way, shape or form. My expression must be a clue that's not enough of a reason to wear it every day.

"What if you were to tell them it is a more

attractive way to add support to your damaged wrist?"

Now that could work. Those in the know will understand what it's really protecting. Me. By hiding Hel's mark. I'll have to tell Dara right away. I don't dare keep another secret from her. Rey and Nys can find out later on. I'm not as worried about them unleashing assassin abilities on me.

Ric nods with a smile. "Teiran is correct; it combines medical reasons and your vanity, leaving no room for more questions."

"Vanity?"

"Admit it or not, Keely, you are a vain creature."

I stick my tongue out at the both of them. Ric's right, I'm vain in my way, but it doesn't mean I have to like hearing it out loud.

"And childish," adds Teiran.

"Whatever." I roll my eyes.

"Point made."

The urge to have the last word bubbles up, but I take the high road and change the subject. "What did your lord and master say when you checked in, Ric?"

"I informed him you were still fighting the headaches, but they were under control now with the help of medication. I am to keep him updated as to when you will be joining him for your missed meal."

"Yay." I can't hold back the enthusiasum.

"You should be honored he wishes to dine with you." The old Teiran has resurfaces and I bite back the words that hang on the tip of my tongue.

I'd love to tell him how this man—I still find it hard to refer to him as a god—he worships is using him, refers to him as a tool at my disposal. It won't do any good when all common sense has fled, and he's in defensive mode.

The gurgle of the coffeemaker is as good a distraction as any as Ric fetches the carafe to fill our mugs. I stick my head in the fridge to cool off, grabbing the cream before rejoining them.

I don't have to ask if he told him about my visit with Hel. It's already been decided it would only get them in bigger trouble for delaying the information about the mark. My one small saving grace.

Who knows how Var would react? Maybe he'd let Vana finish me off. Then again, they might be as nervous about attempting to kill me as they were with Einen.

Why tempt fate? But I do have to tempt something else, a subject I'm not looking forward to bringing up.

"Okay, so on to problem three, Stasia Athory."

"As much as I would like her gone, there is nothing we can do until she breaks a law." Ric hunches over his drink.

"I know, but we need to know what she has

on Teiran that would make her think she can use him to get to me."

"I do not know the woman, nor of anything that she could use against me."

"That's what makes this so tricky. We know she can't kill you and you think you're above being kidnapped, so what does that leave?"

"As I have said multiple times, nothing. She cannot harm me and I will not allow her to harm you."

"Your enthusiasm is to be commended, Teiran, but you do not know Stasia as I do." Ric avoids making eye contact with either of us.

That's right we have our own authority on Stasia Athory. I fidget in my chair, the thought of her and Ric makes me long for the shower.

There's just something so unappealing about the woman beneath the shiny veneer and that was before I found out she was half demon. Now she's just—resorting to childhood verbiage—icky.

"Then enlighten us, Alric." The harsh lines on his face speak a different language than the relaxed, chair rocking on two legs, of his body.

Ric, still hunched over his coffee, lifts his head. Amber eyes darkened to a rich golden brown, jawline tight enough to crack walnuts between his teeth.

Great, there's gonna be a pissing match between them if I don't find a way to intervene. "Anybody want more coffee? Then maybe we can practice my German for a while."

"No, I need to explain the ramifications of not taking the threat seriously."

"Please do, explain how this chit is a threat."

"Not only does she have the cunning of her mother, she was raised by her father's kin. When I met her, she was already formidable, now I can only guess at how her power has progressed."

"What are her Talents?"

"She was able to assume the appearance of others for short periods of time." Ric looks away, clearly embarrassed. I'm not sure if it's because she fooled him into believing she was someone else, or there's more.

Teiran's chair hits the floor and he leans across the table. "What else?"

Ric clears his throat, but the word still comes out like the croak of a frog. "Sexual."

Laughter bursts from Teiran. Only biting my lip, and the shame and fear radiating off of Ric keep me from joining.

"Sex is what you are afraid of?"

"It is not *just* sex," he says, teeth gritted so tightly I can almost hear them protest. "It is the manipulation that comes with the sex. You become a mindless drone. With just one night you will be willing to leave all behind to stay with her. If it continues you will be willing to die for her, and should you survive, you will be willing to kill for her."

"Then I have nothing to worry about, because I shall not be frequenting her bed."

Chapter 39

"Should we be worried about any residual hold she may have over you?" I hate to ask, but it's a legitimate question considering the circumstances. The boy has pretty much admitted they were more than just friends. Again, eww, just eww.

Teiran's laughter and jabs subside, his expression stoic, tinged with concern. I'm not sure if it's over his friend's well-being, or the repercussions of what could happen should Ric fall under Stasia's spell again.

Teiran's all about the keeping to the straight and narrow. I know he'd finish me if I posed a threat, but could he do the same to Ric? They've known each other a lot longer and he actually likes and trusts Ric.His trust in me is a recent discovery. I'm not sure trust is the right word, but he's proven he cares on more than one occasion.

"I do not know. There is every possibility she will try to sway me."

Um, yeah, I've already experienced how much she'd like to *sway* him. I fiddle with the moonstone at my throat. "Is there anything we can do to prevent it from happening?"

"The easiest answer would be, not to leave him alone with her."

"Makes sense. So how about we make a pact to stick to him when he's not with Var?"

"That will not always be so easy; there are times when he sends me on errands alone. I do not think he will allow me to stay here longer than tonight."

"Okay, how about if he sends you on an errand you let us know and we go with you. As for staying here, you're welcome to extend your stay as long as you like. Var Royd may own the loan on the building, but it's my house and I say who stays and goes." I glance over at Teiran. "With the exception of him. Got no choice in that matter."

"Her plan would be sound if it were not for one small detail." Teiran reaches for the coffee pot and refills everyone's cup.

"And that would be?"

"You are not one of us."

I watch the cream swirl through my coffee as I pour. "Guess we should address the elephant in the room."

Silence is not golden. It's not even copper. I wait for one of them to start, but all I get is Teiran's stern gaze and Ric's averted attention as if ignoring it will make it go away.

Fine, if they're not going to say anything, I will. "You both know I was offered the position of Shadow. I know neither of you are too keen on the prospect of partnering with me and I understand."

Ric opens his mouth and I hold up a hand, the one with the shiny new bracelet.

"You both have your reasons, reasons we won't get into, because I don't want to argue about this. I've weighed the pros and cons of taking the job and have come to the conclusion the pros outweigh the cons.

"I get to take this damn thing off and with that the use of my Talents back. I have some protection from those who—as both of you pointed out—fear or hate me. According to Var, the tasks will be minimal and I won't have to give up my business." The biggest perk would be if Vana leaves me the hel alone, but I keep that one to myself.

Teiran may have moved closer to the fence, but Ric is still on the other side as far away as possible. "And the cons? Have you thought them through thoroughly?"

I shrug. "Look, Ric, I know you're not thrilled about me taking this job, but I can't see a way around it. If I don't, I'll never get this thing off. So if you two don't have a better solution. I'm going to have to suck it up and take the job."

Ric shakes his head, but Teiran tips his head to one side, studying me. "There might be a way."

"I'm all ears."

His brows cinch together.

"I'm listening." Should have known better than

to expect Mr.-I-Don't-Pay-Attention-To-Slang to understand.

"If I were to have to accompany Alric, I would have to take you along."

"You know, as well as I, that Lor—Mr. Royd will not allow that to happen. He would not have her placed in unnecessary danger, or privy to the secrets of his inner sanctum."

"Unless I take the job, so that moves us back to square one. I'm sorry guys, I want the collar off, at the very least because of this." I tap the bracelet. "She knows I can't defend myself against her with it on and so does everyone else in the world. I can't keep relying on you two or Dara for protection. Hel, the cat does a better job of protecting me than I do."

"And you think removing that will suddenly make you capable of protecting yourself?"

"I may not be trained like you, Teiran, but I did come out on top with The Collector. He's gone. I'm alive. I think that counts."

A light tap at the front door stops both of them from commenting and sends my mind reeling. Who could that be? Everyone I know should be up to their eyeballs in clients. The knock becomes more insistent and all of us in unison push back our chairs.

"I'll get it."

Teiran practically pushes me back into my

chair. "No, you are supposed to be sick, I will get rid of whoever has come calling."

Peeking around the corner is impossible with Ric baring the way. I know they are only doing their job, but it is my door. Besides these two and Var Royd, only a handful of people are keyed to get past the wards into my inner sanctuary. They don't even take up all ten fingers. What can I say? I don't have many friends.

"Yes?"

"Who the heck are you and where's Keely?"

Chapter 40

"Who are you and why do you need to see Miss Fey?"

"I'm the frickin' Queen of Sheba, now get out of my way."

"You look nothing like her, now tell me who you are and what you want with Miss Fey."

"It's okay, Teiran, let her in." I circle the table, shaking off Ric's hand as I enter the living room.

Even Teiran's broad back can't hide the wild mane of red hair that matches the temper barely contained in her curvy physique. She peeks between him and the door frame and when he moves to block her, she thrusts an overnight bag into his midsection, ducking under the arm holding the door to slip inside. He turns, dropping the bag and reaches for her arm, pulling her back as Ric steps between us.

"I said, let her in." Pushing Ric out of the way as Annya shakes off Teiran's loosening grip, we meet between them and hug like we haven't seen each other in ages. Technically, we haven't, at least not in the flesh. "They mean well."

"What did you do, hire some muscle after that

Collector debacle or are they pretty hair models?"

Laughing, I step back and wrap an arm around her shoulders, not wanting to let go of my security blanket, my touchstone, my best friend. "Not exactly on part one and I wish on part two. Annya, the honey toasted elf is Alric Brand, the Sword and tall, dark and brooding is Teiran Rand, the Shield. Guys, meet Annya Talutah, my best friend. "

Her eyes grow wide and her jaw drops as she looks from me to them. I receive a slow smile and sly wink from Ric and the faintest blush colors Teiran's shocked expression.

"In our last chat, I forgot to mention they're part of the package," I quickly add, hoping to gloss over the slightly flirtatious introductions.

Ric reaches out, taking Annya's hand in his. Bending at the waist, he brushes his lips across it. "It is a great pleasure to meet Keely's best friend."

She turns to me, brows raised, lips twisting in amusement as she pulls her hand free. "He lays it on a little thick, doesn't he?"

I give her a combination shrug and nod. From my left comes a snort of suppressed laughter. "He's quite the charmer, but you'll be lucky if this one acknowledges you."

Teiran's small moment of amusement passes and he frowns at me. "I am not uncouth." He gives his equivalent of a bow by bobbing his head in Annya's direction. "Miss Talutah."

"Shield." She nods in return. "Sword, I'll be holding back judgment on whether our meeting is a pleasure or a pain. Now if you'll excuse Keely and I, we have a lot of catching up to do." Grabbing her bag from where Teiran dropped it, she heads back to the guest room.

Holding out my hand to keep them from following, I quickly turn and chase after her. "Um, Annya, wait."

Swinging the door open, she stands fixed in the doorway. "Looks like you've already got a visitor, which one is it?" She turns to look at me over her shoulder, cognac colored eyes twinkling mischievously. "And please don't tell me you're doing both of them, that's just greedy."

"You can bunk with me." Heat flooding my cheeks, I guide her toward my room. "What is it with redheads turning everything into something dirty?"

"I take it Rey's made a few jabs."

"More than a few. Earlier, Teiran went down to tell them I wouldn't be coming to work tonight, that I'd contacted a bug. Not more than five minutes later, I get a message on the machine wanting to know if it was fleas."

"Fleas?" Tossing her bag in the corner, she sits down next to CC and ruffles his fur. Besides myself and The Sisters, Annya is the only other who's known CC his entire life.

"Yeah, Teiran is the one staying in the guest room and he's a…he's a helhound."

"Helhound? As in one of the goddess of the underworld's pets?"

"Yep." I nod, fondling the bracelet.

"Holy turd buckets. Wait, I thought you introduced him as the Shield, as in the Lord's Shield."

"Yeah, you know all about the Sword and Shield, huh?"

"Girl, I've been dealing with The Sisters for weeks now. Thank you very much." Her eyes roll to the back of her head and she holds out her hands zombie like, in reference to The Sisters' trance state.

"I'm sorry." I truly am, but I'm also grateful that she's been looking after them.

She waves a hand through the air. "No biggie, you'll owe me. They may not remember mentioning those two and that they are somehow tied to you, but they did and then I did a little research. There was no way I was coming down here unprepared."

"What made you decide to come down?" Like I don't have my suspicions.

"Between The Sisters nagging me and our last chat, did I have a choice?" Her eyes focus on the collar for a moment, before meeting mine.

I shrug, sitting down beside her. "You always have a choice." Funny, those words coming from someone who feels like they have none.

"If it had been the other way around, what would you have done?"

"Now that you put it that way, probably the same thing."

"Start filling me in on what's going on around here. Something stinks in the state of Iowa and it ain't just me after a three hour drive."

I crawl up onto the bed, propping the pillows against the headboard and pat the empty spot next to me. "Might as well get comfortable, it's a long story."

She arranges herself next to me, pulling CC up onto her lap. "The kind where we'll need a bottle of wine?"

"More like two or three."

Chapter 41

Removing CC from her lap, Annya slides from the edge of the bed. She does a little shimmy to adjust her skirt as she stands and reaches for the doorknob. "I think I need that bottle of wine now."

I continue to hug my pillow, scrunched up on the bed, unsure if she's just exhausted after my lengthy tale, or disgusted by my actions.

Opening the door, she turns to look at me. "You coming or not?"

"Yeah," I toss the pillow to the side, "I can use a drink."

"I'm surprised you aren't perpetually lit after all that." She grins over her shoulder and heads down the hall.

She's got a point. That's the thing about best friends, no judgment, no matter what you do. They bail you out when you need it, but are more likely to be the one sitting beside you in the jail cell.

Squeals, cheers and laughter fill the apartment before I can walk around the bed. Great, the gang's all here. Here's hoping Annya is enough of a distraction to keep them from being pissed off about my skipping work two nights in a row.

"Why didn't you tell us she was coming, instead of faking that you're sick?" Rey squeezes Annya in a one armed hug and she gives me a sly wink.

I toss my hands in the air. "Surprise?"

"Best ever." Rey gives her another squeeze before letting go to do a little freezer diving. Seems my blender is full of a lovely golden mixture and he's the keeper of the icy concoction. Carrying two frosty glasses, Annya makes her way over to me, with a dramatic wiggle. "Put the lime in the coconut." She hands me one of the glasses and I giggle at the reference to one of our favorite movies. "Drink up sister."

"Just not enough to start spouting secrets."

Leaning in she whispers, "Does everyone here know, everything?"

I shake my head. "Not everyone knows about the job."

She nods. "Got your back."

"And your front."

"And your sides."

"And your head and feet."

We both burst out laughing.

"Do not bother trying to understand them," Dara explains to Ric and Teiran. "They are like silly school children, complete with their own form of language no one, but they can understand."

"Yeah, soul twinsies." Annya giggles and winks at them. "Like soul mates without the mating part."

I choke, holding back the spit-take as Teiran's cheeks take on a faint reddish glow above a twitching jawline. Is it bad that I take a sadistic pleasure in his embarrassment?

"Hey," Nyssa takes hold of my wrist, "what's with the new bling?"

"A gift—

Her grin is wider than her hair. "From one of these two?" She runs her finger over the long cuff, flipping my wrist back and forth. "Nah, too expensive—sorry boys, but I doubt you make enough to cover platinum—must be their boss man."

"Absolutely not, it's from Mel."

Rey removes Nyssa's hands, moving in for a closer look. "What have you been doing with Mel to get a gift like this?"

"Not what you're thinking."

"How do you know what I was thinking?"

My brow raises as varying degrees of laughter fill the room. "Need I say more?"

"My mind's not always in the gutter."

You'd swear someone cued the uproarious laugh track on our little pseudo sitcom, complete with a chorus of, "Yeah, right."

Annya pats him on the shoulder. "Don't worry, Rey, we still love you."

He wraps his arm around her waist, dipping her back. "How much do you love me, darlin'?"

Followed with his patented brow wiggle and wink.

She laughs, pushing him back until she's upright. "Not that much, *darlin'*."

He winks and she squeals as he gives her a double pat on the rear. "So why did Mel give you a mistress bracelet?"

"It's not a—she gave it to me as protection."

"Against other suitors?"

Unnecessary anger creeps in, I know he's only teasing, but it's pushing buttons I didn't know I had. One of those lovely moments when everything you've kept bottled up comes to a head. Unleashed by the smallest, most insignificant jab. My friends, including Annya take a step back. Teiran moves to my side, hand hovering over the collar as Dara and Ric assume a defensive stance between me and the others.

"Whoa, I was only joking. Chill out, I'll stop."

I close my eyes and take a deep breath, holding out a hand to stave off Teiran's assistance. I can do this. I can rein it in. I've got to learn to do this. No problem. Right? Letting out the breath I smile at Rey. "I'm sorry."

"No worries." But his eyes and the rise and fall of his Adam's apple say different.

Still on alert, but less aggressive, Dara and Ric fall back while Teiran keeps to his post. I'm not sure if it's to throttle me if I step out of line again, or help. As always, with Teiran, it's a toss-up.

"It's to help close down Hel's open channel of communication. That's why it's so big, to cover the mark."

"She has been drawing you to her." Her expression is unreadable. Have I stepped into something that would trigger her assignment of taking me out if shit gets deep?

I nod. "She appears in my dreams."

"Maybe I can help with that." Annya steps forward, wrapping an arm around me.

"No, I don't want to involve any of you in this; it would just put you in danger."

"What if the bracelet doesn't work? Will you let me help then?"

"I don't know. Let's see if this works first, then we'll discuss the next course of action."

"Do you have any idea of what she wants from you?"

I don't know how to respond. Dara's fishing for answers, answers to the question of if I'm a threat. Do I come clean about the deal I made when Hel healed me? Will it help or hurt to tell everyone about a deal, even I don't know the specifics to? Most likely, hurt. Fear of the unknown may drive three of the people in this room to attempt to finish me off right now. If the collar doesn't get me first.

"No, I wish I did." Better to tell the truth, even if it's not the whole truth.

It seems to appease her for the moment, but

she continues to watch me over the salted rim of her glass.

"Where did Mel get it? She doesn't do metal work." Nyssa lays my wrist in her palm, stroking the smooth metal cuff.

I want to hug her for changing the subject before the bullets I'm sweating hit the floor. "She wouldn't tell me, but I have a sneaking suspicion."

Rey snorts. "Bet it was that crazy old alchemist that's been chasing her."

"That's my guess, so I'm going to owe her more than the damn thing is worth."

"I bet it cost her a date, or two." He chuckles. "Dude's even more perverted than I am."

"Ouch, poor Mel." Annya bumps Rey with her hip.

"Yeah. She figured I could tell anyone who asks, I wear it as support for my injured wrist."

"Good cover, it's much prettier than that nasty ol' brace." Nyssa lets go of my arm and lifts her empty glass. "Who's up for another pitcher of margaritas?"

Chapter 42

"So you don't need to retire to your coffin, like Dara, at the first sign of the sun?" Annya plays with her empty glass.

Last call ended as dawn dared show its face, sending Dara scurrying for the basement. Rey and Nyssa following close behind, to get their much needed beauty sleep, before the Royd empire descends on us again tonight.

"No, nor do I think Miss Kanika sleeps in a coffin." Ric's smile is wide, flirtatious.

A bit of unnecessary jealousy rears its ugly head and I grab their glasses, rinsing them furiously at the sink as Teiran retrieves the rest.

Annya laughs, seemingly oblivious to my childish actions, but I know better. She'll quiz me later when we're alone and I won't have the answers to her questions about my feelings for Ric, or Teiran for that matter.

There's no sane answer to my attraction to them. I doubt I'll be able to get away with telling her they're eye candy and nothing more.

Teiran's hand brushes mine, sending the butterflies nesting in my stomach fluttering, as he pries the glass I've been scrubbing from my hand.

"Are you attempting to rub through the glass?"

"No, I was thinking and lost track of what I was doing."

"What were you thinking about?"

"Nothing in particular, just letting my mind wander." I shake my head and lower it; hiding the blush I feel building in my cheeks behind my hair.

"Do not let it wander so far that you crush a glass and cut your hand."

The ever practical, Teiran Rand. I'm glad my hair hides not only my blush, but the combination of sticking my tongue out and rolling my eyes. Guess I should be grateful he takes things at face value and not sensitive to underlying emotions and cues. "Duly noted."

"You going to spend the morning washing dishes?" Annya sidles up beside me holding a mug of steaming, caramel-tinted addiction. "Your buddy Teiran makes a mean cup of coffee."

"I know." Taking the mug from her, I savor the scent before taking my first sip. "Almost better than Candy over at Midnite Expresso."

"I won't tell her you said that," she says with a wink.

"Please don't, it might put an end to my white chocolate obsession."

I follow her into the living room. The boys having claimed the chairs, I take the seat next to her on the couch, curling my legs up under me. "So what's the plan?"

"Plan?"

"Yeah, how long are you staying?"

"As long as you need me."

"I'll always need you." I preface with an eye roll. "How long can you stay away before your clients come hunting you down?"

"I'm on vacation, as long as my boss lets me get away with it."

Shaking my head, I laugh. "And we both know what a bitch your boss is."

"Yep."

"I take it this visit is not agreeable with your employer?" asks Ric.

She shrugs nonchalantly and I bite my lower lip.

Teiran's head follows the verbal sporting match. A man of few words, but many opinions, I'm surprised he hasn't chimed in with one about taking unsanctioned vacations. Hel, what am I saying? He probably doesn't know the meaning of the word vacation.

"Did your employer give you a specific time allotment?"

"Not really, I pretty much do as I please."

"And they do not fire you?" Ric leans forward, eyes squinted, brow furrowed.

Annya shakes her head. "Nope."

"I do not understand. How is this boss a bitch when they allow you free rein?"

"Ric, she's stringing you along, she's her own boss."

Annya playfully, bops my shoulder with a fist. "Take all the fun out of it, why don't you?"

"It was fun for a while, but you were starting to bore me and I could tell Teiran was bored a long time ago."

"Leave me out of your silly shenanigans."

Scooching forward on the couch she stares him down. "Do you even know what shenanigans are?"

Her answer is the usual brooding expression.

"Damn, he's no fun at all." She slides back. "Thank the gods, he makes a good cup of coffee."

Ric coughs, then clears his throat, eliciting a glare from Teiran.

"I think it wiser to spend our time deciding what is to be done with Miss Fey and her many problems."

Uh oh, Teiran's using Miss Fey instead of Keely, I'm in trouble. Then again, no matter who says it, this never bodes well for me.

"What do you mean, deciding what's to be done with her?" Leave it to Annya to jump to my defense. She pats my thigh, a silent, that's what friends are for.

Ric slides forward in his chair, setting his cup on the table. "He means, what can we do to rectify her problems. I am sure Keely brought you up to speed on what has been happening."

"I meant what I said; someone needs to decide what to do with her." His irritation boils just below the surface.

Are we back to this? I thought we'd moved past his blanket hatred of me, to disliking *what* I am, but understanding it's not *who* I am.

"No one is *doing* anything with her." Annya is now on her feet, hands on her hips, leaning toward Teiran. "Am I clear?"

He doesn't move, but a chill fills the room as he says, "Crystal."

I think Annya's been added to his hit list.

"Miss Talutah, Annya, no one is going to do anything to Keely." He takes her hand, pulling her back to the couch. "We simply need to come to a consensus on the best way to keep Keely and everyone around her safe."

Talk about candy coating. If all else fails, I'll be removed. There might be a teensy bit of regret, but I have no doubts one of them or Dara will step up to the task. The look on Teiran's face is enough to extinguish any hope I might have held.

Annya sits back down, grumbling to herself and shooting Teiran nasty looks. Even she's not fooled by Ric's pretty words. "What are our options?"

Ric and Teiran exchange pointed glances. "The removal of her collar is one."

"Absolutely not." Teiran's voice is soft and cold, a wicked deadly combination.

"You already have the permission to remove it so she can perform services at work."

"And that is the only time it will be removed."

Ric leans back in his chair, smugly. "I think you have already broken that rule."

Fingers digging into the arms of his chair, Teiran's jaw twitches, a flush that has nothing to do with embarrassment lighting his face.

I'm not sure if it's to garner brownie points, or a weird urge to defend Teiran, I have to speak up. "It was a test drive, to see if I could still grow hair."

"Still…" Ric drums his fingers against the chair's arm.

"There is no still, it was a one-time occurrence. One that will not be repeated as per the conditions of the agreement." He stands, cup in hand and stalks to the kitchen.

Sighing, Ric follows. He places a hand on Teiran's shoulder. "We need her, Teiran. We need her Talents to combat what is coming."

"What's coming?" Whispers Annya.

"No one is really sure, but everyone is on pins and needles about—"

"Vereinen," says Ric, looking at us over his shoulder. Damn his supersonic hearing.

"No." Teiran pulls away, shaking off Ric's hand. "We do not need her, or her Talents. We defeated

Vereinen once and we shall do it again, alone." He glares at me with enough intensity I scrunch down into the softness of the couch.

"It is not just Vereinen we have to worry about."

"The Athory bitch can be handled."

"No matter what part she has in this, it is not her I'm concerned with, Hel is my main concern. Whatever game she plays, there is sure to be death and destruction."

Teiran nods and I wonder if Ric knows both Hel and Var have made Teiran a prime game piece. He's in the same boat I am, stuck in the middle of a war, torn between the sides because of circumstances beyond our control. I'm just not in as deep as he is; I have no ties to Var. I've made no vow. The only thing that holds me to him is the necklace of doom.

Chapter 43

"I thought you said Vereinen was locked away, never to see this world again." Annya holds a hand to her head and leans back in a dramatic fainting stance.

"That's what everyone keeps telling me, except Stasia Athory. She told me she can release him, something about a key. This is the first time I've heard anyone admit that it is possible and they're afraid it might happen." I glance at the door, hoping they can't hear me. The last thing I need is Teiran jumping to the conclusion that I'm conspiring against them.

Pausing her random tossing of items from her bag, Annya looks up at me. "Do you want him released?" Her expression is bland, but if you know her like I do, you'd know the wheels are turning in her head. Tossing thoughts left and right as she assesses the situation, then consulting with her gut instinct before coming to any sort of conclusion.

I shrug, not knowing what to say, or even what I want. "No clue, I don't know him anymore. From our recent encounters, I don't think he's dangerous, but everyone else is convinced he's evil incarnate.

I don't know who's telling me the truth, or what really happened. There is no written history and even if there were, history is always written by the winners."

"True. All I have to go on is what Mom told me—unholy turd buckets." She drops a handful of clothing to the floor. "I just realized something."

I reach down and pick it up, adding the items to the pile on the bed. "What? Did you forget your pjs? I've got extra."

"No." She continues to rummage through her bag, the lines on her forehead deepening as she hits bottom. Turning it upside down, she gives it a shake before tossing it to the floor where CC waits.

"Toothbrush?"

"No, nothing like that."

"What then and is it good or bad?"

"If your Var Royd is Frey, that makes his sister…"

"Freya," we say in unison.

"You're right, that is a bucket of turds."

"Mom is not going to be happy that you pissed her off."

"Nope, but on the bright side, maybe I can get her an introduction."

"This is not a laughing or even giggling matter, chick. My mother's first devotion is to her goddess, even dad and I know where we stand on the totem and you're just my skinny-ass friend. This is so not good." She sorts through the pile on the bed, finally finding her pjs. "Frick, frack, fruck."

"What can I say? My life is a big ol' stinkin' pile that keeps getting deeper, but let's not worry about how your mom will react right now."

"Yeah, we'll think about it tomorrow."

"When we're at the plantation, sipping mint juleps."

She grins and gives me a hug. "You certainly know how to keep things interesting."

"At this point, I'd trade interesting for boring any day."

Comfy clothes donned, we curl up on the bed for what will amount to a day of no sleep and much chatter. Including one of our favorites, ways to drive Rey nuts with leading statements about sleepovers. The boy has a serious fetish with pillow fights; maybe it has something to do with feather pillows.

"So what's the deal with Dara?"

We both roll onto our sides, facing each other. CC tired of rooting through Annya's bag, jumps onto the bed and makes his way up the valley between us.

"What do you mean?"

"Is it just me or does she seem angrier and more closed off than usual?"

"There's some weird shit going on there that I don't understand."

"What kind of weird shit?"

"Well, this First Arrow crap for one and I told you about her little channeling session with Sekhmet."

"You've got gods coming out of the woodwork around here."

"Tell me about it, everywhere I look there's a god. Next thing I know you'll be telling me you're a trickster."

Her smile does nothing to comfort me. "So what's up with this First Arrow stuff?"

"All I got out of her is that she was a sort of handmaiden, or personal warrior to Sekhmet and was sent on some mission that scared the crap out of her."

"You do realize that legend has Sekhmet as the beginning of vampires, right? Ra sent her to punish mankind, but the bloodshed got out of control so he got her drunk and she stopped. I'm not sure what First Arrow means, but it's possible that as one of her warriors, Dara was punished for helping her and turned into a vamp."

"How did I not figure this out?"

"I'd say because you didn't put two and two together, it's not like ancient history is an everyday topic."

"Um, you've seen what I've been hanging out with lately, right?"

"Yeah, but besides the intervention of Sekhmet

in the fight between Dara and Frey, how often do you chat about old Egyptian history?"

"Got me there. What else do you know about my friends that I don't, oh, wise one?"

"First off, I didn't know about Dara, I'm only speculating. Second, even if I did know something, it's not my tale to tell."

"Oh, for crying out loud, you sound just like the rest of them." I thwap her with one of the fancy throw pillows that got left on the bed.

"Careful, you're going to make Rey's dreams come true."

Just for that I smack her again. "Brat."

"Yep, don't deny it and will even add spoiled. Now go to sleep, I had a long drive and I'm tired. If I'm not mistaken, you have a busy night ahead of you and trust me, you can use all the beauty sleep you can get."

She may be a brat, but she's right. There's a long night ahead of Roydians awaiting my services.

Chapter 44

I pause at the entrance between my living space and the salon. "Are you a watcher or a worker tonight?"

"Worker of course, why shouldn't I get in on this major tip action your crew keeps bragging about? Besides, you've got Lorelei up first and that woman takes up major time, so you need all the help you can get, gimpy."

"So true. You can use Dara's station until she comes in, then we can figure something out. Maybe you can help Nys with the shampooing and manicures."

"No problem, I wouldn't mind sitting on my butt all night filing nails."

I reach for the knob, then stop, turning to face her. "By the way, our temp receptionist has also temped for Var in the past, so—"

"I know, watch what I say. You're the blonde, not me." She gives me a push toward the door. "Let's go, the Rheine maiden won't wait forever."

"No doubt." I open the door to two giggling sprites and an eyebrow wiggling fox.

"Woop, new chick alert." Rey rushes over giving Annya an exaggerated kiss and pat on the ass, before she can stop him. "You helping or watching tonight?"

"She's helping if you don't scare her off. Win, this is my friend, Annya. Annya, this is Win, our temporary receptionist and a friend of Nyssa's."

Win grabs Annya's hand before it's offered, pumping it enthusiastically. "Pleasure to meet you Annya, Nyssa's told me so much about you."

Trying to free herself from Win's fervent handshake, she glances over at Nyssa "Really? Don't believe a word she says, she's all wet."

Nyssa giggles. "Oh, come on Annya, you know you're the nicest person on earth."

"See what I mean? All wet."

Looking at the clock, I wince and rotate a finger in the air. "Battle stations people, we're about to be invaded."

A gust of air moves hair and clothing as Win pushes past us, her sensible heels making little to no sound. Sprites, they don't always remember to keep their Talents at bay, but much better than when Nyssa forgets. There's nothing like walking through a wall of mist, or worse, a sudden shower. With the exception of Nyssa and her over sprayed, helmet of perfection, we finger comb each other's locks back into place. Once everyone's in agreement of acceptability, we file into the salon to the jingle of the front door, announcing the oncoming horde.

Friday night is a night of regulars. Rey has his

blue-hairs, Nyssa is booked with manicures and her false nail crew and I have Lorelei. Bets are usually made if she'll be early—very rarely a winner—or late. Tonight she would have made us all losers by being on time, a once in a blue moon occurrence.

"Annya, darling," Lorelei leans in for a European double cheek kiss, "no one told me you were coming to visit. I would have brought tickets to this weekend's show."

"It was a spur of the moment decision, no one knew. I'll be better prepared next time and call you myself. It's been a while since I've heard you belt out That Old Black Magic."

Grinning, Lorelei slips into my chair humming the tune. "We have to hustle tonight. I'm breaking in a new bandleader."

An obnoxious snort pulls our attention to Rey at the next station. "You should have done *that* before you got your hair done."

Annya and I glare at him, but Lorelei winks.

"What happened to Sam?"

"He's moving to Chicago." She slouches in the chair, lower lip protruding.

Draping the cape over my arm, I gather her hair back and lift until she's upright and I'm able to wrap the cape around her. "Wow, I didn't think he'd ever leave The Meadows."

Sam had been Moonlight Lake's bandleader since opening night. He has the knack of making even a mediocre musician a master of his instrument. The combination of his Talent with musicians and Lorelei's voice are legendary in The Meadows and beyond. They are the biggest draw to Moonlight.

Lorelei nods, dabbing at the tears gathering in her eyes.

"I'm sorry he's leaving, but maybe you'll get lucky and the new one will be cute."

The tears disappear as fast as they arrived, a dreamy look taking their place. "Dark hair, dark eyes. He's delicious, absolutely scrumptious."

She swivels the chair around and stands. There's a lightness to her steps on the way to the shampoo bowls that screams enamored. I hope she doesn't get so wrapped up in his looks she forgets to pay attention to his ability to lead the band. Glancing over my shoulder, I shake my head. Annya nods, her features twisted in concern. I'm guessing she's thinking the same thing.

Gathering Lorelei's locks against the back of her head, I gently guide her back until she's as comfortable as you can get in a shampoo bowl.

Even with a neck guard, I don't find it a pleasant position. You head is heavy. Dangling it over the edge with no support, kicks in the natural instinct to keep it upright, straining the neck and shoulder muscles. And there's always the threat of someone standing over you with a live hose, one slip and you're drenched.

It always amazes me, the trust clients put in us when they relax enough to fall asleep during a shampoo.

"Wow, I'm getting a Keely shampoo tonight, how did that happen?"

"Just felt like taking a little extra time with my favorite client."

A honey blonde brow rises. "Favorite client, huh?

I grin, using my hand to keep the water at bay around her hairline. "You don't believe me?"

She laughs. "Whatever you say. Hey, when did you get the fancy new brace?"

"You like?" I dangle it over her face, so she can get a better look.

"I do, so much better than the one the doctor gave you." Flipping the cape aside she reaches up turning my arm from side to side. "No offense, but even with my occasional habit of over tipping there is no way you can afford something like this."

Leave it to a Rhine maiden to know her metals and their worth. "It was a gift." I pull away, fill my palm with shampoo and begin scrubbing her head. Lather rinse, repeat.

"Hmm, should I ask who?"

"Sure."

"Who?"

"Mel."

Her head lifts and I push it back down, reaching

for the hose. "I didn't know Mel swung that way, hel, I didn't know you did."

"Neither of us do, it was a gift, nothing more."

"Okay, if you say so." She closes her eyes as I rise away the suds and apply a generous amount of conditioner, beginning the massage portion of our ritual.

After the final rinse, I squeeze as much moisture as I can from her hair and reach for the towels. Three to four usually do the job. Once I've got the moisture level to less than dripping, but still wet enough to work with, I lift her head and she sits up, then stands.

Hand on my shoulder, she pauses on the way back to my station, leaning in close to my ear whispers, "Who or what is it protecting you from?"

"How did you know?"

"I didn't, you just told me, but it's the only logical answer considering who gave it to you. If you don't want people to know it's for protection, you better come up with a better cover story."

I nod, leading her to my chair. I can't afford to get too far behind right off the bat. "So you couldn't *feel* the protection spells?"

"I suppose if I tried I could, but no, they are well done, discreet."

"Good." I lift the cape as she sits. "The plan is to tell people it's a prettier version of my support brace."

"I'd stick with that and don't tell them who gave it to you. It sounds suspicious on many levels if you say that Mel gave it to you. And by just smiling and winking it gives you an air of mystery that will drive the gossips crazy, especially with all the men you surround yourself with."

"Just what I need, more gossip."

"This is good gossip, darling, trust me."

"Yeah, but you're the queen of seduction and I'm…well, I'm me. I can't pull that kind of thing off."

"Think of it as good PR for the salon."

I look at Annya, surprisingly quite through the exchange. "What do you think?"

"I think she's right that you need to keep the story behind the bracelet quiet and by saying nothing you can't get yourself in trouble. No need to keep track of the lies."

Trouble and lies, my constant companions.

Chapter 45

"Miss Fey," Win sidles up beside me, "I'm sorry to interrupt, but there's a woman here who insists on an appointment with you tonight. I told her you are booked, but she won't take no for an answer."

I can't really blame Win for bringing the problem to me, Jenny would have done the same, but the night is almost over and I'm tired. The last thing I want to do is deal with a pushy client. Both Dara and Rey are booked to the bitter end. I doubt either would want to stay late any longer than I do, for whatever it is this woman wants. And pushing her off on Annya is out of the question, with the limited space.

"Tell her to have a seat and I'll be up to talk to her as soon as I've finished curling Mrs. Marks."

Win nods, the panic in her eyes subsiding as she hurries back to reception.

"Sorry about that, Mrs. Marks."

"Don't apologize for being good at what you do, Keely."

"Thank you, but this is your time, you deserve my full attention."

"I've never been unhappy with your work, or

the attention you give me. Others wanting your skills means you'll stay in business and I won't have to search for a new stylist. Finding one I like and who does what I want is difficult."

"Well, if our full appointment book is any indication, you won't searching any time soon."

"That's good, dear. Now don't forget to use the super hold spray, I need this to last all weekend."

Snagging the ultra-hold spray from my vanity, I hold my breath and spray. Between this stuff and the backcombing, her short 'do should stay in place through shear winds, or possibly an EF0 tornado. Unless she gets caught in the rain, then it will be a sticky, ratted mess. I've had clients who ride motorcycles swear by the stuff.

Handing her the mirror, I remove the comb-out cape and turn the chair, giving her a view of the back. "Does it meet your expectations?"

"As usual you've gone beyond my expectations. Thank you so much, Keely. I'll see you next week."

Mrs. Marks might be picky, but she appreciates what I do and that's all I can ask.

Quickly straightening my station, a feeling of dread builds in my stomach at the thought of having to explain that I don't have time for another appointment tonight.

It could go one of two ways, either they are disappointed, but agree to come back, or they throw a temper tantrum. The latter is the least desired and if my luck holds, the one I'll have to deal with.

Catching Teiran's reflection in the mirror, I'm hoping he doesn't think a miffed client is part of his protection duty. That will only make things worse. Unless they get violent, then I'll gladly step aside and let him do his thing.

Rey and Dara are fluffing and spraying clients to either side and part of me is glad they are regulars. Not that I want them to witness a showdown, but the alternative would be scaring off new clients. Regulars are much more understanding.

Nyssa has my next client under her spell at the shampoo bowl, with any luck the sound of water will block out any strong words. Heading toward reception, I mouth, *take your time*, and she nods. A tiny bit of fear glazing her eyes. This must be worse than I thought.

Annya lifts her attention from shaping a set of nails, as I pass, a silent, are you okay in her eyes. I nod, giving her an okay sign as I walk around the dividing wall.

The chairs are filled, one lone figure that had to be my desperate client stands looking out the front window. Flashy shoes. Designer suit. Perfect up-do. This one is not here for an appointment, at least not a hair appointment. Oh, gods, so don't I need or want to deal with this tonight. Frickin' Stasia Athory.

"Ms. Athory, Miss Fey will see you now," says

Win, her tone overly formal, with an underlying anger. Wonder what Ms. Bitch Perfect said or did to the girl.

"Ah, Keely." She comes at me like a perfumed freight train, grabbing my hands and pulling me in for a double cheek kiss, like we're old friends.

"What can I do for you Stasia? I'm booked solid tonight, but we can find a future slot for you." Like the second Tuesday, of the eighth week, of the thirteenth month, a couple of centuries from now.

"I tried to explain to your receptionist that I do not need an appointment, just a moment of your time."

"I seriously don't have a moment to spare. I'm behind schedule as it is and my next client is waiting for me back at my station by now."

"Perhaps we could meet after you are finished for the night." Her attention darts to something, or someone over my shoulder and she licks her ruby stained lips.

Either Teiran or Dara must have walked up behind me, with any luck both. Yay, maybe I can wave my hand and they'll make her disappear. I'll hold that thought as a last resort. "I don't think so. I'll be too tired to discuss anything after work."

"And tomorrow afternoon, will you still be too tired after you have rested?" Her eyes are flint hard and dark, the pupils blending with the deep brown of the iris.

"It's very possible,"—I glance at the clock—"considering a very long night is becoming longer by the second." I'm getting a certain sadistic pleasure out of needling her, especially since I've got backup in the form of a helhound and a vamp. Without them, I probably—okay, no probably about it, I wouldn't be this bold.

Those deep dark and angry eyes narrow for the briefest of moments, quickly becoming friendly. A reaction I can't take credit for, I'm not nearly as scary as what's behind me. There's no way she can threaten me in my own salon, with all these witnesses and my bodyguard in attendance. If it were Ric, I might be a little nervous that she could sway him with her charm, but not Teiran. He seems to despise lidérc as much as he despises schattenkind. Not that I blame him, this half-breed wants to eliminate him.

"If I remember correctly, you were told we did not wish to carry your potions." Yay, me, Dara's done with her client and has joined the fun. Not standing behind me, but at my side, raising my confidence level another notch.

"You cannot blame a girl for trying, can you?"

Oh, I could blame her for lots of things, but trying isn't one of them. I believe everyone should try, but this woman has balls bigger than any of the men in my life and she certainly likes letting them swing in the open. It's about time someone kicks them hard enough she'll finally take the hint. "I've told you more than once that we—I'm not interested, Ms. Athory, now if you'll excuse me, I have a client waiting."

Ruby lips compress into a thin line and her jaw tightens as Dara places a hand on her shoulder guiding her to the door. She stops at the door Dara politely opens for her and turns to face me. "If that is your final answer."

I smile sweetly. "It is."

She gives me a look that would freeze boiling water as Dara closes the door forcing her outside.

I watch her cross the street to her fancy sports car and a trail of icy fingers make their way down my spine.

Chapter 46

"Got to hand it to her, it was pretty ballsy of her to show her face in the salon." Rey fishes round of beer from the fridge, passing them to Annya at the end of the break room table.

"Yeah, and she got them kicked for her trouble." I take the bottle passed to me, waiting for the opener to make the rounds. Teiran takes the bottle for me, twisting off the cap without any effort whatsoever. "Um, you do know those aren't twist off tops, right?"

He shrugs, repeating the action for Nyssa, and Win, who hold their bottles out to him. Guess we've found another reason to keep Teiran around.

Dara declines his offer to open hers, using the old fashion method. "I would suggest you not go anywhere unaccompanied."

"I came to that conclusion on my own, but I think Nys needs to be watched over too. She got a similar offer and Stasia might try taking her to rattle my cage."

"No worries, I'll watch over short and soggy." Rey places a protective hand on Nyssa's shoulder and she reaches up patting it with a smile.

"Thanks, fur ball." Nyssa snuggles in closer to him.

"Of course, staying at your place will make it easier." He wiggles his brow.

"I wouldn't have it any other way."

It's unbelievable that he's oblivious to her crush after all these years, but Rey only has eyes for every female who crosses his path. I often wonder if he'll ever decide to settle down. Then again, I have no desire to take that path, so why should I expect it of him?

"I'll stay with you too," says Win, wrapping her arm around Nyssa. "Although, it will probably be more to protect you from him."

"Woo-hoo, a two for one." Rey wraps his arms around both of them.

As hesitant as I am about what Win sees and hears, she was witness to Stasia's visit and seems just as shaken as the rest of us. I guess she has a right to know what she's getting into working here, even if it's only on a temporary basis. A temporary basis, that if Nyssa has her way will become permanent. So far, I've got to say, she fits in and is efficient at the job. Two pluses in my book, but I'm still holding out, until I make sure she's a perfect fit.

"I think all of you should be vigilant, no one connected to Miss Fey, in anyway, should go out alone."

"I thank you for your concern, Shield, but I believe I can watch over myself."

"Of course, First Arrow, you would be the exception, but the others should not take any chances."

"Agreed."

Wow, Dara and Teiran agreed on something, kind of blows the mind.

"Threat or not, I'm not letting that bitch on wheels ruin my visit. What are we doing this weekend?" Annya polishes off the rest of her beer and points at Rey, then the fridge.

"Being you're my guest, what do you want to do?"

She shrugs, taking another bottle from Rey. "I don't know. What do you guys usually do on a Saturday night?"

"Atramentous?" Rey, Nyssa and Dara, say in unison.

Annya answers with a goofy, upper body dance from her chair.

I have to admit, the idea of getting out and shaking my groove thing holds a lot of appeal. "Atramentous it is."

Teiran signs beside me and shakes his head. I'm not sure if it's because he doesn't like dance clubs, or that we've just made his job of protecting us a whole lot more difficult. Knowing him, it's a little bit of both.

A night on the town is, without a doubt, the pick-me-up I needed. Loud music that makes you want to move and infectious energy that grabs you and reminds you, you're alive.

Nyssa, Rey and Win immediately head to the dance floor, pulling Annya along with them. Dara excuses herself, disappearing into the crowd to do heaven knows what, while Teiran and I look for a place to sit. It touches my heart when I see the reserved sign on our usual table. Not long ago I would have been shunned and probably tossed out the door, but tonight everyone greets us like we haven't missed a Saturday night.

Teiran frowns at the setup. The booth leaves him either squished into the middle, or always having to jump up when someone wants in or out. To pull up a chair would leave his back exposed to the room. A big no, no.

"Want to sit somewhere else?" I yell over the thunderous base.

Shaking his head, he motions to the bar. "Would you like something to drink?"

"Sure."

Grabbing my hand, he pulls me along behind him. I should have known he wouldn't leave me alone. Not that that's all bad, I get a mighty fine view of some painted on black denim.

While he orders our drinks, I scan the room, waving at those I know and moving to the music. Laughter can't be helped as I spy Rey surrounded by the girls doing his best air guitar moves. I point them out to Teiran as he hands me my Black Pearl, the faintest of smiles lighting his dark features. Yes, even Mr. Stoic can find humor in their antics.

Taking a sip of my drink, my eyes close and a smile stretches across my face. Ah, Black Pearls, how I've missed your smooth flavor on my tongue.

To my delight, the D.J. swings into a heavy techno mashup of a Duran Duran classic, and Teiran shakes his head as the crowd roars. "As if most of them would know what it is like to be hungry like a wolf."

I shrug. "It's a sexual thing for most of them, but I bet there's a few therians out there who understand."

"That is the problem."

"What? The sexual thing or that there are therians out there?" A long drawn out an exasperated sigh, as if I'm a trick birthday candle that keeps relighting and he's given up. It suddenly dawns on me that he's not talking about the song and its possible meanings.

"The stalking of your prey."

He takes a step toward me and gods forgive me I cave, taking one back.

"Tracking them."

He takes another step, forcing me back again. "Until you capture them."

Another step in our tango and there's nowhere to run. The bar bites into my back, his arms on either side caging me in, the animal need flowing off him. My head drops down and I close my eyes, swallowing back the urges building in my belly. Prey, yeah, that's just what I'm acting like, dropping my head, baring my neck. Fool. I raise my head and stare him in those I-promise-it'll-be-a-night-you'll-never-forget eyes.

"I'm guessing you're not talking about food."

He shrugs, lowering his arms as he steps back.

I don't know whether to be relieved he backed off or to be offended he didn't take it further. I must look dejected, because he sighs again, takes my drink and sets it on the bar. Grabbing my arm, he pulls me into the crowd of dancers.

Okay, very unexpected, I didn't see Teiran Rand as a dancer and he's not in the conventional sense. There's no bouncing around, shuffling of feet or—thank the gods—fist pumping. There's barely room to floss between us with a hair. We move with the music, but slower, more of a sensual standoff. I match his every step as he circles me around, keeping us face to face. I refuse to be prey.

It's nothing like being around Ric, who seems to see me as a strange combination of damsel in distress and an equal. If I allow Teiran one tiny victory, such as a missed dance step, he will see me as weak. The man simply has no time for weakness.

Somehow he slips behind me. And that tiny space between us? Yeah, that's gone too. I can feel every long, hard muscle pressed against me. His hands guiding my hips in time with the music, sliding down my thighs and back up before his fingers mesh with mine. Our arms raise until they are wrapped around me. His chin rests on my shoulder, the warmth of his breath grazing my neck and ear.

"Would you like me to show you what it is like to be hungry like a wolf?"

I'm glad he can't see my face. I'm a twisted mass of confusion, common sense and bodily need at war. My body screaming, 'yes, please,' with the way it grinds back against him. While my brain screams, 'hels no.'

"All you have to do is say yes, Keely."

"I thought I disgusted you."

"You, as a woman, far from disgust me," he presses a little closer, "I thought that was evident."

Oh, yeah, it's evident. More than evident. What's not evident is if he is talking about sex, or if showing me what it's like to be hungry like a wolf means attempting to *change* me. If it's choice number two…that's, well, it's asking for trouble. The last thing I need is Hel having another kind of hold over me.

I shiver and he pulls me tighter, his lips working their way from my ear to the crook of my neck. Succeeding in pulling another shiver—this time lacking fear—from me.

"Well?"

I hear the intake of breath and feel his body quiver with a drawn out exhale across my neck and shoulder. Teeth clamp down, firm yet gentle. My head grows empty. Fuzzy. Light. I can't tell if it's the bass in the music or my pulse thumping in my ears. Thank the gods, his hands hold me up, or I'd be on the ground groveling at this feet.

Suddenly, I'm a teetering mess on heels as Teiran and I are separated. As I turn, the crowd backs off, encircling one enraged therian and an equally pissed vamp. Crap, what the hel is Ric doing here?

Club bouncers move in, pausing when they see the Sword and Shield are at the center of the commotion. Instead of breaking up a possible fight, they stand arms out in front of the crowd and stare at me. Great. This is how I pictured spending my Saturday night, breaking up a fight between lifelong friends.

I think I'm the *her* they're screaming about, so I guess this is kind of my fault. Vanity rears its ugly head and I have to bite my lower lip to keep from smiling. Seriously, how often have two super-hot guys fought over me? Never. And it feels good, but not so good that I'll let it continue.

Stepping between them, I hold my hands out, palms flat against their chests. "To your corners, boys. There's enough of me to go around." As luck would have it, the music stops just as the words leave my mouth.

My own words swirl around in my flustered brain. Hel's Realm, did I really say there's enough of me to go around? Brows raise and jaws drop. Yeah, I really said it. Question is, did I subconsciously mean it, or was that just a warped attempt at humor to soften the situation?

I may have averted one crisis, but an entirely new one has arisen. One I'm not sure I can handle.

Chapter 47

They both stop in their tracks, everything seemingly forgotten as they stare at me. A jumble of questions flow forth, from what did you say to did I hear you correctly, before Teiran laughs. Not his usual forced laughter, but a full belly laugh. If I wasn't so damn embarrassed I'd enjoy it, just as I'd enjoy Ric's flushed and flustered expression. And to make matters worse, it's not just them staring.

Every last person in the room has their eyes on me and is either snapping pictures with their phones—freakin' social media whores—laughing, or whispering behind their hands. Unholy crap, my inner child wants to run for the hills and my outer adult is inclined to follow.

I push past what was an average girl's dream, turned nightmare and weave my way through the crowd. Adding injury to insult, the door swings open as I reach for the handle, nearly smacking me in the face. I open my mouth to take my frustrations out on the person entering, but am left gaping like a fish as Frick and Frack stare down at me.

"Just the person we were looking for," says Frack, his beefy hand wrapping around my upper arm.

"Keely Fey," says Frick, pulling out a set of cuffs, "You are to be taken into custody under suspicion of activity in the disappearance of Stanley Lewis. You have the right…"

The rest of the Miranda goes fluttering over the top of my head as my arms are stretched behind me and shackled. I search frantically for anyone in my group. I see the top of Teiran's head as he pushes his way toward me and Ric close behind as they break free. Dara flanks in from the side with a trail of vamps behind her. What the hel is she thinking? A jail break before I even get there?

Rey, Nyssa, Annya and Win scramble through the crowd in time for me to shout, "Call my lawyer," before Frack manhandles me out the door.

Frack is taking a little too much pleasure in dragging me across the sidewalk. The sadistic twinkle in his eyes, as he shoves me into the back of the black sedan, brings fear to the surface in the form of cold sweat and goose bumps the size of mountains. My shields rumble inside my head when his attention moves to the collar. A slow, creeping smile lights his face, a child on Christmas morning finding that bonus gift hidden at the back of the pile.

I put as much distance between us as possible in the confines of the car. He's the driver, so I won't have the added benefit of him sitting beside me and I doubt his partner will allow any unsanctioned stops along the way. It's plain to see, he's at a tipping point, I don't think he's as interested in legal justice as much as inflicting pain. The illusion of the hunting down and bringing in the bad guy is a cover for his hobbies. Makes me wonder at what point on the psycho scale does the NTF put its agents out to pasture. One unfortunate slip-up? Two? Does it take witnesses? My mind races with the possibilities. I can only hope Frick is enough of a deterrent to keep him from playing out whatever wild fantasies he has involving me.

Frick says something and Frack slams the door, miffed that playtime is over. His bulk removed from the window gives me a view of Teiran and Frick's mid-drifts, an obvious argument jumbled by my enclosure. Ric stands farther back, his actions animated as he speaks into the phone, Rey, Nyssa and Win gathered around him. Dara and Annya stand off to the side of both groups. Annya points from the car to Teiran, then draws a finger across her throat. She's pantomiming my thoughts about Teiran and I being separated. I catch a brief flood of protesting as the doors open, but none of this matters as the men in black climb into the car and shut the doors.

I huddle in the back seat, as far out of reach as possible, neither of them saying a word as we cruise down Main Street. My fear rises, but the collar stays in place due to the spelled cuffs wedged between the seat and the small of my back, keeping me from any semblance of comfort as we pull onto the highway. One small perk, I won't be decapitated in an NTF sanctioned vehicle, before I can find out what this is all about. They said suspicion in the disappearance, not death, of Stanley Lewis. How could they know I had anything to do with his demise?

It all happened in The Between. No one knows, except those closest to me, Teiran and Ric, the Royds, Hel, and Stanley himself. Oh, yeah, and the dead I called that disposed of him. Had someone done some sort of hocus-pocus to find out? And what proof could they have? It would have to be physical, metaphysical only counts for a portion at trial and a very small one at that. No one has been convicted on metaphysical evidence alone. When they brought me in before, they'd had my old shears, but Jacobs had gotten me off because it was circumstantial, with no real tie to me committing the crimes. What could they possibly have this time? And if there is something, who gave it to them?

Chapter 48

With the exception of the now flourishing plant on the reception desk, nothing has changed about NTF headquarters. It's still gloomy grey, accented with a touch of dread in—you guessed it—more grey, highlighted by flickering fluorescent bulbs. The hall to interrogation seems longer, or I've dipped into a nightmare of walking a never-ending treadmill of doom. Cursed to pass the same windowless steel door over and over as a line of off-set duplicates stretch out before me.

The whole situation is a nightmare, but there's no waking up from this. I'm stuck with no way out in sight. My only hope is that Royd can use his influence to get me out of here. But what if he's the reason I'm here? Would he stoop so low as to turn me over to the NTF because I haven't signed on with him? No, none of this serves his ultimate goal. But his sister, that's another story, Vana's wanted me out of the picture since she laid eyes on me. Then again, if Hel's right, she needs Var to regain his position for her to regain her's. It's a puzzle, within a puzzle, within a puzzle, all with missing pieces.

I bounce off Frick's back as we come to a stop in front of one of the doors. Frack's hand causes me to stumble against him as he pulls me back, giving his partner room to slide the keycard. With a push, I stumble in after him, my feet barely staying beneath me as I quickly move to the other side of the table, away from my tormentor. Frick follows, removes the cuffs and invites me to sit by pulling out the chair.

Once I'm seated, he bends down, clicking the manacles into place around my ankles. A new wave of terror washes over me as my hands are placed in the restraints decorating the chair's arms. Hey, an upgrade, I'm not in the same room as last time. In there my arms would be connected to the table instead of the chair. Like that's any consolation. I am totally and completely at their mercy this time. The chair is pushed toward the table and Frick takes his spot across from me, no friendly, coercing smile this time. He's all business, even removing the dark tinted glasses. Unsettling, cloudy white eyes send a shiver racing down my spine.

"Miss Fey, we have reason to believe you are connected to, or the reason behind the disappearance of one, Stanley Lewis. In conjunction with that the deaths of his parents and your employee, Jenny Abbot."

I shake my head, this can't be happening, they're going to pin *his* crimes on me again.

"Do you have anything to say on this matter?"

I give the easiest and best answer I can. "I want my lawyer."

"Did you know Stanley Lewis?"

"I want my lawyer."

"How about his parents, Estelle and Bernard Lewis?"

"I want my lawyer."

"Jenny Abbot was employed by you for six months before her death. Is this correct?"

"I want my lawyer."

"We're giving you a chance to come clean, Miss Fey, take it, before things get messy." He glances at Frack.

Fear fog rolls in, clouding my mind and my ears begin to ring. "I know you can't touch me without provocation and you've made that impossible." I look down at my restrained hands and wiggle my fingers.

"No one knows what happens in these rooms, Miss Fey, except you and us."

I nod toward the camera, with its blinking light, in the corner of the room. "You're going to tell me that's not on?"

Frick shrugs.

"Let me guess, the camera malfunctioned during questioning and you lost all the footage up until they find me a bloody pulp on the floor, because you didn't feel the need to restrain me."

"It's always possible; technology can be so… touchy."

"Look, I can't stop you from doing whatever you want, but I'm not saying another word without my lawyer."

"And you'll get your lawyer soon enough, but first I'd like to hear your side of the story."

I shake my head and Frack rounds the table, his hand a vise on my shoulder.

"I suggest you start talking, Miss Fey, my associate becomes antsy in silence."

I can hear and feel the joint in my shoulder grind as his grip tightens, pushing me down. If given the right sign, he'd push me all the way through the chair and possibly the concrete floor. "Fine, I'll talk." The grip lightens with a nod from his cohort. "What do you want to talk about?"

Frack's fingers bite into my shoulder and I wince, constraining the cry of pain to a grunt.

"You know what I want, Miss Fey."

Yeah, I know. He wants a confession, and his buddy wants to mangle me if he gets the chance. It doesn't matter if I talk or not. He, unlike his partner, doesn't give a tiny rat's ass what I have to say, evident by the bone crushing pressure on my shoulder.

"I don't know what to say, except, I want my lawyer."

Frick sighs. Gathering the pile of folders into a

neat stack, he pushes his chair from the table and slowly rises. "If this is how you want to handle this, I have no other choice."

If he has no other choice, I have even fewer. It's either incriminate myself, or take a beating and hope the gang gets Jacobs here before it's too late. The flight part of me says, take the fall. Where fight says, give me a fair shot at defending myself.

"Last chance, Miss Fey."

Keeping my mouth shut might keep me off death row, but it's not going to keep me from death. I open my mouth to stop him, then close it and shake my head. There's nothing I can say to stall this out any longer and I refuse to admit to killing the Lewis family and Jenny.

He nods to Frack, tossing him the keys to my restraints before turning to the door and sliding his keycard.

Chapter 49

The keys jingle enticingly behind me. I want those keys. I need those keys if I'm going to have even the smallest chance of survival. All I need is the walking wall of muscle to unlock the bonds holding my arms and legs. Of the choice between death by collar and death by pummeling, I'll take my chances with the collar if it means I have a way of defending myself.

"So, it's just you and me."

Silence, except for his breathing.

"You going to use those keys, or just keep playing with them?" If I learned nothing else from my confrontation with The Collector, it's that sometimes poking the bear puts it off its game.

Still nothing. I try craning my neck around to see what he's up to, the best view I get is his jacket and its removal. I follow his movement around the table where he hangs it and his tie neatly on the back of the chair.

"Worried the dry cleaner won't be able to get my blood out of your jacket? If I were you I'd be more worried about that pristine, white…shirt."

Damn, spoke too soon. He slowly unbuttons

the cuffs, then takes his time working down the front. Shrugging it off, like he's stripping for my pleasure before he takes his in beating the crap out of me. How considerate of him.

"How about you undo these,"—I wiggle my arms—"and make it a somewhat fair fight? Or are you afraid a little girl might get the drop on you, big boy?"

He laughs. The bright shine in his eyes tells me he's no different from any other predator, he lives for the chase and likes it when his prey fights back. I may not be a natural born fighter like him, but I'm sure as hel going to give it my all.

Rotating the key ring around his thick finger, he stalks his way toward me, looking from my ankles to my wrists. Debating his best course of action. If he undoes my wrists first, I can use my hands against him while he undoes my ankles and vice versa, the other way around. I'm almost hoping he frees my legs first. Maybe I can manage one of those cool movie moves, where the hero uses his chair to knock out the villain. As visions of grandeur dance in my head, he's made a decision and my ankles are free.

My muscles tense, readying for my hopefully promising move only to be stanched as the door opens. I sag in the chair, relieved when Frick is shoved through the door by Jacobs, flanked by Ric and Teiran.

The bare-chested, berserker kneeling beside me doesn't stand a chance of climbing to his feet before Teiran launches himself toward us. Momentum sends them tumbling back against the wall, knocking my chair over in the process. I don't bother smothering the cry of pain as my landing on a concrete floor is cushioned by the industrial metal chair. It's a small price to pay for being saved from a savage beating.

"Shield, stop," yells Jacobs. "Sword, do something before he makes a bad situation worse."

Ric bounds across the room, his sword drawn, a blinding light between the fighting men and the rest of us. One of these days, I'm going to find out where he hides that thing.

Jacobs rights my chair with the help of Frick, who has retrieved the keys and works to set me free.

"This is how you treat my client? Leaving her restrained and unattended with an out of control berserker? This is a total violation of my client's rights. I should have charges filed against you, him, and the NTF." Jacobs helps me to stand, putting himself between me, the brawl and Frick.

Not less than a dozen men in black swarm the room, covering their eyes as they converge on the blinding wall of light hiding the sight, but not the sounds of the free-for-all.

Ric's sword dims on a minimum of eight other berserkers holding Frack at bay, the others surround

Teiran, but keep their hands to themselves. I don't know if it's out of respect, or they if they don't find him as big a threat. After looking at Frack, they should rethink that option.

My behemoth attacker is sporting what looks like a broken nose, at least one blackened eye and a collection of rather nasty gashes across his chest and back, under a glaze of free flowing blood.

Teiran's face isn't much better, smeared with blood, I can only hope isn't all his. Claws retract as he presses a hand to his right side, bending forward ever so slightly. Possibly some broken ribs? He limps toward me. A strange, unreadable glint in his eyes makes me glad we're in a room full of people.

"Are you all right?" asks Jacobs.

"Yeah, now that you guys are here. I kept telling him I wanted my lawyer, but didn't think they'd actually let you in to see me."

"They tried to question you without me?"

I nod. "And when I wouldn't talk he,"—I point to Frick—"left me alone with the other on. His parting words were something about not having any other choice."

If those white eyes aren't freaky enough, when he turns them on me, I can feel the hatred riding just below his professional demeanor.

Jacobs turns to Frick and unloads. "Agent Finnly, is this common practice with NTF?

Threats? Torture? Being denied legal counsel?"

Frick—Agent Finnly buckles under the barrage of questions, even taking a step back as Jacobs pushes farther and farther into his personal space. "No, I had gone to contact you as the defendant requested. I did not realize Agent Barns would take such actions."

Agent Barns shoots his partner a menacing look, made more terrifying by swollen features and streaks of blood. Yeah, dude, you just got tossed under the bus. I'd like to say I feel for ya, but well…I don't. As a matter of fact, I hope that bus backs up and runs you over a couple of times.

"You were the agent in charge if I'm not mistaken and I've about had it with how you run your investigations. I want to talk to someone higher up on the food chain. Now."

While Agent Finnly—I'm seriously missing not knowing their real names, I liked mine better— disappears to find someone to appease Jacobs, another agent shows us to a clean room, locking the door behind him.

Jacobs leads me to the corner farthest from the camera. "We need to talk quickly and quietly, before they come back."

I nod.

"You know why you're here?"

I nod again.

"Have they shown you any evidence, or given

you any hints to what they have that can connect you to the crimes?"

"No."

"Damn."

"All they did was tell me what I supposedly did and ask me to come clean."

"Maybe they don't have anything concrete to hold you on." He taps his foot impatiently. "If they don't, I can get you out of here tonight."

"If have something?"

One corner of his mouth tugs downward and he shakes his head. "If that's the case, I'll do my best to get you out on bond. Your job with Mr. Royd should appease any judge and show that you're not a flight risk."

My job with Mr. Royd…I guess no one let him in on the teeny, little fact that I haven't actually taken that job.

Chapter 50

"Director Mather." Jacobs meets the man at the halfway point of the room, vigorously shaking his hand.

"Mr. Jacobs, I understand you're rather upset about the treatment of your client." Mather has the appearance of a favorite, aged uncle, but under that likable persona there's steel. Like a rod running up his spine, keeping him standing straight when he should be bent with age. A face cut with the lines of life. Laughter, worry, and right now irritation.

"Yes." He turns and looks at me and I lower my gaze. The whole, look visibly shaken and afraid for my life, act is a breeze considering it's not a far stretch from the truth.

"Your agents took it upon themselves to forcibly pull a confession from my client for crimes she did not commit."

"I see, and what proof do you have of their actions?"

"Have you checked your video feed?"

"Yes, the camera in room thirteen seems to be malfunctioning."

My head shoots up and my mouth opens, but

Ric places a hand on my shoulder. Keeping me quiet, allowing Jacobs to work his magic.

"That's interesting; according to my client that was exactly what Agent Finnly told her would happen when he left her alone with Agent Barns."

"Agent Barns insists your man," the director points to Teiran, "attacked him."

"Yes, an unfortunate circumstance that we do not deny, but he was only doing his job."

"His job is to attack my agents?"

"No, to protect Miss Fey."

"Oh? She's hired bodyguards? What would a hairdresser need with a bodyguard?"

"Miss Fey did not hire him; he's under orders given by Var Royd. I know it's difficult to recognize him under the blood and cuts, but that is Teiran Rand, Director, one of Mr. Royd's personal guards."

The Director's brows shoot upward. "Why on earth would he loan out one of his personal guards to a possible murderess?"

Jacobs sighs. "Director Mather, we cleared this up long ago, Miss Fey was a victim of Stanley Lewis, not the other way around. That is why Mr. Royd has loaned her the services of Mr. Rand. You still have not caught Mr. Lewis, if I'm not mistaken."

"If we had your client wouldn't be here. Now, why wasn't Miss Fey's run in with Lewis reported?"

"For the exact reason we are here now, the prejudice of your agents. They wouldn't have believed her if she had come forward. Instead she resorted to contacting her employer for help."

"Her employer? She works for Mr. Royd?"

"Yes."

He lets out a slow breath. "Then can you explain to me why we've found evidence against Miss Fey in these crimes? And the even more puzzling, the claim that she wears a collar?"

Aw, shit. Busted. I don't think there's any magic even Jacobs can work that will explain this damned necklace of doom.

"I'd like to see this evidence against my client. As for this collar you speak of, it is a simple necklace, given to her by friends for her birthday."

Director Mather clearly doesn't believe the BS piling up around his shoes as he motions me closer, squinting at my neckline.

Jacobs holds out his hand, stopping me from moving closer.

"If she can prove that this is a simple necklace and not a collar it would go a long way to persuading me to rethink our position on the case."

"She can and she will, but first, I need to see this evidence."

The Director nods. "Fair enough." He leaves the room and Jacobs hurries over, the three of us huddle close, blocking the agents at the door from seeing our pow-wow. I only hope one, or more of them doesn't have supersonic hearing.

"You need to take this thing off for the Director. The stone makes a nice touch; it looks more like jewelry than a collar. "

I have no idea how we are going to get away with this; I thought it was common knowledge around town that I'm collared. Maybe it's not. Maybe, like the bracelet, I can play this thing off as a piece of jewelry.

Teiran winces as he attempts frowning, the crack in his lower lip welling with blood.

"Look, I know you don't want to, but if you don't she's not getting out of here. Do you want her left in here with them? I'd say your earlier actions prove otherwise."

"Seriously Teiran, I'd rather you kill me than them." I wipe the blood from his lip with the edge of my sleeve, giving him a trembling smile that verges on tears. "I promise you get the first crack."

Teiran nods, a softness in his eyes, I don't think I've ever seen before. "Fine."

"He's going have to see her removing it, so you need to be careful how you position yourself."

"If we stand shoulder to shoulder behind her, we can hide his hand," says Ric, softly and Jacobs nods.

"Better yet, I can act all flustered and light headed. You two can pretend to steady me."

"Whatever you three do, do it right, we won't get a second chance."

The door opens and the Director enters, followed by what I assume to be a female agent, from the black suit, high pony and sensible shoes, carrying a box. When she looks at me, I'm surprised by clear blue eyes, not the milky white of a tracker. There is neither a friendliness to her—like I should expect any from an employee of the NTF—nor the barely contained rage of a berserker. Interest flickers as she takes in our little group, quickly veiled by indifference.

"Mr. Jacobs, Miss Fey, this is agent Wilken. She's been assigned to your case."

There's the slightest twitch from Jacobs, I'm not sure if this is a good thing or a bad thing. Personally, I'm not upset to see Frick and Frack go, but Wilken is an unknown, where I knew what to expect from them. I want to ask what she is, but don't want to get off on the wrong foot with the person who might be holding my fate in her hands.

The Director motions for her to set the box on the table, but neither lift the lid. "We'll open this when you've removed the *necklace*, Miss Fey."

Keeping up the appearance of stressed, tired and afraid is no problem. I'm all of the above and a few others. The trick is not letting it get out of control, if my Talents decide I need protecting, the collar shrinks and game over. Getting my knees to buckle at the perfect moment is another hurdle. We need it to look convincing and I've already proven I'm not winning any academy awards in the near future.

Licking my lips, I lock my knees, trusting Ric and Teiran will catch me when I go down. Once again, Var Royd is winning without even knowing it. Raising my hands, I reach behind my neck feeling for a nonexistent clasp. Tiny beads of sweat build on my forehead and upper lip, what if this doesn't work? What if my knees don't—

Hands grasp me under each arm, steadying me as I waver.

"Miss Fey." Jacobs steps in front of me, blocking the Director and his staff. "Are you all right?"

I let out a breath I didn't know I was holding as a finger touches the back of my neck releasing the collar to my fingers. Blinking once, slowly, to let Jacobs know I have it off, he smiles and steps to the side. "A glass of water would be appreciated."

"Water," I hear the Director say. "Get the woman some water."

With my full audience returned, I make a show of fiddling with the closure, before sliding the collar down and holding it in front of me. Someone hands me a glass of water and I hand the collar to Jacobs. "Well, that was embarrassing. I apologize. I'm not usually prone to fainting."

"You've been through a lot, Miss Fey, it's a

wonder you have been as gracious as you are."

I smile up at Jacobs. "I want to cooperate, Mr. Jacobs. After all, I have nothing to hide." Time to dig out the hip waders, because the shit's getting deep in here.

My darling, lying lawyer holds out the necklace for inspection. "Well, Director Mather, satisfied?"

Chapter 51

Director Mather tentatively takes the necklace, turning it in his hands. Having no idea if the magic becomes inert when handled by anyone, other than the handler, or person assigned to wear it, I cross my fingers behind my back. Hoping he can't feel the spells coursing through the thin band of metal.

He hands it over to Agent Wilken, who handles it like it's nothing, but the metal circle it appears to be. Fondling the moonstone, she lifts those piercing, blue eyes and studies me. That's when I realize what she is.

How could I have missed it? The pale skin. Jewel toned eyes. Dark hair with subtle highlights that don't fool those in the know. She's a döckâlfar. I'm really off my game, but her height might be the reason I didn't put two and two together. Most âlfar are around six feet and she doesn't stand more than five-six or five-seven in her sensible shoes.

"It's just a necklace, sir." She hands it back to him, still looking at me. Those jewel colored eyes so like Teiran's. I wonder if he and Ric know what she is. What am I thinking? Of course they do. Slowly, the corners of her perfect, cosmetic free lips turn upward. If I'd have blinked I would have missed it, but I didn't. She knows.

The floor drops and my knees buckle, unplanned this time, but Teiran and Ric still catch me. They guide me to a chair and I don't protest as everyone flutters around me expressing their concern for my well-being.

Let them think I'm a weak female, I don't care. I'm more concerned with why Wilken didn't serve me up on a silver platter. She'd probably get a fat promotion for exposing my lies. Hel, for misleading the NTF they'd probably convict me of the other crimes, lock me away and throw away the key.

Another glass of water is shoved into my hand, along with a stale doughnut. I take a couple of small nibbles to keep them quiet, setting it aside when their interest turns to the box of evidence. Just like everyone else, I'm dying to find out what they think they have on me, but the inner voice of reason cautions me against giving up the weak, female façade just yet. And it's not like I don't trust Jacobs to do what's best for me, after all, he's well paid to keep me out of jail.

Director Mather lifts the lid and tips several plastic wrapped items onto the table. "We received an anonymous tip to check Ledges State park in connection with the disappearance of Mr. Lewis. Along with his car, this is what we found."

Jacobs peruses the items, lifting each in turn,

studying them from every angle, reading the labels before returning them to the table. I can make out a rumpled bit of cloth, probably the skirt he removed to cushion my head in the trunk. A pair of non-off-road, lucite hooker heels. One bag I'd like to get a closer look at to appease my curiosity, but I think it holds some of my hair. My lips and the surrounding area vividly recall the use of the contents of the final bag. Gods, how I hate duct tape.

"There's nothing here that proves Miss Fey had anything to do with the disappearance of Mr. Lewis."

"Perhaps, but it does prove she was at the scene."

"You have no proof she was actually with him. Do you even have any proof this was the last place Mr. Lewis was seen? No? I didn't think so. All this proves is Mr. Lewis's twisted fascination with my client. He could have taken these items to feed this sick obsession. It also leads to my client's statement that Mr. Lewis attacked her. Miss Fey is the true victim here. If this is all you have, I'll be taking my client home now."

Hel's Realm, he talks fast. Must be part of his strategy to keep the opposition off kilter. Director Mather opens his mouth, then closes it with a snap. Leading me to believe it worked, that or they really don't have anything substantial and that's why Frack was going to beat a confession out of me. If I'm not mistaken, Agent Wilken smiled, but it dissolved so quickly I can't be sure. And why would she smile? I mean, if I'm getting this right, I'll be walking out of here any moment. You'd think that would piss her off not make her smile.

"Well, Director Mather, do I take my client out of here all charges dropped, or do I start filing charges of misconduct and attempted assault?"

The corners of his mouth turn downward, his gaze flicking from Jacobs to me and back. "Take you client and go, but know we will continue our investigation."

Jacobs motions to Teiran and Ric, who help me from my chair and guide me out of the room. Agent Wilken's head dips ever so slightly when we pass her and I can feel her eyes boring into my back as we leave. I can't tell what her game is and don't want to find out, I'd rather not push three times is a charm theory.

❦❦❦❦

The long black car is waiting at the entrance and Ric helps me inside, sliding in next to me. Jacobs and Teiran follow, taking the seat facing us. Limos are becoming synonymous with me being in trouble. It's really not fair, one should be able to enjoy the luxury, not be fearful when one shows up.

"You handled yourself very well," Jacobs pats my knee, "worthy of a Royd Industries employee."

"Uh, thanks?" Should I tell him I'm not technically an employee?

Ric clears his throat and I glance over, his eyes telling me to keep my mouth shut. Teiran's expression says pretty much the same thing. Okay, so everyone is lying to the lawyer, not just me. I feel so much better. Not.

If I've learned nothing else, omitting things or flat out lying to Mark Jacobs only gets you in more trouble. He may be one of the best lawyers around, but he can't do his job if he doesn't have all the facts. Not to mention, bold faced lies have a way of catching up to you. Like on the offhand chance, he says something to Var and I know he will.

"So, am I in the clear? For now at least?"

He nods. "For now, they'll keep digging, but with any luck they won't find anything substantial connecting you with Lewis. What I'd like to know is who tipped them off."

"Me too," I answer, but already have a sneaking suspicion, one I think Teiran and Ric share.

"This whole Collector business just won't die."

I glance out the window with the word die, wondering how much he knows. "What I don't understand is how they connected me to his parents. And why Jenny was brought up? I thought it had already been established that I had nothing to do with her death."

"They were grasping at straws, trying to coerce a confession from you."

I shake my head. "It still makes no sense."

"Interrogation doesn't have to make sense, it's almost better if it doesn't, it's a game of confusion. If they can confuse you into slipping up on one little word, they can twist it to fit their purposes."

"So you're telling me justice isn't fair."

"No, not always. I use the same tactics to keep my clients out of trouble."

"Do you think I did it? Killed those people?"

"Does it matter?"

In the end, I guess it doesn't matter what he thinks. He gets paid either way.

Chapter 52

The sun is up and shining by the time we reach The Meadows and I'm exhausted, too exhausted to even protest a little when Teiran replaces the collar, once we're inside the building.

The last thing I want is to deal with the question of what do we do next. But there's no escape in sight, not with both Teiran and Ric following me into the apartment and a trio of Nervous Nelly's waiting inside.

At least I'm spared Mr. Jacobs finding out the hard way, that I've—hel, we've all been stretching the truth. I'm not sure if client, lawyer confidentiality holds when the one paying his bill is a god and I don't want to find out the hard way.

I don't need the extra stress of explaining to Var that I've kept a few details from him. Important details, like Hel's mark.

I struggle to remove myself from the crush of hugs, only to replace them with awkward questions I don't feel like answering. Are you okay? What happened? How did you get out?

"She's fine, everyone," Ric leads me to the couch, "just a little shaken by the experience."

They crowd in around me, Annya taking my hand. "So what exactly is going on here?"

"A simple misunderstanding," says Ric, brushing my run in with the NTF as if it were a nothing more than me grabbing a flat iron instead of a curling iron.

Teiran snorts. "There is nothing simple when it comes to this woman."

And he's right, nothing is simple anymore. Everything I thought I knew is entangled in lies, misinformation and secrecy. Not a single, solitary, simple truth in the bunch.

"Why did the NTF arrest her?" Leave it to Annya to push the envelope.

"It had to do with The Collector again, didn't it?" Rey moves from his perch on the arm of the couch to behind me and begins massaging my shoulders.

Ric nods, his expression solemn. "Yes."

"You may as well tell them everything. They're going to find out anyway." I pat Rey's hand, motioning for him to take a seat.

Teiran opens his mouth to protest, but I hold up a finger, silencing him. They deserve to know and it's the next best option because I know none of them will choose the best option. Distancing themselves from me, not that there's any guarantee it will keep them safe.

If Stasia Athory is behind this—I wouldn't

put it past the bitch—she proved tonight she'll go to any length to get what she wants, including hurting those closest to me.

As Ric gives them a basic rundown of what happened—minus the near beating—Teiran and I continue our little stare down. He's going to win, I know it, but it doesn't stop me from trying to figure out what's going on in his head. He's clearly not paying attention to what's going on with the others since I overruled his objection.

A nudge comes from beside me, shaking loose the list of possibilities from my head and I look over at Annya. "Huh?"

"We asked what comes next, skinny. Any ideas in that blonde head of yours?"

There's one, but I'm not going to voice it out loud, at least not to everyone. "Nope, any suggestions? Besides leaving town, I think they'd frown upon that, not to mention, take it as a sign of guilt."

"True. I say we sleep on it and convene around sixish," she turns to Rey and Nyssa, "what about you two?"

"It would give us a new perspective and she looks beat." Rey nods in my direction.

"Agreed." Nyssa tugs at Rey's hand. "Take me home, big boy."

Annya follows them to the door, closing and locking it once she satisfied they're safely down the stairs. She returns to our little group, taking up her spot on the edge of the couch. Leaning in, elbows on knees she looks from Teiran to Ric and takes a deep breath. "Okay, boys, here's how I see it, she has no choice."

"What the hel are you talking about?" I slide to the edge, grabbing her arm. "I have no choice in what? And why are you talking to them and not me?"

"You have no choice, but to take the job." She turns to look at me.

"Why the hel are you siding with Var Royd? And why don't I have any other choice?"

"I'm not *siding* with anyone. I'm looking out for you and right now, you need what that job can give you."

"What? A lifetime of servitude?"

"No, protection from the law and the removal of that damn thing." She pings a finger off the collar.

I turn toward the boys. "What about you guys, do you agree with her?"

Teiran is, well, Teiran. Unreadable and unresponsive to my question. Ric is the one who surprises me. As much as he's protested against me taking the job, he's suddenly on board. Maybe a little hesitant, but he's agreeing with Annya.

"I don't get it, why are you two of all people urging me to take this job?"

"You have already tried to take it once before, why are you protesting now?"

Ric's question is a good one, why am I? "If you remember right, he turned me down. What makes you think he'll take me on this time?"

"Because we," he nods toward Teiran, "will guide you."

I turn to Teiran, watching his reactions for any sign of his real opinion. "Do you agree with them? Is this my only hope?"

He's stone silent for a moment and then I get a brief nod. "They have convinced me."

"What the hel? Have you guys been discussing this behind my back?"

Guilty looks, guilty silence, all around. Lowering my head, I lick my lips, chewing on the lower as I ponder the situation. I know they're trying to help. I know they think they're doing what's best. Hel, I've even been thinking about it, but I'm not going to admit it to them, at least not right this second. Why the hel should I?

On the plus side, I'll get what I want, the collar off and the extra added bonus of godly protection against the NTF and super bitch, Stasia Athory. On the negative side, I'll be under that godly thumb, forced to do whatever he desires. And oh, yeah, the awesome benefit package of his sister. Then there's Hel, she'll be getting what she wants too, me on the inside of his little organization. I don't relish playing double agent, but the alternatives don't look pleasurable either. Guess I'm screwed no matter what I chose.

"Okay, guide me, oh, wise ones."

Chapter 53

Teiran is already outside waiting for the car as Ric goes over what I need to know one last time. "The words must be said with intent, you must mean them."

I bite my lower lip, a plot hatching that I won't divulge to any. "Will he know if I don't?"

"To be truthful, I do not know. When I recited them there was no hesitancy, I meant them."

"Okay, say the words and mean them, I got it. I'll meet you downstairs. I need to make a pit stop before we leave."

"As you wish." He smiles, giving my hand a squeeze before leaving to join Teiran.

"I know what you are thinking, Keely, be careful. The last thing you need is haveing a god pissed off at you." Leave it to Annya to read me like a book.

"Yeah, I know, but if there's a chance this bond thingy can be broken, or weakened, I've got to take it. What's the worst he can do? Obliterate me? Once he finds out about Hel, he'll do it anyway."

She sighs. "I wish I could be there for you."

"I know, but it's better I do this alone anyway.

I don't want you caught in any fallout if something goes wrong. Look at the bright side; if it works we'll have something to celebrate tonight."

"Whatever you say, Scrawny."

I laugh. "I wish it worked that way. Good luck entertaining the others, especially Dara if we don't get back in time. Oh, and don't forget to feed CC."

She laughs. "Yeah, you'll owe me big time."

"That I will." I give her a hug and hustle down the steps; taking a deep breath I open the door to the street. Teiran, Ric and Jeffery stand chatting in front of Var's sleek black sedan, no limo this time. Can't say as I'm sorry, this car is just as plush and comfortable.

"Miss Fey," says Jeffery, opening the back door for me, "a pleasure to see you again."

"Good to see you too, Jeffery." I climb inside, Ric right behind me. Teiran must have called shotgun, the thought makes me giggle and Ric leans toward me.

"Are you all right?"

"I'm fine, just amusing myself."

His brow crinkles, but he smiles and pats my hand. "It will all be over shortly."

Jeffery pulls us out onto the highway before I even realize we've left town. There's no backing out now. He knows why I'm coming and I know the basics of what to expect. All I need now is to be able to pull off the twist of saying the words and making him think I mean them. Kind of like cheating a polygraph. From what I understand, if you believe what you're saying is true or false you can fool the machine. I know Var isn't a machine, or human, but there's got to be a way for me to put enough truth in the words not to raise any suspicions. Where there's a will, there's a way and I'm going to give it a good ol' beauty school try. In the words of one of my instructors, fake it till you make it.

My door swings open, practically scaring the shit out of me. Why is it when you don't want to get somewhere fast you, end up arriving in record time? I'd been so busy concentrating on how to weasel my way out of committing myself fully to His Lordship; I hadn't noticed we'd pulled into the parking garage.

I lag behind Teiran, Ric continuously stepping on my heels as I drag my feet down the long corridors of the skywalk. Again, there's no turning back, I don't know why I'm fighting. I made the choice and now I have to live with it, no matter how much I want to turn tail and run the other way.

Teiran slides his keycard, opening the super-secret entrance to Royd's inner sanctum. Wonder if I'll be getting one of those, since I'll be part of Royd Industry's inner circle. Ric stands so close behind me; it feels like I'm walking on his toes as we enter.

The man sits behind his desk, the pile of paper work forgotten when I enter. A wide smile stretches across his face, a warm, loved feeling floats over me. Pulling me into an invisible embrace. "Keely, what a pleasant surprise."

Who's he fooling, he knew I was coming. "Mr. Royd, or do I call you Lord Royd now?"

His laughter fills the room, heightening the feeling of being loved and wanted. "Var will do, my dear."

"Whatever pleases you." What the hel? I really hate it when he uses whatever mumbo jumbo this is to manipulate me. I'd much prefer if he turned it off. It's like being on antidepressants, pleasant on the outside, with your true self banging on the walls wanting to be set free.

If it's possible, his smile grows. "I understand you've decided to join us."

If ya can't beat 'em, join 'em. The words are right on the tip of my tongue, but I bite it and nod.

He comes around the desk, taking my hands in his. "I cannot tell you how much this pleases me."

I know they're all just pretty words, but I don't care how much it pleases him. I'm not pleased with the situation at all. Sadly, I'm sure he'll find a way to communicate his pleasure, probably in ways that will make me less than happy.

Chapter 54

"You have made up your mind and come of your own volition?"

Retaining eye contact, I lift my chin a little higher. "Yes, I've decided working with you is a better alternative to working against you." I so hope he takes note that I said with and not for, but with an ego like his it's all one and the same.

His laughter floats along my skin, but now that I know what he is I'm prepared. Shoving everything I've got against my shields, keeping them tightly in place. I should be okay, unless he pushes it, then I don't know what will happen. I'll probably be on my knees begging for any scrap of attention he'll toss my way.

"My dear, Keely, we've never been working against one another."

I shrug, trying to keep a cool, calm and collected demeanor on the outside while I shudder and shake on the inside. "If you say so."

"I do," he comes around the desk and takes my hands in his, "I did. Are you sure this is what you want and not a choice made by outside influences or foolish fears?"

"Yes, this is my choice." If I continue concentrating on keeping all my bricks in place, I can play this as stoic as Teiran and the lies will fall from my tongue with ease. If he's too self-absorbed to realize fear and outside influences are the only reason I'd take this job, then that's too bad. "You said there's no contract, so what do I have to do?"

He snaps his fingers and just like the good dog he believes him to be, Teiran approaches. "Remove her collar."

Teiran looks from Var to me and back, hesitation and doubt written all over his face. Even though we'd all agreed this was the best course of action.

"Remove her collar, Shield."

He steps between us and raises his hands to just above my shoulders. Our eyes lock, a mutual placing of trust. I'm trusting he won't tell Var the real reason I want the job. He's trusting that I won't become a threat. Slowly, he lowers his hands onto the collar, until they're draped over my shoulders. He could easily strangle me from this position. Again, I have to trust him, just as he has to trust me. I feel the circle of living metal spread as he slides his hands forward and then his touch is gone, along with the collar.

I let out a breath I didn't know I'd been holding. It's gone. It's finally gone. Teiran hangs his head, hands still clutching the collar as he steps away, bringing Var back into view. And I'm reminded, like a fist to the gut. Nothing is truly gone. I'd just traded one type of shackle for another.

"Now, I need you to repeat after me. Your words must match mine and you must place intent behind them." A smile lifts the corners of his lips, but never makes it to his eyes. "No deviations, intentional or not, you must repeat the words exactly. Do you understand?"

"Yes, repeat after you. No deviations. Place my intent behind them."

He nods, placing a hand on my shoulder. "Good. Now kneel."

His hand guides me, until I'm out of reach, moving to rest on the top of my head as I rest on one knee. I refuse to be on two knees in front of him, it's too degrading. The last thing I want is to place unreciprocated, inappropriate ideas in his head, not that I live under the illusion that he doesn't already had them.

"I, Keelyna Monday Fey."

"I, Keelyna Monday Fey."

"Pledge my service to Lord Ingvarr."

"Pledge my service to Lord Ingvarr."

"My mind, body and soul are his to use as he sees fit."

"My mind, body and soul..." I stumble; fear closes my throat, as flickers of the dream come tumbling in. *"Say the words, Keely. I belong to..."*

No one, I belong to no one. I repeat to myself.

His impatience shows in the tapping of his toe and the tightening of his grip on my skull. "My mind, body and soul are his to use as he sees fit."

I let the pressure of his hand push my head down as I try to pull myself together. If I don't do this, don't choke out the words, everything is lost. He's never going to believe me again and I'll be stuck with that damn collar forever. Taking a deep breath, I slowly let it out, raising my head against the pressure of his hand. The swirling blue and gold of his eyes is mesmerizing and I pour myself into securing my wards.

"My mind, body and soul are his to use as he sees fit," he repeats, for what I assume is the last time. My last chance.

With all my energy centered on my metaphysical wall, there's none left to give meaning to the words. I'm nothing but a parrot. "My mind, body and soul are his to use as he sees fit."

Impatience and beginnings of anger dissolve into a smile that lights him from within, as I finish the phrase. Var helps me to my feet and from the corner of my eye I see Ric visibly relax, but Teiran, that's another story. He stares at the collar as it shrinks in his palm.

Var wraps me in a tight embrace. By the time he sets me free, there's no sign of the collar, but Teiran is pulling his hand from his pocket. Sneaky bastard.

A one armed embrace keeps me glued to Var's side. His eyes bright with unshielded power gaze down at me. "Sword, Shield, come welcome our new Shadow."

Acknowledgments

DL Editing, thanks for helping me take this book from meh to readable. Saturday Writers, thanks for keeping me on track. Much love to my family and friends for understanding and keeping me grounded. Rachel Aukes and Tamara Jones, your encouragement and guidance meant so much when I was struggling with my inner demons. I can't thank you enough.

Last, but certainly not least, I have the best readers a writer could ask for.

About the Author

A.R. Miller writes urban fantasy for grown-ass women (and men) who are still too young to care.

She lives in Iowa with an accommodating husband and their four-footed companions. When not testing the patience of readers with cliffhanger endings, you might find her wielding a makeup brush or curling iron as a freelance stylist.

To find out more about A.R. or the Fey Creations series, visit www.feycreations.com.